SEEING THE TRUTH

A novel

By

Faye Rogan

Best Wishes,
Faye Rogan x

SEEING THE TRUTH

SEEING THE TRUTH

Contents

SEEING THE TRUTH

Chapter 1

Karabulut, South-East Turkey, December 1968

The pains had come on suddenly while she swept the yard outside. The recent rain had made puddles on the uneven ground and she swept the water away from the house so that visitors could get to the door without splashing through the dirty water. The baby was due but the pains had taken her by surprise. She gasped and doubled over as the first pain stabbed in her abdomen. She dropped the besom broom and held her stomach, panting to regain her breath. The pain subsided and she straightened up, looking to see whether anyone was watching. One of their workers, busy repairing the tractor at the far end of the yard, was unaware of her predicament. She did not attract his attention and was glad he was distracted by his chore.

Having regained her composure she picked up the broom and continued to sweep the water, hoping that the pains would not begin in earnest. She had been present while her older sister had given birth so knew what to expect. The memories of the still-born baby and then the death of her sister from a massive haemorrhage made her shiver and she prayed to Allah that she and her baby would survive.

The entrance to the house cleared of water, she propped the broom against the wall, slipped off her shoes and went into the house. She went to the kitchen, took a glass from the wooden cupboard on the wall and filled it with water from the large, plastic drum in the corner. She sipped the cold water and sat down on the rickety wooden chair by the sink. Should she send the worker to fetch her mother? Her husband would be home soon, but giving birth was women's work and he would be no help to her.

As she wondered what to do, there was a sound at the door and she heard her husband kicking off his shoes and entering the narrow hallway between the kitchen and the front door. At the door, he had put slippers on his feet so she was unable to hear his footsteps, but watched the doorway expectantly. He smiled as he saw her and she glowed. He was fifteen years her senior and, at thirty years of age, he carried the weight of grief at losing his wife and first child so tragically. She had been flattered when he had asked her parents for permission to marry her, their younger daughter, after their loss. She had known him all her life and had admired him from afar, never dreaming that one day she would become his wife.

She got up from her chair and went to the stove to heat water to make him some tea. She knew what he expected and was happy to oblige. He took her place on the chair and asked her how she was. She smiled and said that she was fine. She reached into the cupboard for a tea glass and grimaced as another pain caught her by surprise. He noticed her look of discomfort and told her to sit down. She shook her head and carried on making the tea. Another pain, more severe than the last, gripped her body and she staggered back from the sink. Sweat appeared on her brow and she began to tremble.

Looking concerned, he took her arm to lead her to the chair. As she sat down heavily, the chair wobbled and she altered her balance to steady it. He left the kitchen abruptly, went to the door and shouted,

'Musa, run to Zehra hanım's house and tell her the baby's on its way. She'll know what to do.'

As the pains became more frequent, the girl made her way along the corridor to their bedroom. She lay down on the mattress on the floor, trying to stay calm, despite the panic welling in her. She hoped the labour would not be long and silently prayed to Allah to give her strength. She was devoutly religious and read the Koran at intervals throughout the day, gaining comfort from the words and vowing to be a good Muslim. She hoped that her mother would bring food for the evening meal as she had not had time to prepare anything. Her husband would not be pleased if a hot meal was not laid before him.

Her mother arrived thirty minutes later, bearing a basket full of food, towels and soap. Her mother had the reputation of being a good cook and her *güveç*, a lamb stew and vegetables, was much praised by visitors to her home. She immediately took out a clay cooking pot from the basket and laid it on the stove in the kitchen. Her son-in-law could smell the aroma of cooked lamb and smiled in anticipation of a tasty meal. He went to the living room, where a tablecloth was laid on the carpeted floor and sat down on a floor cushion. His mother-in-law brought in the food and they exchanged nervous glances. Both of them were remembering a similar situation just over two years ago and hoping the outcome of this one would be happy and not end in tears like the last.

Over the course of the next few hours, the family and close neighbours gathered to give support in the living room of the single storey, mud-brick house, waiting for news. They sat huddled on cushions on the carpet covering the earth floor, sipping tea in small, tulip-shaped glasses, trying to keep warm against the chilly winter air. A coal fire had been lit but provided little heat. Women brought food: cooked dishes, fruit, cheese, olives, bread and an array of biscuits and desserts. Men came to calm the fears of the anxious father-to-be and kept him amused with funny stories and discussions on local affairs. They knew that if the baby was a boy, he would be promised in marriage to the daughter of the Aga, the village headman, in the neighbouring village, who had been born last year. It was to be an important alliance between two powerful families and would give added status to the both families. Their land adjoined and in future years it would be possible to merge all the land to form one huge empire.

In the larger of the two bedrooms, the young girl gripped her mother's hand as she tensed for the next contraction. Her face was bathed in sweat, she fought the urge to scream. The light from the oil lamp was dim and the room had become airless and rank. The experienced midwife issued orders, while her mother uttered words of encouragement and comfort.

Eventually, the girl felt the urge to push and guided by her mother, her mother-in-law and a neighbour who was experienced in birthing, mustered all her energy and pushed with all her might. There was a loud squelch and the baby was out.

'It's a boy!' exclaimed her mother in delight.

The baby's first cry was heard by those gathered in the living room and the father-to-be rushed to the corridor. The bedroom door opened and his mother-in-law poked her head round and shouted,

'Praise be to Allah, it's a boy!'

Feeling immense relief and joy, the father ran back to announce the arrival of his son and received congratulations. He knew the future of the family lay in the hands of this newborn child and prayed that they would all be safe from harm.

Chapter 2

Marmaris, Turkey,

August 1999

Sitting under a straw parasol, shaded from the searing sun, Kaye Knowles was enjoying the break from her frenetic life and allowed herself to wallow in the moment. Visiting Turkey had been on her wish list for many years and she felt the tension in her body ease in the heat, soaking into her bones and relaxing her muscles. It was rare that she had time between her work as a Year One classroom teacher and creative arts specialist in a primary school, her musical activities, her passion for pottery and her social life to take time out. Being able to do nothing was a luxury.

During the long summer holiday, when thoughts about school matters began to subside, she always reflected on the previous year: the highs and the lows, and after reminiscing, sometimes painfully, she made a mental plan of how to move forward. She took her job seriously, but made time for singing in several choral groups and attending pottery evening classes to maintain balance in her life and to allow these creative outlets to divert her attention away from work. In all, she was happy with her life, though sometimes wished she had a significant other with whom to share it.

Heaving her fuchsia pink patterned swim suited body over on her sun bed Kaye pondered on this very issue. Her skin, damp with sweat, made an embarrassing noise as she peeled her ample thigh from the plastic mattress where her towel had become scrunched up and turned onto her side. She could see the waiters in their hotel from the beach and, watching them at work, thought that finally the foreign men fixation which had dominated her choices in men so far must have dwindled, as none of them appealed to her.

Her fascination with dark, Mediterranean-looking men had been part of her life since her parents had brought home a friend's Italian boyfriend one New Year's Eve when she was about six and she was instantly smitten. His dark good looks, his wavy, dark hair caressing the collar of his shirt, the way he took an interest in her and the way he spoke English had shaped her interest in men ever since.

During the past few years she had managed to learn from past mistakes and was able to select men on merit rather than looks. However, none of her past relationships had been successful or long lasting and she regarded the fact that she was a forty year old spinster as a failure. When aged relatives seemed intent on reminding her that she was 'still not married', for a few moments she thought that maybe there was something wrong with her. But then she remembered that she had a good life and one envied by several married friends. She was free to come and go as she pleased and yes, it would be lovely to have someone to go home to after a hard day, but perhaps she was destined to make an impact in other areas of her life. She was a dedicated teacher and gave her all to the children she taught. At times, she gave up hope of ever finding Mr. Right and resigned herself to settling for Mr. He'll Do. She had seen too many of her friends, who had married their supposed Mr. Right, end up in the divorce courts several years later. Would settling for a much more stable relationship with a less dynamic man be so bad?

Kaye's attention then turned to her sister, Jan, who was asleep on the neighbouring sunbed. Her heart went out to her. A month earlier, Jan's fiancé had moved on, leaving Jan with unpaid mortgage payments and had made it clear that he could no longer bear the responsibility of their relationship and being a home-owner. They had been together since they were nineteen and he felt he had missed out on life and wanted his freedom back. Jan was heartbroken and, also being a teacher, was dreading the long school holiday where she would have to cope with constant reminders of broken plans and memories of past happiness. Kaye had suggested this last minute holiday to do something to lift Jan's spirits. She hoped that Jan would appreciate the change of scenery and being anonymous for two weeks, away from other people's expectations and prying eyes.

The next day, as Kaye and Jan neared the end of their jeep safari, Kaye was reminded again of her disappointing love life. Dusty and tired from the endless jostling and jolting in the jeep, they were taken to the one of the oldest trees in Turkey. It was an old custom to dance around the tree to a drum beat provided by a local musician and make a wish. Despite knowing that it might be a tourist ruse, she joined the line of dancers and made a wish to find the man of her dreams soon.

Later, as the heat of the day diminished, they returned to their boutique hotel. They were staying at the quieter end of Marmaris, where the beach narrowed until there was just a small strip of sand in front of huge rocks which jutted out into the sea. It took three showers to clean away the dirt from the safari but after their exhausting day, the two sisters were hungry and made their way to dinner in the outside eating area in front of their hotel.

Kaye and Jan usually sat at the same table to eat from the running buffet which was the standard arrangement for each meal. The hotel was small, with just twenty-eight rooms and as most of the guests were on two-week holidays, everyone quickly established routines of sitting at certain tables.

Kaye and Jan were enjoying a vodka, soda and lime before fighting their way to the evening buffet table. That day was changeover day at the hotel and there were lots of new people to view. Nonchalantly, glancing around the restaurant, she spotted a handsome man, presumably Turkish, helping himself to the food. He was very dark, average height, well-built and having helped himself to a plateful of food, sat down at the next table. Kaye was unable to help looking at him again and as her heart did a little flutter, she reminded herself that she was not interested in this kind of man any more. She convinced herself that he probably would be joined at any moment by a ravishing girlfriend. He was far too attractive to be dining alone.

The queue for the buffet lessened and, as Kaye's stomach gurgled, they decided to join the line of diners. The selection of salads was overwhelming: dishes piled high with vivid coloured vegetables, some smothered in creamy yogurt and others in olive oil, fresh green leaves glistened among plates of cold meats and cheeses. A tempting array of cooked meat dishes, plump rice and pasta steamed in silver salvers, kept warm from underneath by small gas rings. Eager to sample all that Turkish cuisine had to offer, Kaye took advantage of the buffet to try something new every night.

She arrived back at the table first and noticed that the gorgeous man was still alone. Feeling self-conscious, she fiddled with her napkin, took a swig of vodka, and almost sighed with relief when Jan joined her. Kaye sensed that someone was looking at her. She took a sideways glance and met the man's gaze full on. She quickly took another mouthful of food and in as nonchalant manner as she could muster, let her eyes settle in his direction. He was definitely looking at her, but as soon as their eyes met, he quickly looked away.

'Pull yourself together', Kaye thought to herself. 'He was probably daydreaming and didn't realise he was staring. There's no way someone like him would give you a second glance'. She continued eating and decided not to get excited. She was not about to set herself up for another romantic disappointment.

The plates were cleared away and the waiter did not miss the opportunity to flirt with Jan. He had become more daring over the past few days and was obviously smitten with her. Jan ignored him and did not even raise a smile. As Jan began to reminisce on the day's events, Kaye's eyes strayed once more to the handsome Turk on the next table. This time there was no mistaking his intent. He winked at her, causing Kaye's cheeks to burn and she knew it was not from sunburn.

She looked again to make sure she was not imagining his interest and was rewarded by a smile that would have any beautiful

Hollywood actress weak at the knees. He had a dazzling white set of teeth and the sexiest smile. She guessed he was in his late thirties. She was now tingling from head to toe and struggling to keep her breathing regular.

Kaye wondered how long she should leave it before looking again. She looked. He was looking. They held the stare for what seemed ages but could only have been a few seconds. Kaye could not help smiling and felt like a nervous teenager. Every time she looked, her eyes met his. With mounting excitement, questions began to float around her brain, 'How long will he sit there? Is he staying at the hotel?' He seemed to be on friendly terms with all the waiters. Perhaps he was the local gigolo and this hotel was one of his pick-up points. He lit another cigarette and settled back in his chair, seemingly totally at ease with the situation. Kaye noted that he must be used to this kind of thing, whereas she was a quivering wreck. With fingers fumbling to open the packet, she pulled out a cigarette and took a long drag. She took another swig of vodka and in an attempt to calm herself, decided to go to the toilet.

Kaye left the table, smiled at the Turk on her way past and headed for the toilets. She pulled her stomach muscles, trying to walk tall without her bottom looking huge and nearly wobbled off her high wedge-heeled sandals. She tried to look confident but inside she was wondering whether seeing her large shapely body would cause him to lose interest.

Wandering through the beautifully landscaped hotel garden on her way back to the table, Kaye admired the palm trees and tropical flowering plants dotted along the well-tended lawns. The grass had just been watered and she felt the damp tendrils of grass brush her toes. The sweet scent of jasmine wafted on the gentle breeze, without which the humidity would have been unbearable.

'Aaaagh!' she screamed, seeing him suddenly step out from behind a tree. 'What are you doing here?'

There was no reply. He continued to stand, smiling, looking at her. He seemed not at all bothered by the fact that he had obviously scared Kaye to death. Her heart pounding, she repeated,

'What are you doing here?'

He shrugged his shoulders. Kaye was unsure whether to be frightened or pleased. 'He might be Turkey's answer to the Yorkshire Ripper,' she thought, but when she looked at him he had such a friendly face and cheeky smile that somehow she instinctively knew that she was not in any danger. Giggling nervously, Kaye wanted to continue walking but he blocked her way. He saw her dilemma and moved aside to allow her to pass. Before she knew it his hands were around her waist and he was nuzzling her neck. She was torn between surrendering to his hot breath and righteous indignation. The spot just behind her ear took control and for a moment she was in total ecstasy. Her knees wobbled, she could hardly breathe and just as she was closing her eyes he said,

'Çok güzel bir bayansın.'

'Pardon?' Kaye replied, looking puzzled.

'Çok güzel bir bayansın'

Now giggling with embarrassment, she asked if he spoke English.

'No' he replied shaking his head.

'Français?'

'No'.

'Deutsch?'

'No'.

'Espanol?'

Her supply of languages was running dry, except for Greek, which she knew would not be a good question to ask a Turk. So she threw her hands up and babbled to herself that this was hopeless. She could see that he was becoming nervous and there was an uneasy silence. He took her hand, kissed it and pressed it to his forehead. Kaye assumed this was a quaint Turkish custom and smiled. He then leaned forward, embraced her and kissed her with such tenderness that she was hardly able to breathe.

He looked straight into her eyes and said,

'I love you'.

'Oh please! Why did you have to spoil it?' Kaye gasped as she moved away from him, knowing that he couldn't understand what she had said, but hoping that he could understand her frustration from the tone of her voice. Her heart sank as she realised that she had been taken for a fool.

He saw the expression on her face and laughed, 'English!' and Kaye understand that this was the full extent of his English repertoire and began to laugh too. He then produced his room key from his pocket and showed her the number 413. There was no mistaking his intent.

'Do I look like that kind of woman?' Kaye raged, pushing past him, feeling utterly stupid. Thinking that he must definitely be a gigolo or perhaps a frustrated businessman looking for a bit of fun while he was away from home, she berated herself at her naivety. She gave him a look of pure disgust and in as dramatic style as she could muster, flounced off, leaving him standing there.

Her arrival back at the table was met with puzzlement.

'You've been a long time,' Jan stated. Kaye quickly lied that there had been a queue for the toilets and she had been chatting to a woman they had met previously. She continued to relate an imaginary story about the woman but out of the corner of her eye spotted Gigolo coming back to his seat. She quickly suggested that they took a stroll along the promenade. In agreement, they gathered their belongings and made their way out of the restaurant and onto the road. Kaye could not resist a backward glance and was rather pleased that Gigolo had a hurt expression on his face. Served him right!

The next day the sisters had booked to go on a whole day boat trip around the bays. They had an early breakfast and Kaye was relieved to see that there was no sign of Gigolo. She wondered whether after her refusal he had picked up another unsuspecting hotel guest and was now in post-coital slumber.

They had an enjoyable day lazing on the boat and swimming in the azure sea at designated stopping points. Although it was still hot, the weather was unusually overcast, due to the solar eclipse taking place that day. Many of the passengers had come prepared with special glasses and they hoped to see the eclipse from the boat at around midday. Kaye tried to look interested in the once in a life-time event but her mind was occupied with the events of the previous night. It had been a long time since she felt really attracted to a man, but at her age she was determined to let her head rule her heart and not make any rash decisions. Besides, she was here for Jan, not trying to find the love of her life.

They returned to the hotel with just enough time for a shower before the evening meal. Jan made her way to an empty table which happened to be the same one they had sat at the night before. They ordered drinks and it was only a few seconds before Kaye spotted Gigolo heading for the table next to them with a plate of food. He smiled at her and sat down. Kaye tingled from head to toe and tried hard to focus on listening to Jan's conversation. It took every ounce of effort to pretend that he was having no effect on her. Gigolo was just as attentive that night and every time Kaye looked over he was looking her way. They exchanged friendly smiles, he blew kisses and when Kaye needed to go to the toilet at the end of the meal she knew he was going to follow her.

This time, he sat waiting for her on a wooden bench placed in front of a beautiful fuchsia rhododendron bush. Kaye hesitated, wondering whether to walk past but it seemed impolite to refuse his gesture to sit next to him. He offered her a cigarette, which she refused. Her normal reaction would have been to speak, but knowing that he couldn't understand a word she said, she fidgeted on the seat, looking into the distance. His hand reached for hers. For a moment Kaye thought about protesting but allowed him to take her hand and gently stroke it. She noticed his well-trimmed nails and the few short black hairs on the brown skin on the back of his hand. He said something to her in Turkish but when it seemed futile to speak he enclosed her in a bear hug and kissed her tenderly.

After a few minutes, she pulled away, not from any distaste, but because she could hardly breathe. She was terrified by the intensity of her feelings. Remembering that she had left Jan sitting at their table alone, she made a move to stand up. He then showed her his room key again and put his hand on his heart which Kaye took to be a gesture meaning that she could trust him. Using hand gestures and pointing at her watch Kaye agreed to meet him later at 11pm.....in his room.

Hurrying back to the table, Kaye bumped into one of the waitresses, Carol. She was English and Kaye had chatted to her several times during the past week. She looked intently at Kaye and asked,

'You look a bit sheepish. What have you been up to?

Kaye nodded coyly to where the Turk was still sitting and asked,

'Do you know who he is?

'No, I don't but I can ask Mehmet. Wait here.'

She disappeared for a few minutes and returned with a smile on her face. Gigolo was Mehmet, the head waiter's, cousin.

'What do you know about him? Is he married?' Kaye asked. 'Is it safe for me to meet him? What do you think?'

Carol said as far as she knew he was single, here to see Mehmet for a few days but that was as much as she knew.

Jan's anger at being abandoned was evident. She rolled her eyes at Kaye's feeble excuse and suggested that they retired to their room for an early night. Kaye realised that she was going to have to tell Jan about her planned assignation in case her sister woke up and discovered that Kaye was not in the room they were sharing.

'You must be crazy! Jan exclaimed in horror. 'He could be a rapist. If he'd done that to me I would have called the police!'

Kaye laughed. Jan had led a much more sheltered life than her and she knew that her sister would never do anything like what she was planning. Kaye assured her that she could look after herself and that she would be careful. Jan did not look convinced but shrugged her shoulders and got ready for bed.

'Look, if you're worried, I'll call you from his room to tell you I'm alright. He's in Room 413 and if something happens here you can call me there.' Jan did not respond and went into the bathroom.

Kaye now had an hour to kill before her rendezvous and picked up a magazine. She soon realised that she had read the same paragraph at least five times without processing it. The mounting excitement inside her was affecting her concentration. When Jan had finished in the bathroom, Kaye cleaned her teeth, fluffed her hair, took off all her make-up and re-applied it with a precision not normal to her routine. The humidity played havoc with her fine, blonde hair and in spite of huge quantities of hairspray, still managed to wilt under the stifling heat.

With half an hour still to wait, Kaye became unsure about the clothes she was wearing. She opened the wardrobe, pulled a few things out but then decided to stick with what she was wearing. Trousers seemed to be a good idea in case he made a grab for her. The white trousers were fairly tight too so access was not easy. Her black T-shirt was sexy without being too revealing. Even though she had prepared herself for a night of passion she was not going to be an easy conquest.

With ten minutes to go, Kaye was flushed and shaking with nerves. The three huge vodkas that she had downed in the previous hour were working their way through her. She mentally planned what she would do when she reached his room. Room 413 was on the top floor of the hotel at the opposite end to the lifts. She didn't want anyone to see her entering or leaving his room and hoped that the other guests would either still be out on the town or already tucked up in bed.

A hotel guest had been stuck in the lift for an hour the day before, so she decided to walk to his room using the stairs. It was a couple of flights so when she reached the top she was gasping for breath. She walked slowly along the corridor, hoping to regain her composure. His room was at the far end near the fire escape. 'Hope I don't need to use that!' Kaye giggled. No one was about and it was deathly quiet. She continued until she reached room 413 and put her ear to the door. Nothing.

Hesitating, considering whether to make two quiet raps or one big thump on the door and if, in fact he was even in the room, Kaye took a deep breath and knocked, then quickly stepped to the side so if the door opened it looked like no one was there. The door opened, a face peered around, spotted her, took her hand and pulled her into the room. She noticed that it was a smaller room than hers with one single bed, but was very tidy inside and the only evidence of occupation was a water bottle, a packet of cigarettes, a lighter, an ashtray and a newspaper on the dressing table. The air conditioning hummed quietly, providing a cool waft of air. She was ushered to the bed and invited to sit down. He offered her a cigarette. Kaye politely refused, preferring to smoke her own low tar menthols, which she had brought in her bag. Not a word had been said and Kaye felt the urge to giggle to break the silence. He laughed too. The whole thing seemed ridiculous.

'What are we going to say when we can't understand a word the other is saying?' Kaye wondered.

'My name is Vedat.'

'You do speak English! My name is Kaye.'

'My English very bad.'

She was so relieved that he knew any at all.

'You English?'

'Yes. Are you Turkish?'

'Yes. I am Kurd.'

Kaye's heart began to pound. The Kurds had threatened to bomb Turkish holiday resorts that summer and many tourists had been put off visiting Turkey because of it. Her mind whirred into overdrive.

What if he's a terrorist? What if he wants to hold me hostage? How can I have been so stupid?

As these frantic thoughts whirred round her head he continued….

'No bombs.'

It was almost like he could read her mind and she reddened.

'I am farmer.'

Kaye drew heavily on her cigarette. She had always wanted to be a farmer's wife and in her youth had dated several farmers. She gained some comfort from this and began to relax.

'What kind of farm?'

He shrugged. He didn't understand her question. She said it again and received the same response.

'Mooooo! Baaaaaaa! Farm?'

'No!' he laughed. He mimed that he could not say the English and reached into the drawer of the dressing table for a pen. He found a scrap of paper and began to draw plants. Kaye went through all the cereal crops she could think of but he said no. He then touched her trousers. He saw her look of horror and touched his shirt and then the sheet on the bed. Kaye suddenly realised that he was touching the material.

'Oh, you grow cotton!' Kaye said with relief.

'Yes. Pamuk.'

Pamuk was obviously the Turkish word for cotton.

He drew a diagram of his farm and shaded fields in different ways to denote different crops. After some time Kaye learned that it was a large farm with fields of wheat, oats, maize, barley, various vegetables and orchards growing every fruit imaginable – even bananas. She was impressed. He also told her how much he made from his cotton crop - in Deutsch marks so it meant nothing to her, as she had no idea of the exchange rate. Kaye saw that he wanted to impress her, so looked suitably impressed. She told him she was a teacher and he looked similarly impressed.

Vedat offered Kaye a drink. Having already had enough vodka she pointed to the water bottle. He already had a half-empty glass so went to the bathroom to fetch another one for her.

Kaye could tell he was as nervous as she was, despite the fact that they were managing to communicate better than she had predicted. He drew a map of Turkey and showed her where he lived. It was miles away in the far southeast, near Iraq and Syria.

'I was born in a small town in Derbyshire called Bakewell,' Kaye responded and at his puzzled expression, explained that it was in the north of England and not near London. He had heard of London. 'It's famous for its pudding,' Kaye added, miming eating. 'But I live in small town near Birmingham now,' she clarified, turning over his piece of paper and drawing a rough map of the United Kingdom and marking on the relevant places. Engrossed in making an accurate representation, she jumped, startled, as the phone on the bedside cabinet rang. Vedat reached over her to answer it and proceeded to take his identity card from his shirt pocket and give the details to the caller.

'Police,' he stated, placing the card on the cabinet and shrugging his shoulders and aware that Kaye looked worried, added, 'No problem. Just control.'

Kaye remembered that she had told Jan she would call her, so gesturing to Vedat that she wanted to use the phone, she picked up the receiver and dialled their room number. 'Everything's fine,' she told Jan. 'Don't worry. See you in the morning.'

Placing the phone back in its cradle, she sat down on the bed. The next thing she knew was that she was flat on her back and being smothered in kisses. She tried to sit up but he pinned her down. The realisation that he was much, much stronger than she was and the realisation that she could not move alarmed her. She looked straight into his chestnut brown eyes and asked to sit up. He let her. He smiled and touched his chest, obviously sorry and Kaye breathed a sigh of relief. She quickly thought of something to ask to resume the conversation.

'How long are you staying here?'

'I don't understand.'

'Here (gesturing the room) how long?'

'Tomorrow, tomorrow.'

Kaye understood that he meant he was there for another two days. She knew by this time that she liked him – a lot. He was the most handsome man she had ever met. She told him she was leaving next Tuesday, in another five days. 'Are you married?' she asked, pointing to her ring finger.

'No. You'

'No I'm not married.'

'Why?'

'I haven't met a man who I wanted to marry yet.'

'I don't understand. You beautiful woman. Why not married?'

Kaye didn't know how to explain so she just shrugged her shoulders.

He looked into her eyes, 'Kiss?'

It was the tenderest of kisses and Kaye felt her whole body melting. They continued to kiss. Vedat stroked her neck and face. He kissed her lips, moving onto her nose, chin, cheeks, forehead and ears. He gently took her hand, kissing her fingers, and when his hand moved to her breast she did not object. Kaye knew that her make-up was smudged but was enjoying herself too much to care. She stroked his jet black hair, so thick and wavy, raking her fingers through it, revelling in its texture, which was so different than her own fine, straight hair.

His lovemaking, though enjoyable, was also clumsy and as he threw her around the bed, it occurred to Kaye that he was not as experienced as she had presumed. They were a tangle of limbs and the sheet was so tightly wrapped around her neck, it threatened to strangle her. She fought him off to regain her composure and straighten the sheet. They were both bathed in sweat and he rose from the bed to turn the air conditioning up to its maximum level. She swigged water from the now almost empty bottle, not bothering to use one of the glasses and was aware of him looking at her. He wiped sweat from his chest and gesturing to the bathroom, she understood that he was going to take a shower. As she waited for him to return, Kaye noticed his identity card and picking it up, learned his full name, Vedat Erdem, that he was thirty three years of age, the names of his parents and guessed that the word *bekar* referred to his marital status. She must remember the word so that she could check what it meant later. Feeling guilty at sneaking a look without permission, and conscious that she, too, was in need of a wash, she threw off the sheet and tiptoed to the bathroom door and knocked quietly. He looked startled, but beckoned,

'Come!'

She stepped into the bath and under the spray from the shower. 'Oooh! The water's freezing!' Kaye shivered.

Vedat took the tablet of soap in his hands and worked up a lather. He then began to apply the soapy suds in gentle strokes to her whole body. Kaye's body trembled from his touch and it was not long before they were engaged in kissing and stroking every part of each other. He wanted to enter her again, but not wanting her to be uncomfortable, he took her hand and helped her step out of the bath. He pushed her back onto the bed but still being wet, she slid off and ended up on the floor. He was too impatient to care and pulled her down until she was lying flat on her back on the carpet. He entered her carefully and looking deep into her eyes moved deep inside her gathering speed until with a shuddering moan, he removed himself from her and disappeared once more into the bathroom. Kaye found this behaviour quite strange. Was it a Turkish thing to jump off you immediately after sex? What about cuddles and enjoying the afterglow together?

After yet another shower, Vedat joined Kaye in bed and snuggled into her. His body was cold and he shivered as he pulled the sheet over his body. The black curls that covered his whole chest, stomach, arms and legs were still damp and Kaye could not resist the urge to play with them, gently straightening the hairs and letting them spring back into tiny coils lying on his brown skin.

'Me chocolate. You chicken' Vedat stated, looking at the differing skin tones of their bodies. Kaye giggled,

'I love chocolate!'

'Me too. I like chicken more good'

'Better,' Kaye corrected.

'Anlamadım', he said, puzzled.

'More good is better', Kaye explained.

'Ah, I understand. Tomorrow I buy Turkish/English word book'

'You mean a dictionary?'

'I no understand.'

'Okay. You buy,' Kaye agreed with a quiver of excitement, realising that he obviously wanted to see her again tomorrow.

By then it was late and he looked sleepy. The single bed was a tight squeeze for two well-built people, so he spooned her body, wrapping his arms around her and was soon snoring softly. Kaye lay awake, afraid that if she moved she would fall out of bed. She was usually a restless sleeper and flung herself around during the night. In this bed there was not enough room even to turn over. She listened to his snores, gauging his breathing, feeling the warmth of his body next to hers, unable to drift off to sleep.

When it became light and she heard the first call to prayer of the day, she decided to leave and return to her own room. She tried to wake Vedat by shaking his shoulders and whispering in his ear. He was sound asleep.

'Ooof!' Kaye exploded as she put two feet in the same leg hole or her trousers and nearly fell over. 'Well if that didn't wake him up, nothing will!' She made her way to the door, unlocked it and closing it quietly behind her, made her way down the corridor. She was not expecting to see anyone at this hour, so gasped in surprise as she crossed another hotel guest, the worse for wear, on the stairs. He gave her a questioning look and when she was sure he had gone past, she skipped the rest of the way to her room.

Chapter 3

Having had barely three hours' sleep, Kaye was woken by Jan saying,

'If you don't hurry up you'll miss breakfast. Shall I see you down there?'

She would happily have gone without food, but the thought of Jan eating alone, prompted her to throw off her bedcover and stagger to the bathroom. 'I'll just have a quick shower and then I'll be down,' she replied as Jan picked up her bag and left the room.

The powerful jet of steaming hot water prickled her skin as she shampooed her hair – a startling contrast to the soft caresses it had received only a few hours earlier. Still not fully awake, Kaye let her mind drift to the previous night and felt her heart quicken as she tried to remember every inch of Vedat's body. What a magical night it had been! She wondered whether dancing round that old tree and making a wish had really worked or whether there was something special about it being the day of the solar eclipse. Whatever the reason, she knew she would remember that night forever. Even after one night, she had developed feelings for Vedat and hoped she would see him that day.

After breakfast, Kaye and Jan returned to their room to change and get ready to go to the beach over the road. The beach was quiet, so finding empty sun beds was no problem. They quickly lay their towels down, took off their sarongs and slathered their fair skin with high factor sun cream. They took it in turns to do each other's backs and then settled down to read.

'So what happened last night?' Jan's curiosity had finally got the better of her.

'It was nice,' Kaye replied, downplaying how she really felt. Too many times she had gushed about a man after a first date, only to be embarrassed when she had to admit later that she had never heard from him again.

'So are you seeing him again?'

'We'll see.'

'Well things must have gone well – you didn't come back until it was light and you have that gormless smirk on your face!'

'I don't!'

'Kaye, you look like the cat that got the cream!'

'Ooooh, he's lovely!' she let out and instantly bit her tongue. So much for playing it cool.

'Oh no! Please don't fall for him. Holiday romances never last. You'll end up getting hurt.'

'Okay, Miss Doom and Gloom, I'll keep my sensible head on and just enjoy it while it lasts.'

Talking about him, sent Kaye into another reverie and she threw her book down, unable to concentrate. It was another scorching hot day and her gaze was drawn to a family playing by the water's edge. The father was teaching his son to swim, while the mother knelt in the sand, making sandcastles with her baby daughter. A stocky, tanned man sauntered past them, scuffing his feet in the sand as he walked and smiled as the baby girl squealed with glee as she smashed the sandcastle her mother had just built. Kaye squinted against the glaring sun's rays – was she dreaming? Could that be him? She hauled herself into a sitting position to look more closely. Just as she thought he was going to walk past and not see her, Vedat turned his head and recognising her, waved.

Kaye waved back and was delighted as he made his way towards her. Her heart pounding and feelings of panic about to overwhelm her, she greeted him,

'Hi! How are you?'

'I'm fine, thanks,' Vedat replied in heavily accented English. 'You?'

'I'm fine too. This is my sister, Jan.'

Vedat stepped around Kaye's sun bed to shake Jan's hand.

'Pleased to meet you,' she said.

'I go to market,' pointing to the small corner shop across the street, he walked away.

'Well he didn't stay long!' Jan scoffed.

Kaye tried to hide the disappointment she felt inside. She knew that he felt awkward at his lack of English. How she wished she knew some Turkish so that their conversations were not so stilted. She was just settling back down to read when someone standing behind her sun bed thrust a small green book in her face. Vedat grinned as he showed her a Turkish/English pocket dictionary.

'Now we speak,' he said, pulling an empty sun bed alongside Kaye's. He perched on the edge of it and began to thumb through the pages, looking for a particular word.

'Why you leave me?' he asked looking forlorn.

'You were sound asleep and I couldn't wake you.'

Vedat mimed himself waking up and finding Kaye gone and his sad face. Kaye, in turn, mimed him snoring in deep sleep and her trying to shake him awake. He looked at her in disbelief.

Kaye said, noticing the grazes on his knees. 'What happened?'

Laughing, Vedat miming said, 'Jiggy-jiggy on carpet!'

Kaye burst out laughing and then covered her face with embarrassment.

With the aid of the dictionary and hand gestures, they exchanged personal information by taking turns to find words in the dictionary. Kaye's had surreptitiously discovered that *bekar* meant 'single' and had inwardly breathed a sigh of relief. She would never enter a relationship with a married man.

Vedat asked Kaye if she wanted to go for a walk with him. She would have liked nothing better, but felt she could not abandon Jan, so suggested they meet that night in the bar. Jan had refused all Kaye's attempts to go out at night to any of the numerous bars and night clubs along the promenade, preferring to sit in the hotel bar and retire to bed early. Kaye did not see any harm in meeting Vedat that night. This was her holiday too and she deserved to have some fun.

Vedat and Kaye met that night and the following two nights too. He had called his family to tell them that he would be staying an extra three days, so that he could spend Kaye's remaining time in Marmaris with her. His English vocabulary expanded and he taught Kaye some basic Turkish, which she found very hard to pronounce. They walked hand in hand along the promenade, sat on the beach looking at the stars, watched holiday makers make fools of themselves at Karaoke bars, gazed into each other's eyes over drinks at a variety of cafes and skinny dipped in the sea in a secluded spot hidden by rocks. The next day would be their last full day together and in his limited English, Vedat explained he would like to take her on a boat trip and spend the whole day with her. Feeling like a teenager, Kaye wondered what Jan would say, but throwing caution to the wind she kissed Vedat and said that she would love to.

Kaye broached the subject with Jan during breakfast the next morning and to her surprise, Jan, saying she would welcome some time on her own, told her to go. Kaye signalled an okay sign to Vedat who was eating breakfast alone at a nearby table and he held up ten fingers to tell her what time they would meet.

They spent an idyllic day cruising around the coast on a small tourist boat that Vedat had rented for the whole day, with the owner acting as captain. Narrow wooden bench seats covered in long, spongy cushions lay along the sides of the boat, while most of the middle shaded section of the boat was taken up by an enormous mattress, where they chose to lounge. It was far too hot for Kaye's sensitive fair skin to be exposed to the sun and Vedat, too, preferred to be in the shade. The boat chugged away from the beach and out into open water, where they gazed at the shimmering azure sea and the rocky headlands of the tiny islands they passed. When they became too hot, they leapt from the boat to swim in the deep water away from the other tourist boats doing their daily tours around the bays. No longer in the dim lighting of Vedat's hotel room they revelled in looking at each other's bodies, examining their fingers, toes, comparing sizes and shapes, and Kaye asked about an ugly jagged scar on Vedat's forearm that she had noticed a few days before.

'I had car accident. I was twenty-one years.' He mimed his arm going through the windscreen and made scissor-like movements so that Kaye understood that all the nerves and tendons in his arm had been severed. He picked up the small pocket dictionary to look for a word and continued. 'I had… operation, but no good. Now this hand very weak.'

Kaye listened intently.

'Before accident I was write like this,' he mimed writing with his left hand, 'but now I learn write with other hand.'

'Wow! That must have been a challenge,' Kaye sympathised, taking his hand and planting a soft kiss on it.

The captain had a ready supply of cold drinks in a cooler and had insisted they stop for lunch at Işmeler, where his cousin had a restaurant. After a tasty lunch of calamari and salad, they meandered through the narrow streets of Işmeler, enjoying each other's company and laughing at the misunderstandings their language barrier created. They returned to the boat, sweaty and hot and asked the captain if they could find somewhere to swim. As the boat left the beach, they lay in each other's arms, both fully aware that their remaining time together was dwindling.

'I love you, Kaye,' Vedat said, looking deep into Kaye's eyes.

'I love you too.'

'Really?'

'Yes, really.'

'Short time but true love.'

Kaye's eyes filled with tears. She had known from the beginning that she felt something for Vedat, but over the course of the last four days she had realised she had never had such intense feelings before. It seemed like madness that she could fall in love so quickly but she had always been a hopeless romantic and now firmly believed in love at first sight. Vedat seemed so perfect for her and she had waited a long time to find someone like him. She could not contemplate being apart from him and dreaded the moment she would have to say goodbye.

'Why you sad?'

'We are going home tomorrow and I don't want to leave you.'

He hugged her until she gasped for breath and releasing his hold on her he then kissed her entire face with light butterfly kisses. She felt her body melt and her face flush and it took every ounce of self-control not to rip his shorts off and ravage him. He laughed as she struggled to gain control.

That night Vedat joined the sisters at their table for dinner. He was unable to understand most of the conversation, but Kaye made an effort to say things in simple sentences so that he got the gist of what was being said. As they were walking along the beach later, he told Kaye he thought her sister was very unhappy. Kaye agreed that he was right and briefly told him that Jan's fiancé had recently left her.

As the hours ticked by they made a pact that they would not sleep that night but would make the most of every precious minute they had left together. The last of the bars and cafes were closing as dawn broke when Vedat and Kaye arrived back at the hotel. They were surprised to see a number of people still up and gathered in front of the television in the bar. From the anxious looks on their faces, they knew something was wrong. One woman held a handkerchief to her eyes, stemming the flow of tears and another gasped in horror as the story of a huge earthquake, seven point four on the Richter scale which had hit Adapazarı, a city in the Marmara region of Turkey, one hundred miles from Istanbul, unfolded. Vedat made his way towards the television and listened carefully to the reports and then tried his best to relay to Kaye what he had heard. Thousands of people had died as they lay sleeping in their beds and many more lay under the rubble that was once a thriving industrial centre. The emergency services were overwhelmed by the devastation and the darkness of night made their efforts doubly hard. They stayed glued to the screen for twenty minutes, until the reports were repeated and nothing new was said. In sombre mood, they bought a bottle of water from the bar and made their way to Vedat's room.

'What time are you leaving?' Kaye asked.

'Half past nine o'clock.'

'Oh, you leave before me. We're leaving at ten.'

‘No speak. Just kiss.’ Vedat spluttered before bursting into tears and turning away from her in embarrassment.

Kaye had only ever seen one man cry before – her father, when Jan was a baby and seriously ill with pneumonia. She remembered the agony of his sobs as he thought his daughter was going to die. It was difficult to know how to handle a situation with someone you loved and knew well, let alone someone you had only known for a few days, but she let her instincts take over and wrapped her arms around Vedat, rocking him as she would a child. She was unsure whether his tears were the result of the disturbing scenes they had just witnessed on the television or whether it was the thought of their parting that had caused them. Neither of them spoke for some time and feeling calmer, Vedat searched in the dictionary and said, ‘Special. You are special for me, Kaye.’

‘Thank you,’ Kaye was unused to men paying compliments but was becoming accustomed to the open and easy way Vedat expressed his emotions.

‘Don’t forget me,’ he added.

‘Of course I won’t. Will you give me your address so I can write to you?’

Vedat took the foil paper from his cigarette packet, turned it over and wrote down his address and telephone number.

‘Have you got an e mail address?’

‘No e mail.’

‘Okay then, we’ll write to each other. I will try to learn Turkish when I get home.’

Vedat smiled and said knowingly, 'Turkish difficult.' His mother tongue was Kurdish and he had not started to learn Turkish until he went to school at six years old.

They spent the next few hours making love until it was time for Vedat to pack and go for breakfast.

The time for goodbyes had finally come and Kaye struggled to breathe evenly. The lump in her throat felt like it was cutting off her airway. Vedat was going to walk to the bus station where he would catch a bus and begin the twenty hour journey home. He had said goodbye to Jan at the breakfast table, so that he could have a private moment with Kaye. They clung to each other and Kaye studied Vedat's face so that she would be able to remember every detail of it. Over the past five days she had taken many photos, but wanted to have a lasting memory in her head. He stroked her face and her hair, looking deep into her blue eyes and as his bottom lip began to tremble, he kissed her one last time, picked up his holdall and walked away from her. Kaye stood rooted to the spot. She would have liked to go to the bus station with him to wave him off, but there was not enough time before she too, had to take the coach to the airport. Sobs of anguish broke loose and all the pent up emotion she had been keeping inside, burst forth like a torrent. Her chest heaved and her eyes, misty with tears, were glued to his back. He turned around at the corner, waved and blew a kiss, before disappearing out of sight.

Kaye had been sceptical that love at first sight really existed but now believed it did. She had fallen head over heels with Vedat and had forgotten the angst of recent years at not finding 'The One'.

Now she knew she had found him and hoped with all her heart that she would see him again.

Chapter 4

Karabulut, South-East Turkey,

May 1975

'Go on, hurry up! They're waiting for you,' the boy's mother said as she gently pushed him out of the door and sent him on his way. She had arranged everything and did not want his dawdling to delay the proceedings.

The boy had no idea why it was so important to go to his aunt's house today and grudgingly walked slowly to the end of the garden, before turning right onto the lane that ran along the family land. He would much rather be playing with his friends, who, at the moment were probably waiting for him to return after lunch so that they could continue their game of cowboys and Indians. They used the rolling hills and rocky crags behind the village to hide and seek out vantage points. They were a gang of five, ranging in ages from six to nine, and the boy was the natural leader. Being seven years of age, he was not the oldest among them but his family was influential and due deference was made to his being the family's only son.

He walked slowly, shuffling in the plastic sandals that were too big for him. He wiped the sweat from his top lip. The weather was hot and the air dry, making any physical exertion an effort. The boy said a silent prayer to Allah that it was Saturday and he was not at school today. He passed the neighbour's house and tutted to the dog lazing in the sun near the gate. He loved animals and fondly cared for the rabbit which his parents had said he could keep as a pet. He was allowed to keep in it in a small fenced–off part of the garden where it would not eat his mother's vegetables.

He lived on the outskirts of the village and usually enjoyed going to the centre of the village where it was busy with people going about their daily business. However, today he felt apprehensive. It was rare for him to go to his aunt's house unaccompanied by his mother. This made him suspicious but going against his mother's wishes was not an option. He loved her dearly, but being a rebellious soul, he had too many memories of his previous disobedience to want to risk her wrath today.

The village buzzed with life. The boy was tempted to join in with a small band of giggling children who were tormenting a shepherd herding his flock along the rutted road. They knew he kept sweets in his trouser pocket and ran alongside him snatching at his hand. Deciding not to participate, the boy carried on past noisy teenage boys who were playing football on a piece of open ground next to the mosque, shouting at the injustice of an own goal. He greeted two men playing backgammon on the step in front of a flat-roofed mud-brick house, while in the garden the wife of one of them was bathing their son in a large plastic bowl – he protesting loudly at the chill of the water. The boy felt sorry for the child but knew he could not interfere and walking on, a warm, yeasty aroma filled the air as a head scarfed girl took out loaves of bread from the *tandır* oven which stood in the yard next door. An old, flea-bitten dog was sprawled on the pavement and an old man in traditional baggy *şalvar* slowly stepped around it and acknowledged the boy with a smile and a nod of his head. Scraggy hens scratched the dry earth and were free to wander where they chose. As he passed a gaggle of geese honked savagely and waddled towards the wire fence where they were enclosed and he hurried on.

The call to prayer began and soon the menfolk would make their way to the mosque in the square. The boy knew all of the villagers as they were regular visitors to his family home. His father was the Ağa, a religious and well-respected member of the community and it often fell to him to sort out disputes about land rights, financial difficulties and negotiate between families on matters of marriage and family honour. That day, his father had been called upon to give advice to a recently bereaved neighbour and the boy knew his father would probably not return until sundown, when he would lead evening prayers with the rest of the family.

The boy could now see his aunt's house at the far end of the village square. All seemed quiet there and he smiled to himself as he thought about the biscuits and sweets his aunt would have on offer. He stepped over the weeds and stones which led up to the door of the house and tentatively knocked on the door. It was immediately opened by his aunt, who ushered him inside, where he saw that there were several other women sitting on the mismatched cushions on the carpeted floor. They greeted him fondly and offered him *ayran*, a drink made from yogurt, salt and water, and home-made biscuits. His sense of apprehension went as he found an empty cushion and enjoyed the refreshments. The women chatted amongst themselves in rapid Kurdish, making ribald comments and giggling as they shared anecdotes.

His aunt seemed restless and urged him to finish his drink. She asked him if he wanted to pee and led him to the outside toilet. She was waiting for him with a grubby, much-used towel when he had washed his hands at the tap on the wall. Without a word, the women rose and followed as his aunt led him to the bedroom. The boy saw a mattress covered with a sheet on the floor and before he could protest, the women held him, took off his blue cotton shorts and underpants, pushed him down and knelt beside the mattress, pinioning him by his arms and legs. He started to panic, having no clue what was happening. He tried to shout but a cloth was put in his mouth and he was told firmly to be quiet. One of the women took hold of his penis in one hand and, intoning, 'I do this in the name of Allah', with a flash of the wrist of her other hand, sliced off his foreskin with a razor blade. The boy groaned and wriggled but was held tighter to prevent any movement. His eyes flashed with terror and his cheeks flushed with embarrassment at what was being done to him. The woman put the foreskin on a saucer, to be discarded later, and pushed the sheath back to reveal the head of the penis. She directed another woman to pass ointment and a muslin bandage and after covering the penis with the ointment, began to wind the bandage around it. Another of the women quietly cooed comforting words in the boy's ear. She had eight sons and had seen the procedure many times.

Their work done, his aunt told him to sit up and to sip a prepared tincture to ease his discomfort. He refused to drink – afraid it might be poison. What else were they going to do to him? She assured him it was only an herbal drink and that he could go home soon. Reluctantly, he drank the bitter liquid, eager to leave. The women helped him to get dressed and stand. His legs felt weak and he wobbled as he tried to walk so they helped him to a chair in the kitchen. He sat there, dumbstruck. Had his mother known what they were going to do? Did this happen to all boys? Why? In his seven years of life he had grown quite attached to his fore skinned penis. What did it look like now? How would he pee? He could feel his eyes welling with tears and to spare himself the indignity of crying in front of women, he summoned every ounce of his strength and got up from the chair. He told the women he had to go – his mother was waiting for him. They offered him more biscuits but he had no desire for them now. He politely said goodbye and walked towards the door. They congratulated him on becoming a man and wished him well. If he could have, he would have run, but every step he took sent a wave of pain to his groin. He held himself stiffly and trod carefully on the rutted path, avoiding any jolting movement which would cause more discomfort.

It took twenty minutes for him to reach home and he was greeted at the door by his mother. She smiled knowingly and patted him on the head, before congratulating him. His temper flared and he shouted, 'I hate you!' He pushed past her and went as quickly as his wound would allow to his bedroom. He slammed the door and eased himself onto his bed, where he burst into tears. His mother could hear him sobbing from the kitchen where she was preparing the evening meal. Her son had become a man.

Chapter 5

Greenhill, England,

August 1999

The tears Kaye had shed at leaving Vedat behind in Turkey had been replaced with a sense of elation. She felt like she was walking on a cloud and had been impatient to tell her friends about her wonderful holiday and, of course, Vedat.

Her parents were not in the least bit encouraging about her relationship with Vedat, sneerıng that, at forty, she should know better and that she would probably never hear from him again. Kaye hoped her friends would be more understanding.

As she opened the door to the pub where she was meeting her friend, Anna, and other friends, she could hear loud, raucous laughter, which meant Anna was already there. She was greeted affectionately by the group who commented on her honey-coloured tan.

'Wow! You look great!' Anna said, hugging Kaye tightly. She was six foot tall and had a big personality to match, making her the centre of attention in the group. 'Is there a reason for your glow?'

'There might be,' Kaye grinned.

'Come on! Spill the beans!'

'Oh Anna, I've met the most gorgeous man!' Kaye proceeded to tell Anna how she and Vedat had met and how they had spent the last five days of her holiday.

'Wow!' exclaimed Anna. 'Any photos of him?'

'I got them developed today,' Kaye replied, taking an envelope from her handbag.

'He's very handsome – looks like a movie star!' The other girls in the group also wanted to look and agreed. He was definitely a looker.

'So when are you going to see him again?' Anna asked.

'I don't know. We're going to write to each other but that won't be easy as his English is not great and my Turkish is non-existent. I bought a Turkish course today from Waterstones, with a book, four tapes and a Turkish/English dictionary. I can't wait to start learning Turkish. It sounds so exotic when you hear it spoken.'

'Well, with your previous knowledge of languages, it should be quite easy,' Anna said. 'I've never heard anyone speaking Turkish. What does it sound like?'

'It's a bit like Arabic – guttural but softer. Hard to describe really. Give me a couple of weeks and I'll speak to you in Turkish!' Kaye enthused.

'I can't believe you've met someone. Remember on New Year's Eve and you said that you felt that you were going to meet your Mr Right this year? Do you think he's the one?'

'Honestly, Anna, I've never felt like this before. Even though we couldn't really talk we managed to exchange so much information about each other and of course the body language was electric! I just wish Mum and Dad were a bit more supportive. They keep making comments like, 'You don't know him! How can you be in love with him?' and 'Kaye, pull yourself together, it's just a holiday romance. You'll never hear from him.' Don't they realise how hurtful they're being? Mum actually said that at my age my behaving like a love-sick teenager was embarrassing!''

'They'll come around,' Anna said soothingly.

'I hope so. I'm going to write to him tomorrow and send him some of the photos. I love the ones that Jan took of the two of us on our last night.'

'Well, I really hope you hear back from him but be prepared in case you don't. Long distance relationships are never easy'.

Kaye spent the following three weeks before the start of the new school year, poring over the Turkish grammar text book and listening to the first tape trying to get her tongue around the strange sounding Turkish vowels. She realised that learning a new language at forty was more difficult than learning at a younger age but, knowing that her relationship with Vedat would never progress without an effective means of communication, she was determined to tackle the new vocabulary and put her heart and soul into the task. She put Post-It notes on the fridge and bathroom mirror with lists of new vocabulary and every time she passed the lists practised saying the words out loud. She also bought a book about Muslim beliefs and had researched on the Internet about Kurds living in Turkey. She was alarmed to learn about the curfews that were in place in South East Turkey and the human rights' issues that affected the Kurds in that area. Vedat had told her a little about the PKK, the Kurdish Workers' Party and that most men walked around armed with pistols for protection. She found it hard to imagine the gentle, caring man she had fallen in love with carrying a gun. She carried a photograph of Vedat in her purse and had bought a new black picture frame to display her favourite photograph of them together. It now had pride of place on her coffee table. She wondered how long it would take her letter to reach Vedat and whether he would reply. Waiting for the post to arrive every day had become a torture.

After a busy first day at school, where she had done her best to settle an excited class of thirty Year One pupils back into school and introduce them to their new routines, Kaye arrived home to find a letter with a Turkish postmark lying on her doormat. With her heart pounding, she kicked off her shoes, threw her school bag down and grabbing the letter, sat on the bottom step of the stairs, tearing open the envelope to read it. She was surprised to find that the letter was in English and as she read discovered that Vedat had dictated what he wanted to say to a cousin who knew English. He thanked her for sending him the photos; he was pleased that she was learning Turkish and said that meeting her had changed his life. After he left Marmaris, he had gone to Adapazarı, where the earthquake had struck; to make sure his brother, who was studying there, was safe. His brother was unhurt but his house had been destroyed so Vedat had taken him back home to the family. Kaye was amazed that he had not mentioned to her at the time that his brother lived there. No wonder he had been so emotional!

As she read on, Kaye became breathless and she had to reread certain paragraphs to make sure she had read them properly. Vedat's language was very affectionate and he said he hoped they would meet in Marmaris the following April where they could make a decision about the future. At reading this, any doubts that she had been harbouring, disappeared in an instant. She now knew he felt the same way as she did and that this was not just a holiday fling. Bursting with joy, she ran into her lounge and picked up the phone. She hoped Anna would be home from work. After four rings it was answered and she shrieked,

'Guess what? I got a letter today!'

'From Vedat?'

'Yes! Oh Anna, it's such a sweet letter! He calls me 'my love' and wrote that we should meet in April to make a decision about the future! I'll read it to you.' Giggling as she read the stilted English, Kaye continued, 'Can you believe it? I'm so excited!'

'That's wonderful!' Anna responded.

'He said he's going to call me in a few weeks, when hopefully my Turkish will be good enough for us to talk.'

'How's the Turkish coming along?'

'The grammar is fairly straightforward but I'm finding the pronunciation very challenging. I have to keep saying the same word over and over again to make it sound like it does on the tape.'

'I'm sure you'll master it. It's a shame we don't know any Turks who you could practise speaking Turkish to.'

'I've almost had a panic attack at seeing his letter. Can you imagine the state I'll be in when he phones?'

'You won't be able to rely on body language then will you?' Anna teased. 'I'm so happy for you, Kaye. I was worried you might not hear from him. I'm glad you did.'

Kaye needed the positive encouragement from Anna, as many of her other friends had been very sceptical about her having a relationship with a Turkish Muslim, asking her how she would feel about wearing a headscarf and not drinking alcohol and had surprised her with their racist comments. She had replied that Vedat had no problem with her drinking and had in fact ordered vodka for her every night they were together. Maybe he would feel differently if they were married but that was something they would have to discuss in the future.

Vedat's next letter arrived after just three days – this time written in Turkish. It took Kaye two evenings of searching through her Turkish/English dictionary and grammar book to go through the two A4 pages of his small, neat handwriting to work out what it said. He said he wished he knew more English as he had so much he wanted to say to her but hoped that her Turkish would soon be good enough for them to communicate better. He hoped she knew someone who could help her translate his letter into English because his cousin had returned to Istanbul and he could only write in Turkish. He told her he was missing her, thought about her constantly and that waiting to meet her again in April would be unbearable as he was longing to kiss her. He said he kissed her photograph every day and told her he had been to a wedding. Many of his relatives were there but even amidst the crowded gathering he felt lonely and missed her. He repeated twice that the five days they spent together had been the best days of his life and he was so distracted by thoughts of her that he was unable to concentrate on anything else. It was as if he had been hypnotised. He went on to say that the weather was still very hot and that the repercussions of the earthquake were being felt economically, with trade almost at a standstill and the exchange rate being halved. He concluded by saying he would write every ten to fifteen days, he hoped her next letter would be in Turkish and that he loved her.

Kaye, too, found herself thinking of Vedat whenever her mind was not focussing on teaching, planning lessons or participating in staff discussions. She felt more confident and knew she held herself more upright. Strangely, she had been making even more effort than usual with her appearance, reflecting the sense of well-being she felt inside to the outside too. It was as if she wanted to look good for Vedat, even though he could not see her. She spent hours imagining what life with him would be like and was pleased that she had told him of her infertility so that not having children would not be an issue further down the line. He had asked her about the scars on her abdomen and she had explained they were from surgeries she had undergone to treat severe endometriosis. She had made it clear to him that if he wanted children, she was not the woman for him. She decided that to be certain he had understood, she would put it in writing in her first attempt at a letter to him in Turkish. There was no point in continuing their relationship if he wanted children.

In his next letter, Vedat said that he was delighted by her letter written in Turkish and said it was a shame that when he had called her they had been unable to understand what the other was saying. His letters were becoming increasingly longer and he said he was writing from the heart and as if he were talking to her. He spoke of his family and explained about them being very strict Muslims and how he had never had the freedom to take a girl to a café or restaurant. They were from very different worlds. He wrote that he had told his family all about her and his father was strongly against the relationship, saying he could choose from a myriad of local girls from good families and that, if Vedat continued with this affair, he would be disinherited. A foreigner and non-Muslim was not acceptable. Vedat had argued with his father and replied that he would choose who he wanted. He wanted Kaye's opinions about where she thought their relationship was going, what they had to do to be together and whether she really loved him. There was no mention of Kaye's infertility.

Kaye had been extremely frustrated that Vedat had not understood her Turkish on the phone. She had written down what to say and questions she wanted to ask and had practised saying the sentences out loud so she wouldn't stumble over them. He did not seem to understand even the most simple of her sentences, though she knew they were grammatically correct. Her pronunciation presented a real problem that she had no idea how to solve. She had understood some of what he had said but had to keep asking him to repeat himself and after several attempts to try to make her understand, he resorted to 'I love you', 'I miss you' and 'I kiss you' and the sound of kisses being blown onto the handset, which made Kaye's heart soar.

She felt so lucky to feel so loved. It was just a shame Vedat was so far away.

Chapter 6

Greenhill

December 1999

'He said what?' Anna screeched down the phone, disbelieving what she had just heard.

Amid sobs, Kaye explained, 'He says he has to end our relationship and doesn't want to hear from me again! I can't believe it.'

'What reason did he give?'

'Actually, I'm not sure. There are two letters and I'm in such a state that I haven't translated the second one yet. The first one took me hours but it began with, 'This is a letter of farewell', so that's fairly clear. He told me he would never forget me and something about him not ever having a job and everyone would tease him if his father disinherited him and he had to get a job. He couldn't sacrifice everything to be with me. He asked me to forgive him and wanted me to know that he hadn't played with my feelings – he really does love me.'

'It's better you know now though, isn't it? It would be worse to hear this months down the line when your feelings have intensified.'

'You're probably right, but I was so sure that this would work and I had found the man I wanted to be with for the rest of my life.'

'It's a good job it's a Saturday too and you don't have to go to work feeling so upset.'

'Yes, true. My eyes are like slits from crying and I feel so embarrassed. Everyone said it would never last and it seems they were right.'

'I'm so sorry but I'm also glad you're not going to be disappearing thousands of miles away. Where would I be without my Friday night drinking partner?'

Kaye sighed and could feel the tears welling up again so she hastily said she had to go and made arrangements to go to Anna's that evening for a girlie night in. She knew she could not face anyone else at the moment but Anna was used to seeing her without makeup and not looking her best.

She spent the rest of the day looking back over Vedat's letter to make sure she had translated it accurately and tackling the second letter, which, though shorter, gave more of an insight into how he was feeling. He wrote that he was from a feudal family and their reputation would be at stake if he married a foreigner. His philosophy on life was that everyone should live how they pleased but he lived in an environment where tradition and cultural considerations had to be obeyed. He emphasised that his decision was nothing to do with Kaye; he thought she was wonderful and hoped she would find happiness in the future.

A week later, Kaye was persuaded to wear something dressy and attend the staff Christmas party the Head teacher was holding at her converted barn nearby. As Kaye lived only a five minute drive from the party venue, five of her colleagues, including Anna, were staying the night at Kaye's home and coming for drinks prior to going out. They would leave their cars in her drive and take taxis to and from the party. Their Christmas parties were a time for serious drinking and no one would be in a fit state to drive home afterwards.

Kaye was adding the finishing touches to her makeup when she heard a car door slam. She looked out of her bedroom window and saw Simon, her close friend at school, striding down the drive. Running down the stairs, she shouted,

'Coming!'

'Hiya gorgeous!' Simon greeted her with a huge hug. 'You look fabulous!'

'Thanks. It's just a little something I found at the back of my wardrobe,' Kaye fibbed, having spent at fortune at Next the previous weekend. She felt the need to look good to boost her confidence and was determined to enjoy herself that night.

Amidst the buzz of chatter, the clinking of glasses and the soft strains of jazz in the background, the cavernous, yet cosy barn, decorated with antiques and carefully chosen textiles, gave Kaye a sense of well-being. She loved seeing other people's interior design ideas and happily pored over magazines for hours to gain inspiration. Wandering around this newly refurbished home, she noted the use of tweed, cashmere and velvet cushions and throws in muted shades of green and brown, which contrasted with the rich tan of the wooden floor and the rusty coloured leather settee. There were shelves full of an eclectic mix of books and beautiful Italian glassware in rich jewel colours, which sparkled in the ambient lighting. The room was bursting at the seams with the staff and their partners squeezed side by side along the long oak dining table. Kaye looked forward to these events, knowing that the food would be delicious and where she was able to chat with colleagues at leisure, rather than the snatched opportunities during breaks at school.

Despite the copious amount of alcohol consumed during the night, the Head's husband, knowing that Kaye had people staying overnight, insisted that she take some of the left-over bottles of wine and spirits home with her.

'Who wants what?' Simon asked back in Kaye's kitchen.

'Let's make a punch!' Anna suggested, she was famous for her mind-blowing concoctions and ran to the kitchen to make one.

'Cheers me dears!' she cried carrying a tray full of glasses containing a ruby red liquid. 'This'll put hairs on your chest!'

Music was soon pumping from the stereo system and Simon pulled Kaye up from where she was sitting on the floor and urged her to join in with his crazy dance moves. Rosie, the quietest of the group had chosen to be in charge of the music and sat surrounded by empty CD cases. She was unaware that she had spilled her drink in her lap and was sitting in a puddle of drink which was seeping a red stain into Kaye's carpet. It was not until Anna went to choose a new track that Rosie saw what she had done. She stood up and the puddle of wine that had collected in her diaphanous skirt dripped onto the carpet. Anna was mortified. She knew how house-proud Kaye was and apologised profusely. Handfuls of kitchen roll were brought and furious dabbing began but there was a huge red stain which would not budge.

'Don't worry,' Kaye said sincerely. 'My dad will be able to get it out'. She was far too drunk to care about anything and in the dim candle-lit room she could see nothing clearly. She felt very carefree and the alcohol had numbed the pain of her rejection, restoring her to her usual bubbly self.

The next morning, Kaye went downstairs to find Anna and two other colleagues making bacon sandwiches. 'Ugh! How can you bear the smell of food? I need water – gallons of it!'

'Did you sleep well?' Anna inquired, seeing the puffy bags under Kaye's eyes.

Kaye dragged Anna into the lounge as what she had to say was not something she wanted spread around the school staff room. 'Where did you end up sleeping?'

'I slept down here on your settee,' Anna replied. 'Why?'

'So you don't know who slept where upstairs?'

'No.'

'I had planned that Paul and Simon would sleep in the bunk beds in the second bedroom but it didn't happen.'

'What are you saying?' Anna knew Kaye was hinting at something.

'Well, just after you collapsed on the settee, I went upstairs to the toilet. Simon and Paul were on the landing talking and when Paul went into the bathroom, Simon grabbed my hand and pulled me into my bedroom. He kicked the door shut and we fell on my bed. I thought it was very funny and started laughing but he said he's been waiting to do this for years.'

'No way!'

'Really. Anyway, nothing happened. I don't want to ruin our friendship with drunken sex. We just cuddled and fell asleep.'

'I'm flabbergasted! I had no idea what was going on. I wonder whether he planned it?'

'I don't know but we've just had a chat and it's fine. Pretend you don't know.'

'Okay. Mum's the word.'

Kaye was making her way to inspect the stain on her carpet, when the phone rang. 'Who's ringing me at this time on a Sunday morning?' she picked up the receiver to hear a hissing sound on the line and then someone said,

'Hello!'

'Hello,' Kaye responded.

'Kaye?'

'Yes.'

'This is Vedat.'

'Oh my God! Vedat? How are you?'

'I'm fine, thanks.'

Kaye grasped the phone and tugged the cord to allow her to sit down on the settee. She wished she was more clear-headed and able to get her thoughts together. Anna returned to the kitchen to help Rosie with the breakfast to give Kaye some privacy.

'Good,' Kaye said. She really was at a loss what to say. She was far too hung over to think of anything to say in Turkish and her immediate thought was that she had just spent the night with another man. Had Vedat sensed something?

'I love you, Kaye'

'Oh, but you finished with me!'

'Sorry, speak slow. I don't understand.'

'Your letter made me very sad,' she said, hoping Vedat would make the connection.

'I miss you!'

Kaye was bewildered and words would not come.

'Kaye, are you there?'

'Yes, I'm here.'

'I made mistake. I want to see you again.'

'In April?'

'Yes.'

'Oh, now I'm happy!' Kaye burst into laughter.

'You happy, me happy.'

Simon chose that minute to enter the lounge and looked at her questioningly. Kaye quickly gestured for him to be quiet. Now that Vedat was back in her life, she did not want him to hear a male voice in the background and change his mind.

Having said goodbye, Kaye skipped to the kitchen to announce that everything was back on. She saw Simon's look of disappointment so hugged him and told him to be pleased for her. He smiled and helped himself to a cup of tea from the pot on the worktop and joined Rosie, who was now tucking into a bacon sandwich, at the dining room table. He treasured Kaye's friendship but even though he had no wish to spoil their friendship, harboured a secret desire to make their relationship something more.

'That's put the smile back on your face!' Anna commented, handing Kaye a cup of tea. 'What did he say?'

'Oh, just that he's missed me and had made a mistake,' Kaye summarised, not wanting to gush too much. 'Isn't it weird how he phoned this morning? It's as if he realised I was with someone else.'

'Yes, spooky!'

'I hardly know him but there is something special between us. I can feel it.'

'Well, you are very intuitive, so go with your feelings. Who knows where it will all lead?'

Kaye sighed and let herself drift away into an imaginary world where she and Vedat were married and living happily ever after.

Chapter 7

Karabulut,

October 1979

It was a sunny but chilly Saturday in autumn and the gang of boys had just finished a game of hide and seek, noisily running around the streets of the village to find each other. The boy was now bored of this game and gathered his band of friends together to decide what to do next. Some suggested they played football, which the boy did not particularly enjoy, so when one of them said, 'Let's go fishing for eels!' he readily agreed. One of the boys lived close by and said his father had fishing line and hooks and the boys set off for his house.

With everything they needed stuffed into their pockets, the gang made their way to the river, which ran along the edge of the fields near to where the boy lived. Carefully watching their footing to avoid treading on the cotton crop growing in the field, they took a short cut to the river. The boy could not resist picking a ball of fluffy cotton and pulled the silky strands apart, dispersing them into the breeze. The cotton would be harvested soon and the field was alive with soft, puffy orbs, blowing in the wind as though any minute they would take off to some far away planet. The boys found a place where they could slide down the sandy riverbank and stood on a flat piece of dirt at the edge of the water. They helped each other attach hooks onto the nylon line, while others searched for sticks to hold the line. They tossed the hooks into the water, taking turns to hold the sticks and crouched down to wait for a bite. After, reeling in the line many times to find the hooks either empty or having caught a limp piece of weed, some of the boys proclaimed boredom and ran off to play football. The boy was enjoying the stillness of the water and his attention was taken by the men on the other side of the river, who were inspecting their crops and preparing for the harvest. His three remaining friends had found some small stones and began to lob them into the water, competing on how far they could throw them. The boy chastised them and told them they were scaring the eels away, so with a shrug, the older of the boys said, 'Well, if you don't want us scaring away your eels we'd better go!' And off they ran.

The boy, now alone, also decided that this was a pointless exercise and reeling his line in, unravelled the line, detached the hook, threw the stick on the ground and pocketing the line and hook, walked back through the field. There was at least an hour before it began to get dark, so he took a longer route back home. He climbed onto higher ground and went to a rocky crag, where he often came to think. He was a sensitive soul, who thought about things deeply. He knew he had a privileged childhood and had none of the problems of poverty or harsh living conditions like most of his fellow classmates. Though he was an only child, he lived in a very busy household where there was a continuous flow of visitors, giving him little time on his own. This rocky hideaway had become a haven for him when he wanted to enjoy some privacy and solitude. His love of nature meant that he preferred to be outdoors rather than staying at home, watching the black and white television, a rare commodity in this area. His favourite programme was 'Tarzan' and he adored Cheetah, the chimpanzee, whose antics made him laugh, but it was only when the winter weather was too cold to go out that he chose to stay at home and watch television.

He sat on the edge of an outcrop of rock with his legs dangling and swung them to and fro, gaining momentum with every swing. He built up such a rocking motion that suddenly he lost his balance and nearly catapulted himself over the edge. He laughed and let his imagination run away with him. What if he could fly? What would it feel like? He envisioned himself with powerful, white eagle wings sailing high over the village and fields, above his home and waving to his mother as he flew overhead. He would try! He stood up and opening his coat took his arms out of the sleeves, making a cape. He flapped it behind him, seeing if it would billow out like wings. It did! He took a few steps back from the edge ran forward and leapt off. For a few seconds it felt like he was flying and he whooped with joy, before hitting the ground, twenty feet below, with a heavy thud. His eyes were closed and he dare not open them for fear of what he might see, but stayed still, trying to breathe. He was badly winded and the intense weight going through his back to his chest made it almost impossible to take a breath. Gradually, his breathing returned and he looked around to see where he was. He had just missed a pile of sharp, grey stones and had landed on a patch of heat-seared grass. He was aware of an increasing pain in his right arm and moved to release the pressure on it. He tentatively moved each leg and was mightily relieved that he there was no discomfort in either of them. He sat up and examined his arm. There was no blood and it seemed undamaged but hurt if he moved it. His coat flapped in the breeze as he stood and slowly staggered down the hillside towards home.

His mother looked at him in horror as he entered the house. His trousers were torn at one knee, his cheek was grazed and a trickle of blood ran down onto his chin and he appeared pale with shock. 'What on earth has happened to you?' she inquired, trying not to panic at the state of her son. She quickly led him to the kitchen and sat him down on a chair, where she bathed his face with warm water and a cloth.

The boy began to shake, not so much from fear at what his mother would say if he told the truth, but from delayed shock. He knew his mother would be furious at his attempt to fly and would probably give him a good slap for being so stupid. He would have to invent a story that would gain her sympathy. 'We were playing hide and seek up the hill and I was running and tripped over a large rock,' he said. He made no mention of the long fall or the injury to his right arm, which was now throbbing badly.

Later, he sat through supper and a game of chess with his father, trying his best to give no indication of the pain in his arm. His mother noticed that he moved his arm awkwardly but he shrugged and told her it must be bruised from when he fell.

It was the next morning, following a sleepless night, when he was unable to get himself dressed as his wrist, hand and fingers were severely swollen that he had to tell is mother that he thought his arm was broken.

Chapter 8

Greenhill

April 2000

In the middle of January, following a few weeks without letters as Vedat was fasting for Ramadan, Kaye had received a letter from him saying that he would have to postpone their meeting in April. He had commitments that meant he would be in important negotiations, helping to set up a new political party, during April and May but promised that they could meet in either July or August.

Kaye had been furious. She knew that Vedat was heavily involved in politics and he had said that this was the reason he had never married, but she had been counting down the weeks until they would be together again and she was gutted. She wrote a letter to him in English so that she could vent her feelings. Let him make the effort to translate it! She told him that if this relationship was going to work he needed to put effort into it and at the moment she felt she was no more than a pen friend. She said that to wait another six months to see him was intolerable and the emotional strain of waiting to see what would happen was affecting everything she did. She questioned why he had restarted their relationship, if he was unable to give up his life there, as he had also stated in the letter. She said that they would both have to make sacrifices to have a life together and if he was not willing to do this, how could it ever succeed? She decided she had nothing to lose at this point and said in her opinion he was afraid of commitment and was obviously easily influenced by what other people said. If he knew in his heart that this relationship was right, he should show maturity and strength of character and try to make it work. She realised that he might react badly to what he had written but sent it anyway.

Vedat rejected her criticism and replied that he was worried about loving such a strong woman. He had understood that she was very upset but he, too, was disappointed not to be meeting her in April. He wrote that she was judging him unfairly and continued to tell her at length about life in his environment. However, the grammar was far too complex for Kaye to understand most of it. She gathered that life for her there would be almost impossible and the community would reject her. She would have to be extremely strong to withstand the abuse and treatment she would receive. He urged her to trust him and look to the future with hope and, whatever happened, they would meet in the summer. He was free for the whole month of August and knew she would be on holiday from school then. He explained that if he booked the hotel room, they would have separate rooms but if she, as a foreigner, made the reservation, they would be able to share the same room. Initially, Kaye had wondered whether this was a ploy so that she would have to pay for the room, but then remembered that while she had been in Vedat's room, there had been calls from the police to check who he was and the Manager of the hotel had quietly told Vedat that if Kaye was caught in his room, he could be arrested.

Kaye had made the reservation at the same hotel where they had met and had booked her flights. They would have four weeks together and she was counting the weeks. Her Turkish was improving and their phone calls were easier now that she could understand more of what he was saying. Vedat's letters were full of how he yearned to hold her in his arms, stroke her hair and kiss her and she was now becoming familiar with his terms of affection – no longer needing to look up every word in the dictionary.

In his last letter, Vedat had written that receiving letters from her gave him great happiness and he jumped for joy like an excited child when Kaye's letters arrived. He said he had become a different person and thanked her for the excitement, pleasure and delight she had brought to his life. He was impatient to see her as they needed to talk about so many things so that he could take steps to be with her forever. He said that he hoped his family would come around and accept Kaye, but, if they did not, he would remain single for the rest of his life. He went on to tell her in detail about how much land he had and how much of each crop he grew. It was interesting to Kaye but she was unfamiliar with the metric measurements he used and could not gauge how big a *dekar* was, although selling three hundred and fifty tonnes of cotton each year seemed an awful lot. He was obviously not the poor farmer she had originally presumed.

His letters this month had been considerably shorter, due to him spending much of the time in Ankara attending various meetings. He apologised for not having time to translate her letters and asked if she could write completely in Turkish from now on. Up until then,

Kaye had begun her letters in Turkish, using the language that Vedat used as a guide, but changing the pronouns and person. However, when it came to asking questions and new topics of conversation she was forced to write in English as her grammar as still at an elementary level. She could look up new vocabulary but complicated verb tenses and phrases were beyond her. She was eager to comment on the religious beliefs he had expressed in great detail and it was so easy to turn a verb unknowingly into a negative, with the addition of a 'mi' in the middle of the verb, that she did not want to run the risk of offending him or writing the opposite of what she felt. Vedat had been very concerned that she described herself as an atheist and, while he had no intention of forcing his religious beliefs on her, he asked her to think seriously about adopting a religion. In his opinion, not having one meant that she had no one looking after her. It was also an alien concept for him that she was a woman living alone. Women in his culture were taken care of by their families, even if single or widowed and it was a matter of family shame to allow a woman to live alone. He had been puzzled why she did not live with her parents, especially now that her father's health had deteriorated.

Kaye had been on playground duty, wandering around talking to the children and keeping an eye on a group of boys whose game of 'Tick' was in danger of becoming aggressive, when she noticed a colleague coming towards her.

'Kaye, there's a phone call for you in the office. I'll stay here while you go and deal with it.'

'Thanks. Who is it?'

'I think it's your Mum.'

Kaye had never had a call from her mother while she had been at work, so with a rising sense of panic she gained pace and headed inside to the school office.

'Hello, Mum. Everything alright?'

'No, love,' Nora's voice shook. 'I'm afraid your Dad's had a heart attack. I'm calling from the hospital. It's all been such a shock!'

'Is he okay? What happened?' Kaye said, trying to stay calm.

'He was up a ladder fixing someone's roof, when he felt breathless and his arm went numb. It's a good job he came down the ladder but instead of telling someone he felt unwell, he drove home! He even insisted on driving to the hospital. Can you believe it? The daft sod was having a heart attack and didn't know it!'

'So is he in intensive care?'

'Yes, he's in ICU with wires coming from everywhere. He's not unconscious but looks terribly pale and shaken.'

'Shall I come, Mum?'

'I don't know, love.'

'I'm coming. I'll just sort out cover for my class and then I'll come straight over.' Kaye was used to taking control in family matters.

'Drive carefully, then. You know your Dad – he's as strong as an ox. He'll be fine. He works too hard and is getting too old to do all these heavy jobs. I've told him time and time again but he's so bloody stubborn!'

'I know. This is probably a warning for him to slow down a bit. How are you?'

'I'm just a bit shaken. I'm going to get a cup of tea from the machine before I go back to your Dad. I'll call Jan and Donna too to let them know what's happened.'

'I'll do that for you. You look after yourself and get back to Dad. I'm going now and I'll be there in about an hour.'

Kaye's father, Frank, made a good recovery but the shock of the heart attack had been a severe blow to his morale. Heart disease ran in the men's side of his family and at sixty-six years of age he was nearing the age when most of his male ancestors had died. When the doctors firmly told him he should retire and take it easy from then on, Frank responded, 'I'll give up smoking and watch my diet. I can take on lighter jobs too as I'm self-employed, but if you think I'm going to stay at home with Nora all day, think on. I'd either die of boredom or be nagged to death!'

Chapter 9

Marmaris

August 2000

The lights from the harbour flashed by as the coach entered the holiday resort of Marmaris. Music pumped from the many bars along the main street and, despite the late hour, the streets were still buzzing with drunken tourists falling out of nightclubs and teenage girls wobbling on too high stilettos, making their way back to their hotels and apartments. Kaye tried hard to contain her excitement and the increasing nervousness she had felt since landing at Dalaman airport. Anxious thoughts filled her head: What if he didn't find her attractive when he saw her again? What if his feelings had changed? What if he didn't show up? Their letters, recently, had been full of anticipation and she hoped that after such a big build up, their reunion would not be a disappointment. She sat up straighter in her seat and gave herself a mental prompt to think positive. Vedat was probably sitting in the hotel foyer waiting for her with exactly the same thoughts running through his head.

It was nearly four o' clock in the morning when she finally reached the hotel and while the hotel staff greeted their guests and unloaded the luggage and took it inside, she looked around to see if she could see Vedat. There was no sign of him. The hotel was very quiet, with only the newly arrived guests queuing at the reception desk, handing in their passports and being handed their room keys. After completing the formalities, she asked the receptionist if her friend had arrived and was told he was in their room. With mounting trepidation she followed the porter as he led the way upstairs to her room. He knocked but there was no response, so using his master key, let her into the room. It was pitch black inside, so Kaye felt her way past the bathroom and around the bed, unable to believe that Vedat was asleep. The air conditioning was on full blast and Kaye shivered at the air change from the warm humid air of the hotel to the chilly temperature of the room. She shook Vedat gently, whispering his name and with a snort he opened his eyes and sat up, looking very groggy.

'Kaye! Welcome!'

'Hi! I can't believe you were sleeping.'

'Sorry, I was very tired from the long journey. Did you have a good flight?'

'Yes, thanks. Oooh, I can't believe we're here!' Kaye shrieked, flinging her arms around Vedat's neck and kissing him. They engaged in a passionate kiss and Vedat pulled her onto the bed. He embraced her tightly and Kaye snuggled into his body, relishing the comfort of being with him and feeling his warm breath on her cheek. There was no need for words as they made love with feverish intensity, shedding the months of longing and waiting in rapturous abandon.

Kaye felt tired but was far too keyed up to sleep. Having taking a shower, which Kaye had learnt was an important Muslim ritual after sex, they sat on their tiny balcony sharing a cigarette, watching the sun rise and not able to stop touching each other. Kaye, still uneasy speaking Turkish, was forced to express herself in the foreign tongue but Vedat did his best to understand her attempts and prompted her frequently with vocabulary and finished her sentences when he sensed she was struggling for the right verb ending.

When Vedat went back into the room, Kaye presumed he had gone for another cigarette but he came back holding something in his hand. Opening his palm, he presented her with a very ornate gold ring, with a deep blue central sapphire surrounded by small diamonds.

'This is for you,' he said, smiling.

'Oh, Vedat! It's beautiful. Thank you!'

'It's a traditional design from my area. I hope you like it.'

''I love it!' unsure which finger to try it on. 'Shall I put it on this finger?' Kaye asked, gesturing to the ring finger on her left hand.

'As you wish. It's for friendship and my love for you'

Kaye's heart sank a little as she had momentarily thought it might be an engagement ring, but she put the ring on the ring finger of her right hand and was amazed that it fitted perfectly. 'How did you know the right size?'

'I just imagined your fingers and hoped it would fit,' Vedat replied proudly.

Kaye felt her heart would burst with happiness as she admired the ring sparkling in the early morning sunshine. All of the waiting and frustration of the past year seemed a distant memory – for the moment at least.

After unpacking her suitcase and showing Vedat all of the new clothes she had bought especially for the holiday, they decided to go down early for breakfast. Vedat had smiled politely as she paraded each item of clothing but showed no enthusiasm for any of them. Kaye was too animated to pay attention to his apathetic response but was surprised to see no evidence of Vedat's clothes as she hung hers in the wardrobe. She presumed he had not had time to unpack yet. When she asked he shrugged his shoulders and, taking her hand, led her to the door.

They helped themselves to a traditional Turkish breakfast of cheese, boiled eggs, black olives, tomatoes, cucumber, fresh bread, butter, runny pine honey and sour cherry jam, together with cups of tea, and sat down at an empty table. Kaye noticed that Vedat's face had changed from the earlier euphoric glow to a troubled, uncomfortable expression. Her first thought was that his feelings for her had changed and he had realised on seeing her again that the imaginary Kaye he had conjured in his mind during the past year, was a very different one in reality.

'What's wrong?' she asked tentatively.

'I've got something to tell you.' Vedat began taking a deep breath.

Kaye's heart was pounding as she waited for him to continue.

'Yesterday, as I was packing my bag in my bedroom, my father came to talk to me. He begged me not to come and said that if I came I could not return – he would disown me. We argued fiercely, yelling at each other, both standing up for what we considered to be right. I told him that I love you and that I want to be with you, but he just laughed and said I was being ridiculous and asked how I could throw away my life for a woman. I was so angry I just left with only my identity card, my wallet and my flight tickets and drove to the airport.'

'That's why there were no clothes in the wardrobe!' Kaye interrupted.

'Yes. I arrived here late in the afternoon and sat down in the hotel foyer to wait for you. At eleven o'clock last night I received a phone call from my mother, sobbing uncontrollably, saying my father had suffered a massive brain haemorrhage after I left and was being flown to Ankara for treatment.'

'Oh no! How awful!'

'I have to go, Kaye.'

'You mean to Ankara to see your father?'

'Yes. It's my fault. He might die because of me.'

'It's not your fault,' Kaye said indignantly. 'It's just terrible timing.'

'While I was waiting for you I booked a flight and I have to leave in an hour.'

'What? But I've only just got here! How long will you be gone?'

'I don't know. Maybe I won't come back. If my father dies I can't come back. You should go home too. You shouldn't be here on your own.'

'I'm not going home! Kaye shouted, as her mind raced with the horror of the situation. I've paid a lot of money to come here for a month. I can't go home! What will everyone think?'

'Well, it's your decision, but I don't feel comfortable about leaving you here on your own. Please go home,' Vedat pleaded.

'No! I'm staying for at least a week to see how it goes. I'll be fine on my own,' she said, sounding more confident than she felt. 'You might be able to come back in a few days if your father responds to the treatment.'

Their appetites gone, they left their food and returned to their room. In the lift, Kaye's could not control her tears and back in the room, flung herself onto the bed and sobbed. Vedat, too, was near to tears and lay down next to her, stroking her hair and wiping away her tears with his thumb.

'I'm very sorry, Kaye. I don't know what to say.'

Kaye was too emotional to think in Turkish and let forth a torrent of English, expressing her frustration at the situation. She did not care whether he understood or not. She just needed to vent her anger and disappointment.

'What have I ever done to deserve this? I've looked for forty years to find someone like you, waited a whole year to see you and now, after a couple of hours together, you're leaving me on my own in a foreign country for four bloody weeks!'

From the embarrassed look on Vedat's face, she knew she was wrong to blame him but at the absence of anyone else, she could not help herself. He watched her raging and waited for her to calm down, before hugging her and trying his best to make her feel better. He never wore a watch but knew that he would have to leave soon. He turned Kaye's wrist over to look at her watch and with a sigh, got up from the bed. 'I must go,' he whispered, his voice breaking with sadness. They embraced each other tightly, not wanting to let go of each other, but eventually he released her and picking up his wallet, making sure his identity card and ticket were in his shirt pocket, headed for the door. He opened it, looked back at Kaye, still sitting on the bed with tears trickling down her face, black smudges ringing her eyes and her nose running and went back to her. She knew it was pointless to try to make him stay. She knew he had to go, but welcomed his arms as he held her again. She hoped that he would miss his flight and have to come back, but then thought how dreadful it would be if his father died before he arrived. She would have to be strong and let him go.

On his second attempt, Vedat made it out of the door and halfway down the corridor, before turning back and taking her in his arms again. Kaye almost laughed at the farcical state of affairs but was eager to savour every available second with Vedat. When he realised he would have to hurry to catch the flight, he successfully made it out of the hotel and glancing back, saw Kaye waving to him from their balcony. His heart ached with desire for her but he was used to putting duty before pleasure and signalling to a taxi driver, got into the car and was driven away.

Kaye stayed on the balcony, looking out to sea, wondering how she was going to manage on her own. The disappointment she felt was crushing down on her chest and she fought to control her breathing. The closest thing she had experienced to this was when she woke up on her eighteenth birthday, sure that her parents had bought her a car, only to find, as she eagerly opened the small box expecting to find the car keys, a silver bracelet lying on a bed of cotton wool. But what she was feeling now was a lot worse, much worse. She wondered whether she was strong enough to cope. She desperately wanted to talk to someone but knew that with the two hour time difference it was too early to call anyone back home. She found her cigarettes and sat chain smoking, letting the racking sobs come, not caring whether anyone heard her. The sight of Vedat in the taxi, disappearing into the distance would remain etched in her memory forever. She felt sorry for herself but felt even sorrier for him. Not only did he have to face a difficult meeting with his family, but was fighting inner demons with the guilt he felt for having caused his father's collapse.

Two hours later, after taking some Rescue Remedy, which she always carried with her and doing a few calming techniques, she tried to call Anna but there was no reply. She called Ellen another close friend, and Kerry, her cousin, but had no luck getting through to them either. By this time, even though she had not wanted to call her mother, she felt she would have a complete panic attack if she did not talk to someone.

'Hi, Mum, it's me,' Kaye said, trying not to cry.

'What's the matter?' Nora could tell immediately something was wrong. 'Didn't he show up?'

'He came, but had to leave,' amid sobs, Kaye explained what had happened.

'You must come home. You can't stay there on your own. Go and see the tour rep and explain the circumstances. I'm sure they'll be able to change your return flight.'

'I don't want to come home!' Kaye screamed, losing control. 'I want to be here in case he comes back.'

'He might not come back. What will you do for four weeks on your own? How do you know he's telling the truth? This might be just a story he's invented. You don't know him, Kaye. He could be married with kids and spinning you a whole load of lies.'

'Oh, I should have known there would be no sympathy from you. You've been against this relationship from the very beginning. I'm really upset and just wanted some comfort but I should have known better than to phone you. You're always so quick to judge and jump to negative conclusions!'

In the earpiece, Kaye could hear Nora relaying the story to Frank and she took the opportunity to blow her nose. The tissue was sodden and disintegrated in her hand. She leant back over the bed to reach into her bag for another.

'Your Dad says you should come home,' Nora announced, 'and that you should find someone to help you there.'

'Okay, I'll talk to the tour rep and see what she says. I'll call you later to tell you what I'm going to do.'

Kaye put the phone down and went to the bathroom to wash her face. She knew she must look awful, but was unprepared for the sight that met her when she looked in the mirror. Her eyes were puffy and red, her face was blotchy and a few black smudges of mascara under her eyes were the only trace of the makeup she had applied so carefully at the airport, what seemed like days ago.

In the hotel foyer, people were clustered in groups, listening to information on the area and local customs and deciding which trips to book with various holiday reps. Kaye looked around and was relieved to see only one couple talking to the rep from the company she had booked her flights with. She waited until they had concluded their business and approached the friendly-looking rep, who she saw from the name badge on her T-shirt, was called Sandy. She tried not to cry as she described her predicament, but when the rep told her not to worry and was very sympathetic, Kaye's tears flowed again. Sandy could not guarantee that Kaye would be able to change her ticket but would talk to her supervisor later in the day. She told Kaye that she was married to a Turk from the South East of Turkey and that the culture there was very different. Her husband's family had not approved of her either initially, not attending her wedding and refusing to speak to her, but after she had given birth to her eldest son, they had acquiesced and now accepted her. She felt genuine sorrow for Kaye and said that she was at the hotel every morning and if Kaye needed to talk to her at any other time, the receptionist knew how to reach her. She reached out and gave Kaye a hug, before she left to visit another hotel.

Chapter 10

'Slow down, take a deep breath and start again from the beginning,' Anna said in her best teacher voice, as though calming an hysterical child.

Kaye, again sobbing, explained to her friend what had happened since her arrival in Turkey.

'Poor man. Have you heard from him since he left?'

'No. Today has been the longest day of my life. I was so happy when I saw him and since he went I've not known what to do with myself. I couldn't face going to the beach so I've just stayed in the room all day.'

'Well, as long as you're there, you might as well get a tan. Tomorrow, get your swimming cossie on, slap on your sunscreen and enjoy being in the sun. I'd offer to come out there to be with you, but I've got a hospital appointment next week.'

'That's sweet of you, thanks. I know you'd come if you could. Oh, I never dreamed I'd be here on my own,' Kaye broke down yet again.

'When will you know if you can change your ticket?'

'Tomorrow, I think, but honestly I will feel so embarrassed coming home.'

'Don't be silly! When have you cared about what anyone thinks? It's not your fault his Dad had a stroke. Just take it day by day and see what happens.'

Kaye woke up early the next morning to the sun streaming through the thin muslin curtains. Her stomach gurgled with hunger and she realised that she had not eaten since the few mouthfuls of food at yesterday's breakfast. She decided to take a shower, put on a sleeveless sundress and her flip flops, grabbed her handbag and went to the dining room.

Kaye had always felt sorry for women dining alone and now had joined their ranks. One of the waiters, who she remembered from the previous year, came over to talk to her. He was surprised to see her sitting alone so Kaye quickly filled him in on events, trying hard to stem the threatening tears from running down her cheeks. He was very sympathetic and told her to be brave. He was sure Vedat would return soon.

After managing to eat a few rounds of toast with some sickly strawberry jam, Kaye headed for the hotel reception, where she saw that Sandy was organising a group of tourists setting out on a day trip to the mud baths in Dalyan.

'I'm sorry, Kaye, but if you want to change your ticket you'll have to pay for a new one,' Sandy explained later.

'I see.'

'What do you want to do?'

'I don't really want to spend any more money, so I'll stay, at least for another week. Maybe by then Vedat will be back.'

'I hope so. I've got a few hours free tomorrow afternoon, shall we meet for coffee? Sandy offered.

'That would be lovely. Thanks.'

Kaye appreciated Sandy's kindness and was grateful that she had something to look forward to. A day of loneliness and misery stretched ahead of her, so taking Anna's advice she prepared to go to the beach. She sat under a thatched umbrella, watching the antics of a Turkish family who were trying to master a surfboard. Unable to concentrate on her book, she was grateful for the distraction.

That night, after dining alone and returning to her room, rather than sit in the bar looking like a sad spinster, and attracting the stares of other holiday makers, Kaye resumed reading the bestseller that she had eventually begun on the beach. She was an avid reader and feeling a little calmer, was able to immerse herself in the light-hearted tale of unrequited love. She jumped when the telephone next to the bed started to ring.

'Hello,' she said, picking up the receiver.

'Hello. It's Vedat.'

'Vedat! Are you OK?'

Proceeding in Turkish, he continued, 'My father is very ill. He needs surgery to unblock an artery in his neck but because of his previous bypass operation, they don't want to take the risk.'

Kaye frantically searched the Turkish/English dictionary to find the medical terms so that she understood.

'He's totally paralysed and can't speak. He can't even eat. The doctors say he has nine or ten weeks to live. My family hate me and I feel so guilty.'

Kaye could hear him crying as he spoke and her heart ached for him. She tried to comfort him but he was inconsolable. She knew it was insensitive to ask but she needed to know,

'Are you coming back?'

'I can't leave my father. Please Kaye, go home.'

Kaye told him about her meeting with Sandy and reassured him that she would be fine. She did not want to add to his troubles, even though the thought of endless days alone, frightened her.

'Remember my cousin, Mehmet? Well, he and Carol have a new restaurant in Marmaris. The waiters at the hotel will tell you the name. Go and find them and they will look after you. I'll phone Mehmet and tell him to expect you.'

Kaye agreed that she would and felt relief that at least there was someone she knew there.

She had booked only for bed and breakfast at the hotel. Vedat had suggested this so that they would have the freedom to choose where to eat each evening. He said he would pay for all their expenses while they were there if Kaye paid for the room. Kaye had happily agreed but this meant that she had not brought much spending money with her. She would have to be careful with her money, in case Vedat was unable to return and she had to buy food for her remaining weeks.

That night she gave the name of Mehmet's restaurant to a taxi driver and her spirits lifted as Mehmet and Carol welcomed her with open arms. She cried again as she filled them in on the details and was relieved when Mehmet said she must not be on her own and must come to the restaurant whenever she liked. He insisted she try the house special and she tucked into the tasty food, cleaning the plate. Carol was now pregnant and Mehmet made sure she did not overtire herself so, despite the restaurant being full to capacity, Carol frequently was urged to sit down and rest. She did her best to distract Kaye, by telling her funny stories and introducing her to some of their regular customers – British and German expats who spent their summers in homes they had bought in the resort. Kaye was surprised to find herself laughing as one of the Germans told of his problems trying to get his car through Turkish customs and on reflection, later in her room, she acknowledged that in spite of her underlying desolation, she had enjoyed the night.

Over the course of the next week, Nora, Anna, Ellen, a close teaching colleague and Kerry, Kaye's cousin, had called her regularly to see that she was surviving her ordeal. She had also met Sandy for coffee as planned. They were all heartened to hear that Kaye had settled into a routine of going down to breakfast, spending the morning on the beach, buying a sandwich from the small corner shop opposite the hotel for lunch, returning to her room to read and doze while the sun was at its hottest. She had not been sleeping well at night and in the early hours of the morning had regularly woken up in a sweat, heart pounding as she remembered terrifying dreams of being kidnapped by Vedat's family, being locked in a small cell, being cruelly treated, abuse being hurled at her, trying to escape and running away only to be recaptured. She then lay awake, not daring to sleep for fear of the recurring dream, therefore needed her afternoon siestas to catch up on her sleep. Sometimes, in the cooler late afternoons, she went for a stroll along the promenade and, after being alone for most of the day, looked forward to the company at Mehmet's restaurant, where she spent her evenings.

Her mood was one of resignation and she looked forward to Vedat's occasional calls to update her on his father's condition. She was elated when he said he was hoping to come back to her the following Friday, a week later. Her flagging spirits were further buoyed when Carol said that her three month tourist visa was about to expire and said she had to leave Turkish soil and renew her visa upon re-entry into the country. She was planning to go to Rhodes for the day in three days' time and invited Kaye to accompany her.

The trip provided a welcome break to Kaye's routine and she had enjoyed walking around Rhodes' old town, despite the incredible heat. Carol had successfully acquired another three month visa, with the help of a policeman friend of Mehmet's who frequented their restaurant.

The following day Kaye woke up with a pounding headache. On her way to the bathroom she felt faint and then threw up in the toilet. Her legs felt too weak to hold her weight and she lay down on her bed wondering why she felt so ill. She mentally ran through all the possibilities – she couldn't be pregnant, she had not drunk sufficient vodka the previous evening to warrant a hangover and if it was food poisoning it would have struck last night. Thinking back over the previous day, she remembered the long walk from the ferry port to Rhodes' old town in the baking heat, with no shade, and not wearing anything on her head. She had slathered sunscreen over any exposed skin, but had been aware of the sun beating down on her scalp – her fine hair giving little protection from the searing rays. She thought it likely that she was suffering from sunstroke and spent the day in bed, making sure to drink plenty of water to avoid becoming dehydrated.

Vedat did not return that week. He called to say that his father was scheduled to have an angiogram some time the following week. If the operation was successful, he would be able to leave, to spend Kaye's last week with her. He apologised for not calling, but said he got so upset while talking to her that he wanted to die. Kaye was worried by his words. He kept repeating that he wanted to leave this world and was overcome by his emotions, sobbing down the phone. Kaye, too, could not hold back the tears, but felt helpless to find the right words or comfort him. Knowing that he was deeply religious, and that according to Muslim belief, suicide was a mortal sin, she quelled the anxiety she felt inside and hoped he would be strong enough to conquer his feelings of despair. He was obviously exhausted, spending most of each day at his father's bedside. He told Kaye how much he loved her,

'You are the only woman for me, Kaye and I'll never forget you as long as I live.'

'That sounds like a goodbye speech,' Kaye said, keeping her voice light.

'No, it's not. I told you in my last two letters, I'm not free – everybody wants a piece of me. It's not the same for you…'

'Will you ever be free?' Kaye interrupted.

'I don't know. I love you – don't forget that.'

'I love you too,' she replied and after a protracted farewell, she hung up.

Kaye had exhausted her supply of reading material. She had quickly finished the few books and magazines she had brought with her. The hotel had a minimal supply of novels left by departing guests and she had read any that appealed to her last week. Two girls from Manchester who she had befriended on the beach were going to give her their books before they left. She hoped they would be at the beach tomorrow as she found it hard to sleep without her regular reading habit to switch off her brain and relax at the end of the day. Without a book to immerse herself in, Kaye lay in bed, going over her conversation with Vedat. She hoped he would come next week as she had cashed the last of her travellers' cheques and would soon run out of money.

Chapter 11

Kaye was woken early the next Friday morning by a sharp knocking on the door. She rolled out of bed and, bleary-eyed, went to open the door. She woke up quickly as she saw Vedat standing before her looking very weary.

'Oh my God! You look awful,' she gasped, seeing his bloodshot eyes and ashen pallor.

Vedat all but collapsed in her arms and she supported him until they reached the bed where he could lie down. Kaye lay beside him, stroking his hair and wrapping her arms around him. Words were unnecessary as the weeks of loneliness and sadness melted away and were replaced by physical closeness and relief at being reunited. He slept for most of the day but Kaye was too happy that he was there to care about wasting the day. She had ordered breakfast from room service and had ended up finishing most of it herself, as Vedat picked at the food, too fatigued to eat. Inquiring about the health of Vedat's father, she learned that his condition had slightly improved and he was not in immediate danger. It would take many months before they would know how badly damaged his brain was and whether he would make a full recovery or not. Vedat's family had seen how deeply he had taken his father's sudden collapse and had understood when he told them he needed a break for a few days. Kaye wondered if they guessed he was with her.

Feeling refreshed, Vedat woke up in the late afternoon took a shower and suggested they go for a walk. He had been cooped up in the hospital for three weeks and was eager to get some fresh sea air. They dressed and, hand-in-hand, left the hotel to walk along the long promenade, heading towards the town centre. Although she was relieved and happy he was back, Kaye sensed that Vedat was unwilling to talk about his father, so she kept the conversation light as she told him how she had been filling her days. Her heart leapt as Vedat took the hand she was holding and bringing it to his lips, kissed it. She looked into his eyes and saw such tenderness that for a moment, she was lost. She threw her arms around his neck to hug him, ignoring his embarrassment at such public display of affection. They giggled and almost tripping over each other's feet, resumed walking hand in hand.

They chose to eat at a typical Turkish restaurant as Vedat was not adventurous in his choice of food and Kaye was happy to try new dishes. Kaye had suggested they go to Mehmet's, but Vedat said he wanted only to be with her. He was eager to make amends for the time she had spent alone and wanted to recapture the magic of their time together the previous year. When he suggested they should go on a boat trip the next day, Kaye readily agreed.

Having successfully negotiated with one of the many boat companies, Vedat led Kaye to the boat that was to be theirs for the day. The captain was an elderly man, who, knowing that his tip from a couple would be considerably less than that from a full boat of tourists, welcomed them aboard with a dissatisfied smile. Vedat sensed his frustration and engaged him in friendly banter as they cruised away from the shore, gradually charming the old man and being rewarded with a toothless grin. The gentle rocking motion of the boat soon lulled the two lovers into a deeply relaxed state and they forgot about the trauma of the preceding weeks. Being together was the best feeling in the world.

It was not until the end of the afternoon that the tide turned, when Vedat began to ask Kaye questions.

'Do you still want to be with me?'

'Of course!'

'Do you want me to come to England?'

'For a holiday, you mean?'

'No, to live with you.'

'I want to live with you but I'm not sure you would like life in England.'

'How do you know?'

'Well, what would you do for a job? Could you be a farmer in England?'

'No.'

'I earn enough money for both of us, but what would you do all day while I'm at work?'

'I could never take money from you. It's not right.'

'Vedat, if you came to England, you would end up either being a taxi driver or a waiter in a restaurant. Could you do that? Your English is not good enough for you to do anything else.'

'You don't want me to come to England!' Vedat exploded.

'Calm down! I never said that. It's just that I know how hard it would be for you there.'

'No. You don't want me to come to England.'

'Vedat, it's not that. I'm trying to be practical. Foreigners think that life in England is some rose-tinted paradise, where life is easy and money grows on trees. It's not like that. People work hard and getting a good job is difficult for foreigners.'

'Would you come to Turkey, then?'

'I wouldn't mind, but would your family accept me?'

'I don't know. Could you live in my community where women are covered and stay at home all day? It would be very lonely for you.'

'I could be the one who brings the women into the twenty-first century and shows them a bit of freedom!' Kaye giggled.

'You would ruin my reputation.' Vedat snapped.

'But you like the fact that I am different from all the women you know!'

'Yes, but that's here. No one knows me here. Where I live everyone knows me and they would tease me if you didn't behave appropriately.'

'Could we spend half the year in England and half in Turkey? Would that work?'

'No. If I leave Turkey I would never be able to come back. I would have to wipe away my whole life, my career, and my goals for the future – everything - which would be very difficult.'

'So what's the solution? I'm not giving up on this relationship without a fight. We have to find a way to be together.'

So, reaching stalemate, the glorious mood of the morning, turned sombre and they both sat, not speaking, wrestling with their thoughts, for the rest of the trip. Later that night the topic was raised again and they had their first row, ending with Kaye in tears in the bathroom and Vedat sitting on the balcony wondering if life could get any worse.

Kaye woke up the next morning to feel the warmth of Vedat's body against her back. He sensed that she was awake and hugged her to him, wrapping his arms tightly around her and nuzzling her neck. She turned to face him and her heart melted at the sight of his sleepy smile. They kissed and began stroking each other, frantic for the closeness of their bodies and to become one. They made love for hours until Vedat's stomach rumbled and he said he felt light-headed from hunger. Having missed breakfast at the hotel, they walked along the promenade to find a suitable café where they could eat breakfast. Neither of them mentioned the argument from the previous night and although Kaye was eager to pursue the topic of their future, she was unwilling to spoil the mood and bring it up. They still had several days left for serious talking.

They spent the rest of the day on the beach, enjoying swimming together in the warm salty water, testing each other's strength with underwater breath-holding, diving under the waves and swimming races. They returned to their room to shower and get dressed before heading to Mehmet's restaurant.

Vedat was treated like royalty and the waiters gave him special attention. After filling Mehmet and Carol in on his father's condition, everyone tried to distract him from the sad state of affairs and he soon relaxed, laughing at jokes and anecdotes, complementing the chef on the excellent food and much to Kaye's delight, agreeing to go to a karaoke bar with Mehmet and Carol, when all their customers left.

Karaoke was a new experience for Vedat. He refused to sing but laughed out loud at the amateur singers, as they sang their hearts out, often badly out of tune and not caring that they were making fools of themselves. Kaye loved seeing Vedat so happy and hearing his deep bass laugh as he slapped his knee with glee and rocked with mirth. He insisted that watching was far more fun than singing could ever be and even when the song was in English and he could not understand a word, the antics of the singers and their terrible singing kept him amused for hours.

Many of the waiters and staff at the cafes and restaurants were Kurdish, who came from the south east of Turkey to work in the season, from April to October. The staff at the karaoke bar was from the same area as Vedat so he proudly introduced Kaye to them and caught up on recent events and their family news. It was interesting for Kaye to hear him speaking Kurdish and she listened hard to try to understand but it seemed such an alien language that she soon gave up and spoke to Carol about her plans for the baby.

The manager of the bar, a tall handsome Kurd called Hamdan, proudly showed Vedat the front page of a newspaper, explaining that this was his English girlfriend. Vedat looked suitably impressed and passed the paper over to Kaye. It was supposedly the front page of the Daily Mirror, featuring a headline story about an award winning office manager, complete with photograph.

'Mmm,' Kaye murmured, smiling. 'She looks very pretty'.

'Let's read what it says,' Carol suggested suspiciously.

'It says she works for a successful electronics firm in Brentwood in Essex and has been given an award for reaching sales targets. Oh, look! There's a spelling mistake here,' Kaye added, pointing to the word 'thier'. She looked at Carol, trying to gauge if Carol was thinking what she was thinking.

'Do you think this is real?' Carol asked.

'No. I'm thinking it's one of those mock-ups you can make in card shops or at motorway service stations.'

'Oh my God! You're right! Shall we tell him?'

'I'm not saying a word. If we say anything it'll just look like we're jealous and mean. The poor guy is so proud of her. I don't want to rain on his parade.'

Kaye handed the newspaper back to Hamdan, hoping that he wouldn't ask her opinion. He folded the paper carefully and before taking it to show another customer, announced, 'I'm moving to England in September to marry her!'

Kaye and Carol offered their congratulations, feeling guilty for not being honest. Kaye leaned over to Vedat and explained the situation, hoping that maybe he would say something to his lovelorn compatriot, but Vedat just shrugged his shoulders and turned to watch the next karaoke victim.

The following year, Kaye would learn that upon his arrival in Essex, Hamdan discovered that his girlfriend did not receive any award and was unemployed. He tried to make the best of living in a small, grotty flat on a huge housing estate with the girl, her mother and her brother, but after securing a work visa and a job as a postman, left her to start a new life of his own in London.

The next day, not having slept until dawn, Kaye and Vedat did not surface until midday. The weather was a stifling fifty degrees and so they decided that Vedat should go to the corner shop to get snacks and drinks and they would remain in the comfort of their air conditioned room until the temperature dropped in the late afternoon, when they would spend a few hours at the pool. Kaye asked if there was somewhere with dancing and live Turkish music where they could go that night. Vedat said he would ask the hotel staff on his way to the shop.

They took a taxi to the night spot the waiters had recommended. It was too far away from the hotel for Kaye to walk in her high heels and as neither of them knew Marmaris well, it was a better option than getting lost and walking for miles in the wrong direction. The open air arena with a central dancing area surrounded by tables was designed especially for tourists, which disappointed Vedat. He would have preferred a more authentic venue, but Kaye seemed happy, so he allowed them to be shown to a table. Kaye chose a table near the dance floor and they ordered drinks. Kaye was surprised that Vedat ordered a bottle of vodka,

'But you don't drink alcohol! I can't drink a whole bottle on my own!'

Vedat shrugged his shoulders, 'I feel like getting drunk.'

'Have you ever been drunk?'

'Yes,'

'When?'

'I used to hide bottles of vodka under my bed when I was younger.'

'Really? I'm shocked! I thought you were a strict Muslim.'

'Eh, no one's perfect. I try to be a good Muslim but sometimes I'm not.'

'Cheers!' Kaye toasted as the waiter poured their vodka and added lemonade and ice.

Traditional Turkish fayre was included in the price for the night and Kaye was excited to try new dishes and share the unending array of *mezes* that appeared before them. She loved the yogurty dips and cooked green beans in olive oil. She was eager to learn the name of each side dish and learn which ones were Vedat's favourites. They fed each other mouthfuls of food, taking pleasure in sharing their meal and in between courses, held hands across the table and stared lovingly into each other's eyes. Taped music boomed from speakers around the space and in order to hear, they had to shout which made them giggle and they resorted to gestures and facial expressions to communicate.

As everyone was finishing their main course, a group of five musicians took their places at the back of the dance floor. Kaye loved all kinds of music and had a sizeable collection of world music. She was fascinated by the Turkish instruments and asked Vedat the names of them. She learnt that the lute-like instrument was a *saz*, the one that sounded like a clarinet was a *zurna*, the drum was called a *davu*l and the stringed instrument held between the knees and played with a bow was a *Karadeniz kermancesi* – the Black Sea violin. A group of male dancers dressed in black baggy trousers, loose-fitting white shirts and soft, leather knee length black boots ran onto the dance floor and Vedat explained this dance was from the Black Sea. Kaye was spellbound as, arms outstretched; they shook their upper bodies and then did a dazzling routine of jumps, kicks and twirls, each taking their turn and trying to outdo the previous one. The audience responded with loud applause and the men ran off to be replaced by a troupe of graceful girls, dressed in brightly coloured dresses, soft red pumps and white headscarves, held in place by headbands of jingling gold coins. The tempo of the music changed to reflect the less energetic style of the girls as they portrayed the story of gathering in the harvest.

On hearing the first strains of the *halay,* Vedat grabbed Kaye's hand and led her to join the dancers and other holiday makers who were being urged to join the dance. This was a dance from his region and one he knew well. He had taken a serviette from the table and, waving it aloft, led a chain of people around the floor, doing the complicated steps and hops in time to the music. Kaye was familiar with the moves as it was a similar dance to one she had mastered while living in Cyprus and Vedat was impressed as she kept up with him.

Kaye got her turn to teach Vedat when the music slowed and couples took to the floor to smooch. Vedat refused to get up, saying he had no idea what to do but Kaye ignored his pleas to remain sitting down and dragged him into the middle of the floor, placed his hands on her waist, threw her arms around his neck and gently began to sway to the beat. He soon found the rhythm but laughed as his body felt awkward and he was not used to dancing in such close proximity to a woman. He was worried that someone might see the growing bulge in his trousers as his crotch rubbed against Kaye's hip and held her tighter. Kaye took this is a sign that he felt more comfortable, until she felt the hardness pressing against her. Vedat hid his head on her shoulder as embarrassment overcame him. Kaye giggled reassuringly. Vedat showed no signs of being affected by the alcohol they had drunk. Kaye felt tipsy but knew she had never felt this ridiculously happy in her life. She felt safe in Vedat's arms and consciously stored every detail of this night in her memory bank, fully aware that what she had with Vedat was something very special.

As the pearly white moon cast its glow on the ink black sea, waves gently lapped the sandy shore below where Kaye and Vedat sat on their tiny balcony, savouring every moment of their last night together. They sat next to each other on white plastic chairs with their feet propped on the balcony's ledge, occasionally kissing as they shared information about each other's lives. They enjoyed discovering similarities in being the oldest child in their families, both with a long gap between themselves and their younger siblings and gasped in amazement when they realised they had liked the same television programmes as children. They had a frank discussion about their differing religious beliefs, Vedat being confused by Kaye's certainty about reincarnation and Kaye trying to explain such a complicated matter in her limited Turkish, frustrated at his dismissal of life after death. By now the Turkish/ English dictionary Vedat had bought the previous year was looking very tatty, but without it they would never have been able to have the in depth conversations they needed to get to know each other well.

They had laughed remembering the previous summer when they met and Vedat had held his head in his hands in embarrassment thinking about his behaviour. He had acted like a pervert! It was totally out of character for him to behave like that. He explained that Kaye was like a magnet, drawing him to her and there was nothing he could do to stop himself. What must she have thought of him?

Vedat was intrigued by the fact that at the age of forty Kaye had never been married. Such a thing was unheard of in his culture. Kaye explained that although she had been in several long term relationships, she had never felt that marriage was a possibility. There had always been something missing and she could never imagine herself being with any of her ex-boyfriends for the rest of her life. She then threw the question back at Vedat.

'Why have you not married? Isn't it unusual for men in your culture not to be married at your age?'

'Yes, it is, but I have been so involved in politics that it leaves little time for finding a suitable woman.'

'Isn't it the custom to have an arranged marriage?'

'Yes. My father has tried to marry me off to a number of local girls: a bank manager's daughter, the Member of Parliament's daughter and girls from other influential families, but I refused. I will marry who I choose.'

'Does your father know how you feel?'

'I have told him. If he doesn't believe me, that's his problem.'

Kaye sensed that this was a sensitive subject and so changed the topic to what they were going to do. They reiterated their feelings of love for each other and their desire to be together but were both at a loss when it came to a solution and decided to wait and see what the future had in store for them.

All too soon it was time for them to go their separate ways. This time it was Kaye who would leave first. Her flight back to Manchester was in the afternoon, but she had to leave the hotel straight after breakfast to make the journey to Dalaman airport the required two hours before departure. Vedat had sobbed as they took a final shower together and he had used her nail scissors to snip a lock of her sun bleached hair to keep as a memento. He carefully put the hair in an empty matchbox in his holdall, telling Kaye that he wanted something to remind him of her and that he would stroke the hair every day, remembering their precious time together.

In the foyer, Sandy was ushering several other guests out of the front door and onto the waiting coach. Kaye approached her and introduced Vedat to her.

'Oh, so you finally made it!' Sandy exclaimed, shaking Vedat's hand. 'I'm so pleased. Nice to meet you.'

'Yes, he's been here for the last week,' Kaye replied.

'Well, you make a lovely couple. I can't say you look very happy, though,' Sandy added.

'I've been deliriously happy for the last week but now it's time to say goodbye again,' Kaye replied, smiling bravely.

'Yes, that must be hard. Let's hope it won't be for long.'

'*Inşallah*!' Kaye responded, squeezing Vedat's hand. The conversation had been in Turkish, so she knew Vedat had understood what had been said.

Vedat carried Kaye's suitcase to the coach and placed it on the pavement, along with the others waiting to be loaded by the coach driver. He turned to face Kaye and despite not being comfortable showing affection in public, grabbed Kaye in a bear hug and whispered in her ear, 'I adore you. Kaye. Never forget that.'

Kaye was fighting for breath and holding back the huge sob in her throat. She knew she had to go but tearing herself away from Vedat's passionate embrace was heart-breaking. 'I adore you too, Vedat,' she choked, tears trickling down her cheeks. 'I'll call you when I get home. Goodbye my darling'.

She chose a seat on the left side of the coach so that she could wave to Vedat from the window. He had retreated back to the shadow cast by the doorway and blew her kisses as the bus pulled away. He was dreading going back to Ankara to face his family and having to explain his absence at the hospital for the last seven days. The only consolation was that his father was too ill to shout or make a scene. He had no idea whether he would see Kaye again but hoped with all his heart that he would.

Chapter 12

Karabulut,

March 1983

It was a sunny evening in early spring and the boy's family were preparing to go for supper at the Ağa's house in the neighbouring village. The boy, at fifteen years of age, found these events tedious and would rather not have gone. His parents had insisted he was to attend, so he reluctantly dressed in his best white shirt and black cotton trousers with a light black jacket over the top. He polished his shoes by putting them on and rubbing them on the back of his socks. He could hear his mother fussing over his younger brother and baby sister as she gave instructions to her cousin who was to look after them while the boy and his parents went out.

The boy's father was starting their prized saloon car and revving the engine with impatience. In the yard, eight other cars carrying the senior members of his family were waiting for the convoy to set off. This was an important event for the family and the excitement was tangible.

The boy's mother soon appeared, wearing a full length navy blue dress and white waist-length scarf covering her head and shoulders, carrying his sister. She shouted to the boy to hurry up and got into the front passenger seat beside her husband. The boy came out of the house and, opening the back door of the car, sat with a sigh on the back seat, next to his brother.

They were welcomed warmly at the door of the house by the Ağa and his wife. They slipped off their shoes and were given house slippers to put on. The Ağa shook the boy's and his father's hands and respectfully greeted the senior male visitors by holding their hands, kissing them and touching them to his forehead. Then, with an outstretched hand, ushered the boy, his father and the other men in to a large carpeted salon, where male members of his family already sat. The Ağa's wife, after kissing her on both cheeks, took the boy's mother, her baby and younger son and women into a separate salon.

It was a close-knit community and everyone knew each other. The alliance between the two families would have an effect on the whole community. Local women were busy at work outside, cooking a whole lamb over a spit, tending juicy chicken kebabs on skewers over a charcoal fire and seasoning rice, beans and vegetables in large copper vats. They too, sensed the importance of the evening and were eager to make the food as delicious as possible. Some women were taking bread out of the clay oven at the side of the house, while others were chopping cucumber and mint to make *çacık*, a side dish made with yogurt. The meal was almost ready and they sent a message with a young girl to ask the women working in the kitchen inside the house, to find out if cold drinks had been served. When they received word that the drinks had been served, they then began to carve the lamb, pulling huge chunks off and piling them on two silver salvers.

The boy could smell the aroma of cooked lamb and his stomach rumbled in anticipation. He was hungry and knew he would be able to eat his fill. Soon, young men came with tablecloths, which they spread over the carpet in the centre of the room, along with silver metal water jugs, glasses and paper serviettes. The guests shuffled forward to sit on the edge of the cloths. The silver trays, heaped high with steaming food were placed in the centre of the room, along with warm *lavaş* bread, yogurt and olives. The men ripped off pieces of bread and used them, in a pinching movement, to pick up the meat, beans, rice and vegetables. They continued to talk amongst themselves, sharing opinions and feelings on local issues and the national economy. The recent actions of the separatist movement, known as the Kurdish Workers' Party, the PKK, were also a hotly debated topic. Most of the assembled men were fiercely against any anti-Turkish revolt and shook their heads in dismay at suggestions that this may happen. Some of the men avoided this topic and focussed on the reason for their attendance tonight and the happy union it would bring.

The boy was not included in any of these discussions and concentrated on eating. The food was delicious! He began to daydream. He had recently fallen in love with a girl in his class at school and knew she was interested in him too. They had exchanged furtive glances across the classroom and had met secretly behind the school building at break times. He had not kissed her yet, but lying on his bed at night, fantasised about holding her in his arms and kissing her full pink lips. She was the daughter of a bank manager, so was from a respectable, wealthy family. He hoped his parents would approve of her.

When the men had finished eating, the trays, still bearing small amounts of food, were taken away and were replaced by trays of fresh fruit and *künefe*, a dessert made of shredded pastry with a cheese layer in between, and crushed pistachios on top, served with hot syrup and clotted cream. Hot tea was served in small glasses and bowls of sugar lumps were placed at regular intervals along the tablecloths. The men placed a sugar lump in their mouths and slurped the tea – many of them draining the glass quickly and asking for another. Several local teenage boys rolled cigarettes and handed them to those who wished to smoke.

The boy, still in his own world, was unaware that the focus of the conversation had changed. He craved one of the cigarettes but his smoking habit was still a closely guarded secret between himself and his friends. He wished he could escape outside but knew this would be seen as rude. He was aware that the men were now discussing the forthcoming marriage of the Ağa's elder daughter but was not sufficiently interested to pay close attention and decided to visit the toilet. It was fascinating to him that there was a room inside the house with a porcelain bath, toilet and wash basin. He was used to an earth closet at the back of his home and using a plastic of jug of water to clean himself. Here, there were paper and towels and a scented tablet of soap. What luxury!

Dates were set for the wedding in three months' time, before the fasting month of Ramadan would begin. It would be a three-day celebration and arrangements would have to be made for catering and the formalities which would accompany such an occasion. They negotiated how much gold would be given to the girl's family as her dowry and other items, such as clothes, the weddings rings, household textiles were agreed upon. Following a prayer that Allah would bless the couple and provide a good future for them, there was much shaking of hands and celebratory slaps on the back – the purpose of the evening had been accomplished.

At school, on the Monday morning, two days later, the boy was the subject of much amusement. His friends ran to him as he entered the school yard, patting him on the back and asking him how he felt. He had no idea why they were so excited and looked at them innocently. He listened as they said he was lucky – the Ağa's daughter was very pretty and they reminded him of a boy they knew, who had been married last year to a girl who had, unknown to his family, been swapped at the marriage ceremony for her uglier older sister. It was only when the veil was lifted on conclusion of the formalities, that the swap was noticed – too late to do anything about it. The boy smiled as he remembered the story, but a troubling thought entered his head. What had this got to do with him? Eventually, one of the boys said that they had heard about his forthcoming marriage to the Ağa's daughter. The boy staggered back in amazement suddenly feeling claustrophobic. How had that happened? He had never even seen the Ağa's daughter!

Feeling trapped, he ran from the school yard, out onto the lane and headed for the rocky outcrop that had become his refuge. Lucky? He did not feel lucky. Why hadn't his parents told him? Now he realised the reason for his father's strutting around like a cockerel. He berated himself for not paying closer attention to the conversation at the meal. His life was ruined – how could he be married and still be at school? What about his intended career as a doctor? His head was full of questions and he was overcome by feelings of hatred towards his parents, his culture and the environment he lived in, as he tried to come to terms with what lay before him.

Chapter 13

Greenhill,

May 2001

The frustration of waiting for letters and the hours it took to translate them ended when Kaye and Vedat decided to use e mails to communicate. Vedat still encountered problems with e mailing as there was no internet access in the village where he lived, so he had to drive an hour to the nearest city, Diyarbakır, to go to an internet café. With the help of the café owner he set up an account and was shown how to write an e mail and send it. Kaye had internet access in her classroom so was able to read her emails in her lunchtime or after school.

Their relationship had gone through a sticky patch in the months after their traumatic time in Marmaris. Vedat's father had been in hospital for thirteen weeks, slowly recovering from his stroke and during this time Vedat had mended his broken relationship with his father. He had been made to promise that his relationship with Kaye was over in order to heal the rift between them. He had told Kaye that the psychological strain of loving her amid the restrictions of his life made it impossible for him to continue. He said he would always love her and that she had made an indelible mark on his life. He would never forget her and hoped with all his heart that she would find happiness with someone who was free. Kaye responded with an angry e mail, stating that it was obvious that his family were influencing his decision and that she wished she had never met him, as having discovered that love at first sight really existed, it would be hard for her to settle for anything less in the future. She picked up on every one of Vedat's reasons why their relationship could not continue and argued the case against them. If they were so different, why had they been so comfortable in each other's company, despite the language barrier? If being with a foreign woman was such a problem, why did he even begin their relationship and why did he resume it after their break up in December 1999? She said she regretted being so open and honest with him – the first time she had ever done so – and said she would find it very hard to give herself so freely and be so trusting ever again. Vedat had been stunned by her response and apologised for upsetting her so. After a few weeks of not emailing, he finally admitted defeat and said he could not live without her.

In January, Kaye had bought a mobile phone and suggested that Vedat buy one too, so that they could text each other and have daily contact. The time difference of two hours suited them well as they soon developed a routine of exchanging messages for an hour before they went to bed each night. Sometimes they encountered delays in texts being delivered and Kaye, particularly, felt under pressure when several messages arrived at the same time. She thumbed through her dictionary scrambling to translate unknown words and then hastily constructed a reply in Turkish, knowing Vedat was waiting for her reply. Neither of them used text speak: Kaye had no idea how to do it in Turkish and Vedat was aware that if he abbreviated words or omitted some, Kaye would not be able to understand.

Speaking on the telephone had become much easier as Kaye's Turkish improved. She had been going to a language school in Birmingham once a week for Turkish lessons, where, from the moment she entered the room, only Turkish could be spoken. It was just what she needed to gain confidence in speaking the language. There were only five students in the class, making it easy for the teacher to tailor the course to suit particular needs. The students had been assessed before being placed in the class and Kaye had been pleased to discover her Turkish had progressed to intermediate level. The teacher had encouraged the students to enter for GCSE Turkish that summer but none of them deemed it necessary, only requiring to be able to speak to their Turkish partners.

It gave both Kaye and Vedat a huge boost to hear each other's voices and hear the words of endearment, rather than reading them in black and white. Vedat always asked if she would like him to call, making sure she was available and he was not disturbing her but they knew each other's movements so well that it was rare that Kaye refused his call. Kaye usually had made notes on things she wanted a direct answer to and worked out how to say them in Turkish prior to the call. They talked about mundane things such as the weather, how their days had gone, how they were feeling, and any news which they deemed the other might be interested in and from time to time the issue of their future arose. Vedat assured Kaye that he wanted to spend the rest of his life with her but had no idea how this was possible.

[One day I hope things will change and we can be together. I can't bear this situation and know I want to be with you – only you. On one side is you and on the other my family, my workers, my career, my responsibilities. I don't know what to do. I need to know what you think is possible.]

[I am 100% sure of my feelings for you and because of my experiences of life so far, can be flexible to fit in with you. You have said before that you wouldn't want me to work and I am not interested in furthering my career. I want a simpler life.]

[I am good with people and have tamed some very difficult children. Your parents' attitude towards me doesn't bother me. I'm sure I will win them round. If your father is a good man like you say, he will see me for what I am.]

[He is a good man but he is a radical Muslim and sticks to traditions. He has set ideas and nothing will change them. Oh, I wish I were from a poor family with no expectations and then everything would be so much easier.]

[Calm down. Please try to think of the positives as well as the negatives. My life experience is different from yours. I have met and worked with people from many cultures and backgrounds. I make friends easily and adapt to new situations quickly. It would be better for me to come to Turkey than for you to come to England.]

Kaye had been at the same school for seven years and she felt it was time to move on. She was becoming disillusioned with teaching too, with the endless changes in the National Curriculum and the tedium of rewriting new policies and curriculum documents to fit in with these changes. She was a natural teacher and the strictures of having to teach to a rigid curriculum stifled her creativity. She had loved teaching before when she was able to run with a topic that inspired her students, a newspaper article that had motivated them or plan cross-curricular topics that lasted weeks and allowed the children to explore in depth. Now there was no time to spare and there was a set timetable to adhere to, even down to how many minutes to spend on mental arithmetic every day. She had discussed these issues with the Head teacher who had understood and although sorry to see Kaye leave, would support her in any way she could.

Even before meeting Vedat she had thought about going abroad to work again. Her time in Cyprus in the eighties was the best time of her life but she had not regretted her decision to leave after five years. The island had become claustrophobic and she knew that she must return to the UK if she wanted to advance in her career. Every Friday she looked at the Times Educational Supplement's overseas job section to see if anything appealed. On seeing a position for a Pre-school teacher in Ankara, she went straight home from school, updated her CV and letter of application and e mailed them to the Director of the school.

She couldn't wait to tell Vedat that night,

[*Hi! Guess what?! I've applied for a teaching job in Ankara at a private school called Özkent International School. Have you heard of it?*]

[Really? Yes I've heard of Özkent. It's a private university with an excellent reputation. I didn't know there was a school there too. When will you know if you've got it?]

[I'm not sure. I only applied today but usually you hear in about a week and then if they're interested they invite you for an interview. I hope it won't be long as if I'm leaving my job here I need to give my notice in by the end of the month, which is only three weeks away.]

[Kaye please don't do this for me. You have to want it for yourself.]

[I am doing it for myself! I'm ready for a change.]

The possibility of a total change in direction came from another advertisement in the TES. The BBC was inviting applicants for their trainee journalist scheme. Kaye's interest was pricked. She had always enjoyed writing and found it very therapeutic. Having a complete career change appealed to her just as much as moving abroad. The advertisement asked applicants to complete an online application form including two pieces of writing: one a criticism of a recent BBC early evening news programme in her area and a local story yet to be reported. Ideas for a community website and an explanation on why the applicant's skills and experience would be valuable in a career as a journalist were also required.

Saturdays were usually a day of rest, catching up on housework and seeing friends and family but Kaye had far too much to do to stay in bed. Having filled her washing machine with dirty laundry, hurried around her house with the vacuum cleaner and flitted around with a duster, she settled down to fill in the BBC's application form. The thought of being a journalist excited her and her imagination ran away with her as she practised, 'This is Kaye Knowles, reporting from ….' Chuckling to herself, she opened the form and began typing. She was tasked with writing a piece on a story of local interest and had seen the advertisement in time to watch last night's local early evening news programme and was engrossed in writing her views on it, when the phone rang,

'Hello. Could I speak with Kaye Knowles, please?' an American voice asked.

'This is Kaye.'

'My name is John Da Souza and I am the Director of Özkent School in Ankara. Are you available to talk?'

'Yes. That would be fine,' Kaye said, flapping her free hand in panic and trying her best to give intelligent replies to his questions about her previous teaching experience.

'I will be in London next weekend interviewing. Would you be able to meet me next Saturday afternoon at the Thistle Hotel, Marble Arch?'

'Yes. At what time?'

'Does two o' clock suit you?'

'Perfect!' said Kaye quickly calculating how much time it would take to get to London and find the hotel.

'I look forward to meeting you, Kaye.'

Before resuming her writing, Kaye searched on the internet for a map of central London and tried to work out the best route for her journey. She would ask Ellen's husband, Tom, for advice as he often went to London for meetings.

By late afternoon, her writing assignments complete, Kaye sent off the BBC application, feeling proud that she had been so productive and purposeful on a day that she usually spent shopping, lazing in bed or preparing for a night out with Anna.

Two days later she received another call from Özkent School, this time from the Elementary School Principal, Judy Allen, who had seen Kaye's application and was impressed. She was calling so that Kaye could ask more detailed questions about the job, living in Ankara and any other queries she may have. She also wanted to know Kaye's reason for choosing their school when there were so many schools on the international schools' circuit to choose from. Kaye thought it unprofessional to say that she wanted to be nearer to her Turkish boyfriend so said she had worked abroad before and after a stable thirteen years working her way up to a senior position, she was ready for a change. Working in Turkey appealed to her as it was a similar culture to Cyprus. They chatted for almost half an hour and Kaye felt relaxed. Judy was English and had been at the school since it was first opened ten years previously and she openly said that the pre-school was in need of someone with proven experience who could develop the curriculum and bring in new ideas.

Kaye gasped in amazement when Judy asked her if she would consider being the Head of Pre-School, as well as the class teacher for the pre-kindergarten students. 'Is the current head leaving?'

'No, she will still be there,' Judy replied candidly.

'How will that work then?' Kaye was puzzled.

'She is near to retirement and has been having difficulties with the parents – they are not happy with what is going on. I think she will be relieved if we find someone to take over her responsibilities.'

'It could be a very awkward situation.'

'Well, it depends on how we handle it and it won't be your problem. Let us deal with that.'

'I feel uncomfortable about taking over someone's job when they are still there. If she had asked to be released from her position, that would be fine, but she has no idea you are offering me her position. Right?'

'No, she doesn't know yet but we will tell her when you accept the job.'

'Are you offering me the job?'

'John will offer you the job on Saturday and I will be very disappointed if you don't take it.'

'I'm very interested but it depends on the salary, accommodation and conditions. Talking to you has been really helpful – thank you!'

'Don't let me down, Kaye. I expect to see you here in August.'

Kaye put down the phone, stunned at the turn of events. Not only was she almost certain to get the job but she was being offered promotion too. She had been looking forward to going back to being just a class teacher without the numerous responsibilities in her current senior management position. However, the pre-school at Ozkent was small, with only two classes, and if she had total autonomy, as Judy had said, she felt confident that she was up to the challenge.

'I got the job!' Kaye screeched down the phone, deafening Anna on the other end of the line.

'Well done! I knew you'd get it. Have you accepted it?'

'No not yet. The salary is terrible. I know that I get a flat, tax free status, return flights and free health care included but it's about a third of my present salary.'

'The cost of living in Turkey must be cheaper than here though'. So what are you going to do?'

'I'm going to accept but I have said I need twenty-four hours to make up my mind. It doesn't pay to be too eager. I am sure the Director will come up with a few thousand more to seal the deal.'

Laughing, Anna asked, 'Did you like the Director?'

'I was alarmed at first when he invited me up to his hotel room but he assured me that all the recruiters used their rooms for interviews. He probably thought I was a fruitcake when I insisted he keep the door open but when I saw that the room was set up with a table and chairs and a display of information about the school, I started to relax. He had lots of photos of the school, the campus, the flats and school events which gave me a good impression of everything. There is even a Marks and Spencer's at the shopping centre down the road from the school. Can you believe it?'

'I'd say that is the deciding factor. You'd never survive without your fix of M&S!'

'There'll be so much to do between now and August – signing the contract, applying for a work visa at the Turkish Consulate in London, renting out my house, Jan's wedding and trying to fit in a holiday with Vedat.'

'Don't worry. Everything will fall into place. You're so brave even thinking about moving abroad. I don't think I could do it.'

'I don't feel brave. Living in Cyprus for five years was the best time of my life. I have such wonderful memories of my time there. It's time for a new adventure and I hope you'll come and visit.'

'Of course I will. Have you got your dress for the wedding yet?'

'Yes! Luckily, I found just what I was looking for at Next. It's only a small wedding so I'm not wearing a hat. Of course, Mum's going to be stunning in a matching two-piece with a huge brimmed hat. She says this might be her only chance to be mother of the bride so she's going to make the most of it.'

'And so she should! I'm glad Jan has found happiness with Guy after her heartbreak with the other one. Fancy her meeting her future husband while walking the dog! Perhaps I'll get a dog!'

'I think that's a bit extreme. You'll find your Mr Right when you're least expecting it.'

'Hope so,' Anna sighed. 'Are you coming out tonight to celebrate?'

'Absolutely! I'll pick you up at eight.'

Chapter 14

Karabulut

May 1983

During the past three months there had been many visits to his family home from the girl's parents and senior family members. The marriage was more than building a bond between the bride and groom–to-be. Both families were eager to forge ties and strengthen their relationship with each other. The boy and girl had been present at a few of these meetings but had not had the opportunity to speak to one another. They had exchanged shy glances, trying to make contact and see what the other looked like. He had noticed, with some relief, that the girl was pretty and behaved very politely. She was petite, several inches shorter than him and dressed in a conservative manner, in long dresses with the traditional long scarf around her head and shoulders. He knew that she, too, would have had no choice in this marriage and wondered what she thought of him?

The five day wedding celebration had begun with immediate members of the two families gathering at the bride-to- be's home for the first of the wedding ceremonies performed by the Imam. This was the religious marriage where the young couple were united in the eyes of Allah. It was a quiet, private event and to both families this was more important than the civil union, performed later by the Registrar, as both families were strict Muslims and lived their lives trying their best to obey the word of the Prophet Mohammed in the Koran. Divorce was not an option, although recently, less religious people had begun to separate from their spouses and seek divorce. This was abhorrent to those who were strict Muslims as it meant that a woman was left to return to her own family with the shame, dishonour and stigma of a failed marriage.

The following day, the preparations for the civil wedding had begun. At the boy's home, a small army of local people had set up a huge carpeted area for dining, rows of plastic chairs for their guests and a large tent canopy had been erected at the far end of the yard, where the civil marriage would take place. Tens of thousands of people were expected to attend, including most of the families' villagers, relatives from other parts of Turkey and also a number of important dignitaries from Ankara, so providing food and drinks for such a number was a great feat. The boy's mother had been in charge of the organisation, clucking around the yard and giving instructions and orders to the workers. Groups of men sharpened knives, ready to slaughter the many lambs, calves and hens which would be needed to feed such a number. Women friends and relatives had been busy for weeks preparing butter, cheese and yogurt, pickling vegetables and conserving fruit. Huge amounts of fresh fruit and vegetables were piled high in the kitchen, ready to be turned into sumptuous dishes. The family's reputation depended on this being a superb event.

His mother had also been on a rare shopping trip to Diyarbakır to buy new outfits for herself and her family, as well as clothes for the girl and her family, which would be presented at the henna night held at the girl's family home. Gold coins, bangles, bracelets, elaborate necklaces and rings had also been purchased.

That evening, the women of both families and female friends gathered at the girl's family home for a henna night. They brought presents of gold coins, gold bracelets and necklaces for the bride-to-be and food for the evening. A few of the women mixed together powdered henna and water to make a thick paste which was then placed on a silver tray with some gold coins for wealth, salt and sugar to represent the tastes of life and a mirror to reflect good luck. They added small candles to the tray and then, joined by the other women, processed into the room where the bride-to-be sat. Draped in a red chiffon veil, covering her face and shoulders, the bride sat on a wooden stool in the middle of the room. The women sang a traditional Kurdish song about a girl leaving home to marry. The girl's shoulders began to shake and tears rolled down her face. Her mother and aunts also cried – they were losing their daughter and niece. After she married they would not see her often as she would live with her husband's family. After the song, the women knelt down in front of the bride and took hold of her hands. They smeared the palms of her hands with the henna paste and then wrapped them in red cloth before daubing their own hands with a circular mound of henna on each palm.

Meanwhile all of the men from both families and male friends were assembled at the boy's family home where they danced and sang to music played by a local group of musicians. They boy's mother had ensured there would be an array of tasty food and plenty of soft drinks available. One of the boy's older cousins took the boy aside and confidentially told the inexperienced groom how he should behave towards his wife on their wedding night.

The next morning, the boy was woken to the sound of activity below. Women were chatting loudly in the kitchen as they began to cook, accompanied by the clanging of pots and pans and the banging of doors as endless people traipsed in and out carrying supplies. The pungent smell of frying onions, used as a base for many of the dishes, wafted through the whole house. Outside, guests were beginning to arrive and in the single-track lane next to the family property, cars were parked on the grass verge and doors slammed after unloading the people crammed into each car. Everyone was in high spirits and when the musicians arrived, they erupted into clapping and dancing. The deep pounding of the bass drum, keeping time against the meandering of the *zurna*'s reedy wail, accompanied by the celebratory rattle of the snare drum woke the boy. He turned over in bed and covered his head with the sheet. It was all too unbearable! He knew that today he would be the centre of attention and, being shy by nature, this caused him much anxiety. He had no desire to go downstairs to eat breakfast with all of the women there to fuss over him so, despite his hunger, he stayed where he was.

His peace and quiet was soon shattered as his younger brother, still in pyjamas, burst into the room, jumped on the bed and insisted that he get up. To the four year old this was going to be the best day of his life. He was more gregarious than his older brother and revelled in the attention he received from adults. The boy could not help laughing as he was dragged by his little brother from the bed and pushed out of the bedroom door to the kitchen. He loved his little brother and smiled in amusement as the young boy sat down on the floor to watch as he performed his ablutions.

Dressed in his wedding finery: a new black suit, pristine white shirt and blue patterned tie and new black shoes, and still accompanied by his brother, the boy was greeted by whoops of delight from the women. They stroked his still damp hair and patted his back, before offering him something to eat. He tried to look relaxed but his stomach was churning and he found he had no appetite. After several mouthfuls of bread, a small piece of cheese and a glass of tea, he excused himself and went outside.

A group of local musicians had been hired to lead the festivities and they began to usher people towards their cars. The boy and his father followed by other male relatives, were going in convoy to the girl's home to collect her.

The bride-to-be emerged from her family home dressed in a heavily embroidered, long, white dress, with the traditional decorative silver belt, symbolising chastity, around her waist. A red ribbon was also tied around her wrist and she wore a red veil with intricate yellow and white embroidery over her head and shoulders. Women were wailing as she moved towards the waiting car and men fired rounds from Kalashnikovs into the air. Her head bent and shoulders heaving from sobbing, she left her family and got into the car where her groom to be was waiting nervously. This was the first time they had been alone together and neither of them knew what to say. They were both totally overwhelmed by the situation. He felt sorry for her and told her not to worry – everything would be fine.

On arriving back at the boy's house, as they emerged from the car, they were showered with wrapped sweets and children came running to claim them.

The local Registrar was ready and waiting underneath the tented canopy to formalise the marriage.

Chapter 15

Greenhill

June 2001

Kaye's head was whirling with everything she had to do. Normally extremely organised and adept at forward planning, she was struggling to cope with the usual demands the end of the school year brought: report writing, parents' meetings, end of year concerts, the Summer Fayre, as well as helping to find her replacement. Having accepted the job at Özkent, she had signed the contract and returned it to the school, had made plans to go to the Turkish Consulate in London to apply for her work visa and had begun research on a reputable property management company in her area.

The BBC had sent her a letter to say that she had been short-listed from fifteen thousand applicants to the next round and invited her to London for an interview. As was tempting as it was to attend the interview and see if she would have been accepted onto the course, she had already committed to the Özkent job and had far too much to organise to spend time and energy pursuing something solely out of curiosity.

John Da Souza had sent all of his new teachers a list with contact details and brief personal information of the group of sixteen who would be joining his staff that summer and urged them to make contact with each other. They were a mixed bunch, ranging in age from late twenties to late fifties, some single, some divorced, and three married couples and were from the UK, Canada, The United States and New Zealand. Kaye had noted that Jane Marshall was the same age as her, also from the Midlands, was single and would be teaching English in the High School. She had sent Jane an email introducing herself and was delighted when Jane had called her for a chat. They had instantly hit it off and discovering that Jane, too, was having a long distance relationship with a Moroccan man, found that they had even more in common than they had initially thought.

Jane had been able to warn Kaye of the pitfalls at the Turkish Consulate, having been there a week before Kaye was due to go.

'Make sure you get there before eleven, as there is always a long queue and they close the counter promptly at twelve so if you haven't been seen then you will have to go again.'

'Thanks. I am planning to drive down to Luton, leave my car there and take the train into London. I'll make sure I'm there about ten. How long did they say it will be before you get your visa?'

'They said eight to ten weeks, which is cutting it fine. But Gonca, the administration manager at Özkent said they don't issue our flight tickets until they have the work visa so there's no danger of us entering the country without all the right documents.'

'That's good. What are you doing about your house?'

'I've contacted a letting agency and they seem pretty confident that I can rent it out easily. What about you?'

'I'm thinking of doing the same. Someone is coming from a property management service next week. What'll you do with all your personal possessions?'

'I'm going to put them in my loft and lock it securely. I'll give the key to the lettings agent, in case they need access to the roof space, but the tenants will not be allowed to go up there.'

'That's a great idea. I could do the same.'

'I bet your boyfriend's excited about you moving to Turkey. Are you going to meet him this summer?'

'Yes we are planning to go to Ölü Deniz as soon as I break up from school. I think he's pleased I'm moving to Ankara but to be honest his reaction was a bit of a damp squib. I'm full of excitement and he's saying, 'Make sure you give this a lot of thought' and 'Don't do this for me.'

'He's just being caring and doesn't want you to make a mistake, that's all. I'm sure he's pleased as Punch really.'

But that day Vedat was not pleased. He was extremely angry, but for a very different reason.

[What have you done? Why? Why? Why?] came the first of a series of text messages.

Kaye bit her lip as she read the message and knew from his reaction that she had made a huge mistake.

[What were you thinking? Don't you know my father is not a well man? He threw the letter in my face and slapped me – for the first time in my life. I am so angry. There was no need for you to write a letter to him.]

[Why did you do it? Did you think my father would agree to our relationship? It will never happen now. I've told you before that my father has his own set of values and nothing will change them.]

[You and my father are only thinking of yourselves and are very selfish. I am living between two knives and neither of you is thinking about me. You're only thinking of your own happiness and my father just wants to protect his honour and his radical principles. I feel like a tennis ball being batted between the two of you. You say do this. He says do that. I am trying to do what is right for everyone but no one understands this.]

[I am losing my trust in people because the two people I love most in the world are causing me so much pain. My philosophy of life is live and let live. How I wish I could be allowed to do that.]

[I'm sorry. I can't talk any more. Endless respect .....]

The messages came so fast that Kaye did not have time to respond and when she eventually sent a text to say how sorry she was, Vedat's phone was switched off and the message did not deliver. She had written a letter to Ibrahim Bey with the intention of explaining how she loved Vedat and asking if he would be willing to meet her face to face. She had hoped that by writing in Turkish he would see that she was making every effort to understand Turkish culture and was willing to adapt to their way of life. She had appealed to his better judgement by quoting a verse from the Koran about treating 'People of the Book' with kindness, tolerance and mutual respect. With the help of her Turkish teacher, she had written very respectfully and hoped she came over as an intelligent, sincere and honest person.

Obviously, she had failed and now had to convince Vedat that she was not trying to make trouble for him, but her intentions had been to improve their situation.

Vedat was willing to talk that night but it was to say that their relationship was over.

[I have thought about this from every angle and I have decided that our relationship cannot continue. I have argued with my family and we have hurt each other's feelings. They are unable to understand my feelings for you. I have truly loved you and will always love you – don't forget that.]

[For two years, you have drawn me like a magnet and I have experienced the deepest love, a waterfall of excitement and indescribable respect for you. You have turned my life upside down and you will always be a part of me. I have spent hours daydreaming about a life with you and cried to myself with frustration at not being able to find a solution. I couldn't restrain the feelings inside me but I have responsibilities and ties here.]

[I won't disturb you again and this is my last message. I wish you health, happiness and success. All my love and respect. Elveda.]

Kaye was too stunned to send a reply. The last time Vedat had said, '*elveda*', meaning farewell, had been like a knife in her heart, but this time she felt numb – neither upset nor angry. She sat rereading the messages, waiting for an emotional reaction but none came. Only when she relayed his words to Anna later, did she acknowledge feelings of sadness but also acceptance. The last two years had been an emotional roller coaster and she felt wrung out.

She would accept Vedat's decision and move on. She had a whole new life to look forward to in Turkey and with or without Vedat she was determined to enjoy it.

Chapter 16

Ankara

August 2001

As the minibus climbed the steep winding hill towards the school campus, Kaye's excitement mounted. Despite the nail-biting wait for her work visa to come through in time for her flight, everything had gone to plan. Wiping the sweat from her top lip, she leaned forward in her seat to catch her first glimpse of her new home.

'Welcome to Özkent!' John Da Souza said, helping Kaye with her bags as they climbed the steps up to her flat. He had met her at the airport and given her a detailed copy of the orientation programme for the coming week. As the only member of the new group who was part of the school's management team and the only new recruit who spoke any Turkish, she would be excused from the daily Turkish lessons, deemed essential by the school, to attend meetings with the John and Judy to outline her plans for the pre-school. The rest of the timetable included a guided tour of the school, university and campus, shopping trips to buy essentials, going to the bank to open an account, registering with the local health centre, sight-seeing tours of Ankara, meals out at various local eateries and a formal reception to meet their teaching colleagues at John's home. That night there would be an informal gathering at John's flat for those who wished to go.

Kaye was pleasantly surprised by her flat. It was clean and appeared bigger than on the photos John had shown her in London. She had two large bedrooms, a small kitchen opposite a small bathroom and a light airy living room which formed the centre of the whole space. Everywhere was decorated in neutral tones, which Kaye liked as she could already see what a difference a few splashes of colour and a few plants would make. She had a small balcony which was bathed in late afternoon sun and from where she could see the main university campus in the distance and further out to where purple grey mountains shimmered in the heat. The leafy green campus sat on a hill ten kilometres outside the city and Kaye was comforted to see the surrounding green countryside and rolling hills. She was not a city person and apart from her three year stint at university in London had always lived in rural locations.

As Kaye was chatting to Judy that night at Johns' flat, she wondered whether Jane had arrived yet. They had been unable to find seats on the same flight out of Birmingham. Jane had taken the later afternoon flight via Munich. Judy said that someone was on their way to meet Jane at the airport and she would arrive soon. Kaye was looking forward to meeting Jane in person after their many lengthy phone conversations and e mails. She had a mental image of what Jane would look like and wondered if she would recognise her when they came face to face.

She did not. Kaye paid little attention to the petite blonde woman wearing a faded track suit and trainers, who entered John's lounge about an hour later, looking a little weary and lost. Kaye was enjoying a conversation about alternative therapies with a lady called Julia, a shy American who was also new to the school. Judy, knowing that Kaye was eager to meet Jane, brought her over to introduce them to each other.

'Hi! I'm Kaye. Lovely to see you in the flesh,' Kaye began.

'Hi! Nice to see you too. You're just as I imagined you to be.'

Laughing, Kaye admitted, 'You're nothing like I imagined you to be!'

Jane pulled up a chair next to Kaye and was introduced to Julia. The three of them instantly found a common bond and chatted until John yawned and people began to leave.

Two days later, Kaye had managed to squeeze in time before a mid-morning meeting with John, to visit the Özkent Pre-School, a purpose-built, one storey prefabricated building at the top of the school campus. It was a large, light and spacious building with plenty of windows and the whole building has been painted a stark white over the summer holiday and provided a perfect blank canvas for displaying children's work and visual teaching aids. The miniature white porcelain toilets and wash basins in the bathrooms had made Kaye smile but she had been alarmed to see that boys and girls shared the same toilets with no doors for privacy. The two classrooms led off on the right side of a long corridor and were the largest ones Kaye had ever seen. They were furnished with specially made little wooden tables and chairs, painted in red and white, for the young pupils and larger versions for the teachers. The rooms seemed to be well-resourced, with storage units full of educational toys, puzzles and games but Kaye noticed that there was only one small book case in each classroom with a poor selection of tatty, much-used books. Literacy was one of the areas that Judy had highlighted as a need for development and Kaye knew that without a good supply of reading and picture books, it would be hard to put her plans into action.

As she made her way around the building, noticing the enormous playroom which ran the length of the left side of the building, Kaye heard voices coming from a large room at the far end of the corridor. She opened the door to a large dining room, where small tables were set out, to see three Turkish people having breakfast. She apologised for disturbing them and introduced herself. Immediately, the group stood up, welcomed her and introduced themselves as Sema, the tea lady, Ali, the driver and Sevgi, the cleaner. Amazed that she spoke Turkish, they invited Kaye to sit with them and offered her tea, cheese, olives, tomatoes, cucumber, bread, and honey. She explained that she had already eaten but decided it would be good to share a glass of tea with them as they were an essential part of the pre-school team and knew they would be offended if she refused their hospitality. She laughed as Ali said she looked like Princess Diana and politely replied that she wished she was as slim as Diana. Sevgi was eager to find out all about their new boss and asked Kaye questions about her family, where she was from and how she knew Turkish. Kaye did not mention Vedat but said that she had Turkish friends in England and had learnt the language through them. She was eager to maintain a professional air and not one of a woman who was chasing after someone she had met on holiday two years ago.

The week passed quickly in a blur of activity and by the end of it the sixteen new recruits had become a close-knit group. Within the group, the seven single women had formed an alliance and were eager to travel together and see as much of Turkey as they could. They had all bought a selection of travel guides with them and compared recommendations as they planned their first trip to Istanbul in three weeks' time. Two of the married couples, Jean and Peter, and Anne and Bob, were experienced travellers and had worked in a number of international schools around the world. They proved to be a great source of information and took the younger members of the group under their wings, especially when 'Turkish tummy' struck and the new recruits went down one by one with crippling stomach cramps and incessant diarrhoea. Anne was a walking medical chest and produced an array of suitable medications, remedies and unguents for every possible illness. The group had been warned that they may experience stomach upsets as their bodies adjusted to the different composition of minerals in the water and the high altitude, but none had been prepared for the ferocity of the reaction. A day of complete rest seemed to be enough for them to regain their strength, although all were hesitant about eating any food, in case they suffered a relapse of the symptoms. Jane was the only one to require spending a day in the health centre on a drip, having become severely dehydrated.

A large, bearded Australian man called Lee, a member of the school's orientation committee, had accompanied the group on all their activities and being a gay drama teacher, had entertained them with tales that had them howling with laughter. He had been at the school for five years and had seen enough people come and go to be able to give sound advice on making the most of their time in Turkey. He had been eager to meet Kaye as he had heard through the school grapevine that she had taken over Pam's role in the pre-school.

'Oh, my dear, I don't envy you,' he teased. 'Pam is a big lady too. I can't wait for the mudslinging to begin! Will it be fisticuffs at dawn?'

'Please don't say that!' Kaye begged. She was already nervous about meeting Pam and worried about the reception she would receive. 'Seriously, has she taken it badly? Does she hate me?'

'You'll have to wait and see,' Lee said with a twinkle in his eye. 'There's no way I'm getting involved in this. Me in the middle of two feisty ladies doesn't bear thinking about!'

As Kaye was changing to go to the dinner at John's, her doorbell rang. She opened it to see a friendly round face smiling at her. She was presented with a potted plant and welcomed to Özkent once again. Pam introduced herself and Kaye spluttered, 'Oh, thank you. It's lovely to meet you! Please come in.'

'Thanks. I thought I'd come over to see you before we met at John's dinner. I want you to know I don't bear any grudge against you. The school treated me very badly but it's not your fault.'

'That's very gracious of you. I'm so relieved! I felt terrible about taking your job but they said you might be relieved if someone else took over your responsibilities.'

'Actually, I am. I'm getting too old to cope with all the crap we get from parents. They're a difficult lot and need firm handling.

However, that doesn't excuse the way I was told you were replacing me. It would have been nice to have been asked how I felt first.'

'Yes, you're right. Can I get you a glass of wine?' Kaye offered, putting the plant on the draining board and going to the fridge for a chilled bottle of white wine.

'Thanks. That would be nice. How are you settling in?' Pam asked, joining Kaye in her kitchen.

'Fine. It's been a hectic week but I'm looking forward to meeting the other pre-school teachers tonight. I was dreading meeting you!'

'I can understand that. Now you can relax and enjoy the evening. I'm not the old dragon you expected then?'

'Certainly not!' Kaye admitted, thinking that the plump, motherly figure who stood next to her was the antithesis of the harridan she had been imagining. 'Lee scared me and said he was anticipating fisticuffs. I think he secretly fancied a mud wrestling match!'

'He's a good friend of mine but has a devilish sense of humour. How about we pretend we haven't met and stage a mock first meeting where we look at each other with hatred, build up tension and then walk towards each other and …hug? Are you up for it?'

'Great idea! Let's do it. I can't wait to see Lee's face!'

Kaye was just getting into bed after an enjoyable evening and chuckling to herself as she remembered the priceless look of horror on Lee's face when Pam had advanced towards her and the visible relief when they had hugged, when her phone pinged. It was a message from Vedat asking how she was. Finding time to talk to him recently had been hard and he was feeling ignored.

[I'm sorry but I've been busy with meetings and the days are full of activities. I've been getting home late and going straight to bed. Hopefully things will settle down next week. Are you OK?]

[I'm fine. Now you have your new life and your new friends you don't need me.]

[Vedat, that's not true! This is a stressful time for me and I don't need you giving me a hard time too!]

[Sorry. Let's not argue. I'm just missing you, that's all. I love you, Kaye. I wish we could be together tonight. I can't stop thinking about you and long for your touch, your smell and the warmth of your body.]

[I know my darling. Please be patient. We'll talk properly tomorrow but I have to sleep now – I have an early start in the morning.]

After a protracted goodnight, sending love and kisses, Kaye got into bed. She reflected on their time together three weeks ago. Despite ending their relationship in June, Vedat had been unable to resist seeing Kaye when he discovered she was on holiday with Anna in Ölü Deniz. It had been a last minute booking and initially she and Anna had been concerned by the rustic appearance of the small hotel but after a few days they began to love its charm and the friendly Turkish family who ran it. It was a five minute walk away from the sea and they spent their days either lazing by the hotel pool or at the beach. Vedat had come for their second week and all of the upset and disappointment of the past year had evaporated when Vedat strolled into the hotel and hugged Kaye so tightly she feared he would break her ribs.

Kaye had listened to Anna's suspicions that Vedat was married and was stringing her along but she dismissed them. Kaye was adamant that Vedat would not lie to her and trusted him. They had spent an idyllic time together and their time in each other's company made it worth all of the time they spent apart.

Chapter 17

Northern Cyprus

March 1986

The day began in the same way as those of the last thirteen months, the sergeant came into the dormitory at five o' clock, just as it getting light, hit the beds in turn with a stick and commanded everyone to get up. The forty soldiers in the dormitory jumped out of bed and put on their army issue khaki jumpers, thick serge khaki trousers, socks and heavy black boots. They put the string around their necks on which their small purses hung and helped each other make their beds. Those soldiers who had the top bunks appreciated help from their friends to lift up the mattresses so that they could tuck in the corners of the sheets and blankets. When all of the beds were made, they gathered together their soap, toothbrushes, toothpaste, towels and shaving equipment, and proceeded to the bathroom. Long queues had already formed at each basin, so the soldiers joined the queues to wait their turn.

He returned to the dormitory to finish clearing up his space, put on his khaki beret and waited for the other soldiers to return, before marching for breakfast to the canteen. He had now grown accustomed to the meagre breakfast of two slices of toast, a couple of olives, an egg, a small piece of cheese and the revolting tea, served in metal beakers. At first, he had missed the huge breakfasts he was used to at home and dreamed of freshly baked bread warm from the oven, home-made cheese and yogurt, plump black olives, sweet apricot jam and fresh eggs from his mother's hens. Now he found he had little appetite and, despite losing twenty kilos, had to force himself to eat the army food.

Following the roll call, to check none of them had run away during the night, the soldiers received their orders for the day. He was the General's personal driver and was told to report to the General's office immediately. The many months of physical training and drills made marching an almost natural way to move around the camp. He was told he was taking the General to a meeting in Mağusa, at the far end of the island, so he went to collect his jeep. He checked that the jeep was spotlessly clean, inside and out, checked the oil in the engine and drove over to the building where the General's office was housed.

While he was waiting for the General to appear, he stood by the jeep, reflecting on the last thirteen months. His father had used his connections to change the date on his identity card, to allow his son to be conscripted two years early at eighteen years of age instead of twenty. The Ağa realised that his son was finding married life difficult and thought that doing his military service would give him a break and hoped he would come back ready to face his responsibilities. His son had dropped out of school, as a form of rebellion against being forced to marry at such a young age and spent his days lounging around at home or wandering aimlessly around the fields. The discipline and hard living conditions of national service would be a much needed shock to his system and hopefully, he would welcome the comforts of home and his family life when he returned. Being posted to Cyprus after basic training was considered a softer option than some of the other possibilities, but the Ağa knew that his son would not find the experience easy.

Not being naturally physically adept, the new recruit had suffered much during the first month of basic training. The punishing drills, endless marching, long runs and rigorous bouts of exercise had taken their toll on his morale. He had resented being spoken to in such a harsh manner – his position as an Ağa's son and always being treated with the utmost respect had not prepared him for the abuse he received. To the drill sergeant he was no different than any other rookie and there was no special treatment. He was shouted at, punished for misdemeanours and expected to give his all, just like all the others.

As he had not been to university or graduated from school, he had to complete the full fifteen months of service. He had no particular skills but being brought up on a farm and used to driving a variety of vehicles, he was a confident driver. Being a driver was easy for him and was a far better option than being a cleaner or working in the kitchens, peeling endless mounds of onions and potatoes. He still had to do guard duty, usually in the evenings, but quite enjoyed that. His rebellious nature had not been squashed entirely and he revelled in finding inventive ways of flouting the regulations. His latest venture was to go into Lefkoşa in the early evenings when one of his friends was on guard duty, to buy vodka. This was against the regulations – no alcohol was allowed on Turkish military bases. Instead of smuggling a bottle of vodka in his clothing as others had tried to do, with serious consequences, he bought either a two litre bottle of Coke or Fanta and with a syringe he had purchased from the chemist's, drew out half of the contents and replaced it with vodka, bought from a local supermarket. He then taped up the hole made by the syringe, cleverly hidden underneath the label, with a sticking plaster. Returning to the base, he innocently walked past the guard and went to his dormitory to share the bottle with his friends. He had never tasted alcohol before coming to Cyprus – it would have been seriously frowned upon by his devout Muslim family and was not easily accessible where he lived. Now, though, he loved the effect the alcohol had on him and drank it at every available opportunity. He could forget his troubled life, the disappointment of his dashed dreams and become the clown of the company, by imitating the officers or pretending to be absolutely leglessly drunk.

He made friends easily and had made friendships that would last for life. He loved hearing about his friends' attempts to find women and sleep with them. One friend in particular regularly went into town and bedded Russian prostitutes in a seedy hotel. He had an arrangement with a café owner, who kept his civilian clothes in the back room at the cafe, so that he could change out of his uniform and go unnoticed as a soldier into the hotel. On his return to camp he regaled his friends with stories of the women he met and the details of his sexual exploits. He smiled as he remembered another friend's attempt at a similar escapade, which resulted in total humiliation when he discovered the pretty woman he had paid to accompany him to a room, turned out to be a transvestite. Oh, how they had all laughed!

The days passed slowly but he liked the routine. He had formed a good relationship with the General, who knew his father well and they had interesting conversations while they were driving around the island. Always respectful, and used to having politicians, local VIPs and other dignitaries visiting the family home, he did not feel uncomfortable around those who had important roles in society. The General, too, liked him and behaved in a milder manner towards him than he did to other soldiers under him.

He hated being in Northern Cyprus. The tension on the island between the Greeks and Turks meant that there were continual skirmishes along the Green Line where the United Nations soldiers also patrolled. The locals were antagonistic towards the Turkish soldiers and resented their presence. The Turkish Republic of Northern Cyprus was very run down and in an attempt to create revenue, the government had allowed several hotels to open casinos. This in turn encouraged prostitutes from Eastern Europe to prey on the businessmen who came over from mainland Turkey to gamble. He considered this to be a sin.

Having not used his month's holiday leave to visit his family, he had only a month left to serve and then he would have to return home. This prospect filled him with dread. What was he going to do with his life? He still had yearnings to be a doctor but knew he had sabotaged his chances of getting to medical school by leaving school at fifteen years of age. He had wanted to make a difference in his community by offering free health care to the poor by holding a free clinic one day a week. It hurt him deeply that this was now impossible. He knew his father expected him to take over the farm but he felt no excitement at this prospect. His father was a wonderful man but had no real business sense. His compassion for the people in his village meant that he gave away far more than he should and the farm was only just breaking even.

As much as he wanted to leave the military, he did not relish the thought of returning to his wife and having to face the prospect of starting a family. He hoped he would grow to love her and give her the children she craved. She was a good woman and wanted to make him happy. He still thought of his true love and wondered where she was and whether she was married. With a heavy heart, he gave a sigh and turning towards the building, he saw the General walking towards him.

Chapter 18

Ankara

November 2001

A week after school had begun, the World Trade Centre in New York was hit by planes carrying Al Qaeda suicide bombers. As soon as the news was broadcast, the university and school sent its students and teachers home for the day in fear of other reprisals. The American and British embassies instructed their nationals in Turkey not to travel and all of Özkent's non-Turkish teachers had been urged to be vigilant and stay in Ankara. Özkent, with its affiliation to several of the top American universities and having a large population of foreign staff was an obvious target. The group of new recruits converged at Kaye's flat, watching the television news channels in horror as events unfolded. Amid the feelings of disbelief, there was one of insecurity. They discussed the fact that Özkent campus, sitting isolated on its hill top perch, was exposed and unprotected, apart from a few dilatory security guards at the entrance, and with thousands of foreigners living and working there, it was a prime target for terrorists in Turkey. The newly arrived teachers felt like sitting ducks but agreed that nowhere in the world was safe at that moment and all they could do was to be alert to any possible dangers.

Vedat also shared this opinion as he spoke to Kaye that night. He urged her to be careful and not take any risks by going anywhere on her own or out of Ankara.

[You are a very precious person, Kaye and you are everything to me. Please look after yourself and keep safe. If anything happened to you I don't know what I would do. You have stolen my heart and I think about you all the time. I have become a Kayeaholic!]

[*That must make me a Vedataholic! Don't worry about me. I'm fine.]*

[Of course I worry about you! How can I not? You are living alone in a foreign country. I know it's my country but I'm still so far away from you. I know this love of ours is special and I'll never love anyone like I love you. I can't find the words to say how much you mean to me.]

[*You are everything to me too and I love you with all of my heart. Now tell me about your day.]*

They had resumed their nightly conversations and looked forward to sharing their news, thoughts and feelings. Vedat kept Kaye informed about what crops he was sowing or harvesting, the profit made, what expenses he had, the prices of crops on the market and fuel costs for his many tractors.They still had spats as a result of language misinterpretations and misunderstandings but generally overcame their differences quickly. Kaye's heart still fluttered when her phone pinged with a message from Vedat and when he called her, she could hardly catch her breath, so much was the excitement at hearing his voice.

Two months on, the political situation being calmer and travelling restrictions having been lifted, the group of new teachers decided to make the most of their long weekend celebrating the end of Ramazan and Şeker Bayram. They had taken backpacks to school with them so that they could leave school promptly and go directly to the main bus terminal in Ankara where they would travel to Cappadokia in the Central Anatolian region of Turkey. Jane had asked one of the school secretaries to reserve seats for them so that if they were on the last minute they were still guaranteed seats. None of them had been to this spectacular place before but it was top of their wish list of places to see in Turkey. They had all read accounts in their guidebooks and listened with fascination to colleagues' descriptions of the unusual landscape. There was mounting excitement as they chatted amongst themselves about spending the next two nights in a cave hotel recommended by colleagues at school.

They could not see much of the countryside on the way as, being late autumn, it was dark before they set off. The journey would take them about five hours, with a refreshment stop at a service station after a couple of hours.

'I'm dying to go to the toilet!' Kaye said as she clambered down from the bus and followed the people in front of her to the toilets.

'I'm not, but I'm going to go anyway.' Jane stated. 'I don't want to be caught short and have to ask the driver to stop at the side of the road.'

On reaching the Ladies, the two of them joined a queue of Turkish women. Kaye nudged Jane as she noticed an old lady with her leg over the side of a wash basin, washing her foot. 'No matter how smelly my feet are, there's no way I'd wash them in a public toilet!' she said indignantly.

'She's probably washing them before she goes to the prayer room. I saw a sign for one as we came in,' Jane said.

Kaye's turn came and she went into the vacant cubicle and cringed at the smell as she saw it was a traditional toilet with a footplate around a hole in the ground. Bundled up with extra layers of clothing – they had been warned it would be cold in Cappadokia – she pulled her sweatpants, along with her knickers around her knees and adopted a squatting position over the hole and tried to relax. Nothing happened. She shuffled on the footplate and got into a lower position. Her thigh muscles began to quiver and was relieved hear a tinkling sound as water went down the hole. She looked around but there was no sign of any toilet paper, just a plastic jug next to a tap on the wall. She smiled to herself as she reached into her pocket. Nora had always insisted that her daughters never went anywhere without a tissue in their pocket. You never knew when one would come in handy. Finally, she filled the jug and swilled it down the hole. She presumed this was what the protocol was.

Jane was waiting for her outside the toilets, looking at the nuts, dried fruits and array of sweets for sale at a nearby stall. 'Shall we get a drink?' she asked Kaye, who was shaking her leg in a strange way.

'I'd love one but the thought of having to repeat that toilet episode is putting me off drinking more. I've splashed my trainers. Can you tell?'

'How did you do that? Jane asked puzzled.

'Trying to squat over that hole!' Kaye whispered.

'What hole?'

'The toilet hole!'

'Didn't you go to the proper toilet at the end?'

'I didn't know there was a proper toilet at the end,' shrieked Kaye.' I just went into the next vacant cubicle when someone came out.'

Jane giggled. 'There's always a western sit-down toilet at the end in these places. You'll know next time!'

The group shuffled in their seats towards the windows as they became aware of strange shapes outside. The moonlight highlighted an eerie landscape with hills of what looked like sand-coloured whippy ice cream, dusted with icing sugar. As they entered the town of Göreme, they could see tall conical mounds of stone with small windows and doors cut into them in the distance.

Mehmet, the owner of the cave hotel where they were staying, was waiting at the bus station to meet them. He helped the bus driver drag their bags from the hold and when they were ready, ushered the group along the main street, before turning up a winding cobbled hill. They soon arrived at a cast iron gate, which led to a steep set of narrow steps.

Now tired after a full day at school and the long journey, and struggling to mount the steps, Kaye breathed a sigh of relief at the top of the steps.

‘Hey, look! There’s a pool! Not that it’s warm enough to swim now but it would be brilliant in the summer.’

Mehmet explained that there were rooms on this level and more on an upper level. There were no other guests so they could have the run of the place and choose which rooms they wanted. Some rooms were single, others for couples and a few larger rooms for small groups. Kaye suggested that she, Jane and Julia could share a room and Mehmet pointed to a doorway at the far side of the pool. After arranging to meet at the dining room downstairs at eight thirty the next morning, the others went in search of their rooms.

‘Wow! This is amazing!’ Julia exclaimed, taking in the small sitting area which had been created near the door of the dark, cosy cave room. Two beautifully upholstered armchairs had been placed facing an intricately carved wooden coffee table, all of which sat on a small fringed Turkish carpet. There were three beds in a row on one side, and an elegant mahogany wardrobe set against the wall, next to which was an ornate, full length mirror on the other side. The uneven walls were of bare creamy coloured stone, decorated at intervals with traditional wall hangings, kilims and old fashioned wall lights which provided a romantic orange glow to the room.

‘I bet these things are all antiques,’ Kaye said.

‘Yes, they look like they are,’ Julia replied. ‘This is such an experience. I’ve never been to anywhere like this in my life!’

'I've heard a lot about Cappadokia, but this is better than I ever imagined. Fancy sleeping in a cave!' Jane gushed. 'Which bed do you want?

'I'm not bothered,' Kaye replied. 'I'll have this one if you like as it's nearer what I presume is the bathroom,' she added, pushing open a wooden door to reveal a modern bathroom with small tiled shower cubicle, toilet and wash basin. 'We've got a proper shower! I was imagining having to do a strip wash with a bowl of hot water and a flannel.'

'That's good,' Jane said with relief. She liked her creature comforts. 'These duvets on the beds are really thick. Even though the room is a bit chilly, we'll be as warm as toast in bed.'

A few hours later, Kaye stirred as she became aware of the call to prayer. It was pitch black outside so she had no idea of the time. She found the muezzin's exotic call soothing and turned over in bed to fall back asleep listening to it.

'What the Hell is that?' she muttered to herself, a few seconds later, eyes wide open and alert. The sound of pots and pans being banged was coming closer. She could also hear people shouting. If she hadn't been so alarmed and drowsy, she would have leapt out of bed to investigate, but she was cosy and warm and did not feel brave enough to get out of bed in this unfamiliar place. She looked over to where Jane and Julia lay. How could they still be sleeping with all of this racket going on? She saw Julia turn over.

'Hey, Julia! Are you awake?' she whispered.

'Hmm?' Julia murmured. 'What is that noise?' she asked groggily.

'I don't know,' Kaye replied.

'Do you think we should go look?

'There's no way I'm going out there!'

'Is it some kind of riot?'

'No idea. Why on earth would anyone be rioting in the middle of the night?'

'You speak Turkish. Can't you understand what they're shouting?'

'No. I can't make out any words for all the banging of the pans.'

'How long has it been going on?'

'Well, I heard the call to prayer and then this started.'

'Do you think it's something to do with it being Ramazan?'

'It could be. Well, I might as well go to the loo now that I'm awake. Wonder what time it is?'

'Hey, listen! It's fading away. Whoever it was is going to torture someone else.'

Jane was sceptical about the din that Kaye and Julia described Kay as they dressed for the cold climate and went down for breakfast. If it had been so loud, why hadnt it woken her too?

It was a fine, sunny day with a cerulean blue sky. There was a light dusting of snow everywhere and from their high vantage point they could now see the magical landscape in all its glory. As far as the eye could see, smooth hillocks of pinkish cream stone, some made into homes or hotels or simply as nature intended them, undulated around them.

The rest of the group were already seated when they entered the dining room. Mehmet bustled around and tea was quickly served in small glasses. He had heard Jane's comments about the rude awakening in the night and smiled.

'During Ramazan volunteers take turns in going round the town to wake everyone up so that they can eat breakfast before the sun rises and fasting begins,' he clarified.

'Aha!' Julia said. 'That explains it. Perhaps we should wake Jane up tonight so that she can hear it! We can't have her missing out can we?' she added teasingly, smiling at a scowling Jane.

Mehmet offered them a traditional Turkish breakfast, French toast or cereal and toast. He was used to international tourists and knew that foreigners liked cornflakes, puffed wheat and chocolate rice cereals, rather than cheese, tomatoes, cucumber and olives first thing in the morning. The group ordered their food and Mehmet disappeared into the kitchen to give instructions to his wife.

'The eggy bread is delicious,' Kaye announced, 'particularly drizzled with this local honey.'

'Yeah,' agreed Julia. 'Who'd have thought we'd be eating this in Cappadokia!'

The conversation turned to their plans for the day and Mehmet, overhearing their chatter, suggested that they go to the Göreme Open Air Museum, which was a must see. He asked if any of them were interested in horse riding as his friend had a ranch and horses for every level of rider from experienced to those who had never been on a horse before. Jane and Kaye immediately said they would love to go riding and Julia showed interest too. The others said they would prefer to go walking in Rose Valley as the weather was perfect for a hike. Before they left to begin the day's activities, Mehmet told them about his café down the hill and also recommended a local restaurant where the food was excellent for their evening meal. He asked Kaye, Jane and Julia to stay behind for a few minutes while he arranged the horse riding with his friend.

'My friend Erkan will come and pick you up here at one o'clock to take you to the ranch. That will give you plenty of time to see the museum and have lunch before you go.'

'Thanks Mehmet,' the girls said. 'We really appreciate your help. Let's go and get our things.'

The group made their way out of the town, up a steep hill, following the signs to Göreme Open Air Museum. They showed their Özkent identity cards and were pleased to get a twenty-five percent discount on the admission price. It still surprised Kaye that teachers were held in such high regard in Turkey- so unlike the derision and disrespect for the profession in Britain.

The museum is a World Heritage Site and the group opted to have a tour guide so that they would make the most of their visit. They spent the next three hours, following the guide walking along the pathways, climbing stairways and passing through tunnels to reach the various eleventh and twelfth century churches, frescoes and dwellings. The guide explained that the history of Cappadokia began with volcanic eruptions ten million years ago.The eruptions spread a thick layer of hot volcanic ash over the region which then hardenend into a soft, porous rock called tuff. Over time, wind, water and sand erosion wore away the tuff, carving it into the pinnacles we see today. Boulders of hard stone caught in the tuff were pushed up onto cones of tuff and are known as 'fairy chimneys'. The soft texture of the rock, the magical conical structures, the fact that people actually lived, worshipped and carried out a relatively normal existence in these dark caves was remarkable.

As Mehmet's cafe was on the way back to their hotel, Kaye, Jane and Julia decided to seperate from the rest of the group, who were going to make their way to Rose Valley, and go for lunch in the cafe. They sat down on cushioned pew style wooden seats in front of a roaring fire and asked for the menu. They all chose *menemen,* a traditional dish of eggs, onions, tomatoes and peppers, baked in the oven in clay dishes. While his daughter prepared their lunch, Mehmet sat with the girls and asked them if they knew various people he knew who worked at Özkent. They didn't but as they were new to the university it was hardly surprising.

'So, where are you from?' Mehmet continued.

'Kaye and Jane are from England and I am from Canada,' Julia replied. Kaye and Jane looked surprised at Julia's response but Julia's stern look told them not to correct her. The American community had become almost paranoid about terrorist attacks against them and preferred to say they were Canadian if asked about their nationality.

They chatted to Mehmet until their food arrived and he promptly left them to enjoy their meal.

A small, wiry man, Erkan, the owner of the ranch, dressed in dusty, well-worn chaps, tooled cowboy boots and a dark leather stetson, the colour of which matched his weather-beaten complexion, arrived just before one and helped the girls into his minibus. They went through the same questions again on the journey to Avanos. Erkan's English was fluent and he spoke with a slight American accent. He was eager to get to know his new acqaintances and asked them if they could ride and their proficency levels, mentally deciding which horses he would give them. Kaye said she loved riding but had suffered a nasty fall last time she had ridden and had lost her confidence. She asked Erkan to give her a slow plodder.

Taking a sharp right turn off the main road to Avanos instead of going into the town centre, the minibus jolted along a stony, dirt road which twisted and turned through the countryside until they came to a large parking area. As they entered the ranch, a horse whinnied, sensing Erkan's return. He stopped to pet a chestnut horse in the first loose box, saying proudly, 'This is my prize stallion, Gigolo. No one can ride him except me – he's a real handful!'

Erkan shouted orders to the group of youths who were leaning on the white fence surrounding an outdoor menage. They loped off into a large barn and Erkan urged the girls to follow them. The barn housed forty horses and he wanted to show them some of them. He pointed out the merits of each horse, stroking and talking to each of them in turn. It was obvious he had a great love for his horses.

Suddenly, the sound of approaching hooves on concrete made the girls stand against the wall to let the grooms and horses past. Kaye looked anxiously at the four horses being led out. She really hoped the enormous black one at the back was not her mount. Erkan smiled as he saw Kaye's face. 'Don't worry! He's not yours. I'm going to give him some exercise – he's an ex-military horse and is getting lazy. Jane, this is Sevda, she's yours. She's gentle and obedient but will run like the wind if you want her to. Julia you'll be riding Ceylan. Riding her is like sitting in an armchair but don't get near her head – she bites! And Kaye, here's your slow plodder. This is Rahvan. Let's get mounted and spend a bit of time in the menage before we go out into the countryside.

Even though Rahvan was not a big horse, Kaye had forgotten how high off the ground she felt when on a horse. With her heart racing, partly from nerves and partly from excitement, Kaye urged Rahvan to start walking around the sandy ring. She kicked him on but he barely budged. She moved in her saddle and clicked her tongue, trying to find the right signal to make him walk on. No, that didn't work. She looked around and saw Jane and Julia walking confidently around the menage.

'Erkan, what do I do to make him move?' Kaye shouted.

'Use your heels to kick him,' Erkan replied.

Kaye lightly dug her heels into Rahvan's fat belly and he reluctanly walked forward a few steps, then stopped. Kicking again, Kaye whispered, 'Come on you lump of lard, walk!' Rahvan started walking but not because of Kaye's word, but because he had spotted

Erkan making his way across the ring. He knew who was the boss around here and decided he'd better behave.

'That's it ladies. Now let's try a trot,' Erkan shouted, walking to the centre of the ring. Jane and Julia soon had their horses trotting in an anti-clockwise direction but Kaye was still walking. She kicked hard and Rahvan lurched into a trot. Just as she was falling into the rhythm of a rising trot, he slowed to walking pace. By this time Kaye was beginning to get warm and unzipped her fleece.

'Are we ready to go out? Erkan asked.

'Think so,' replied Jane. 'What about you, Kaye?'

'I'm ready. Now I know there is no chance of this one running away with me, I'll be fine.'

Erkan mounted his huge steed and led the way along a dirt track out of the ranch. 'We'll do the river ride' he said. 'Just make sure you follow behind me.' Jane followed behind Erkan, with Julia behind and Kaye bringing up the rear on the reluctant Rahvan.

The riders were accompanied by Erkan's kangal dog, Khan. He was the size of a calf with a short-haired cream body and black face. His sturdy build made him perfect for his primary job as a guard dog, as his breeding dictated, but despite the fierce looking barbed collar he wore around his neck he was a friendly dog who loved people.

'He won't hurt anyone who is with me but if he senses danger, an intruder or I give a command he will kill,' Erkan explained. 'Kangals are used to protect flocks of sheep and will fend off wolves, bears and jackals. They will protect the people who they regards as their 'flock' and guard them with extreme loyalty and devotion.'

Kaye had petted Khan upon meeting him at the entrance to the ranch and was glad she had not known about this vicious side to his personality then as she would have been forever scared of him. She was suddenly brought back to reality as a branch almost took her eye out. She ducked to avoid another low branch as they rode through a small coppice. The horses picked their way through the spindly trees and Kaye noticed that the river was perilously close on the right hand side. She immediately took a tighter hold of the reins, worried that if Rahvan lost his footing she would be pitched into the freezing water. She looked ahead and saw Erkan lying almost flat on his huge horse's back. There was barely enough room for the horse to make its way through the trees.

'Watch out for low branches!' Erkan called back.

'Too late for that!' Kaye shouted, maintaining a low crouched position over Rahvan's neck. She felt nervous as the ground began to slope down in front of her and gripped with her knees in case she lost her balance and toppled over his head. She was determined she was not going to fall off.

Soon, the riders came out into the open, where there was a dirt path, well trodden by previous riders and Kaye breathed a sigh of relief. Although the weather was icy cold, the pale, watery sun shone in a cloudless blue sky. An eagle soared overhead and Jane quickly took her camera from her pocket to take a photograph. She then, turned around to capture a snap of Julia and Kaye.

'This is to show the others what they're missing,' she said, smiling. 'Who wouldn't love this? It's ages since I've hacked out. I used to ride in an indoor school. I hope we get a chance to canter. That'll blow the cobwebs away!'

'Oooh! I'm not sure I want to do that,' Kaye hesitated. ' I'm only just feeling safe at walking pace.'

'Don't worry, Kaye,' Erkan shouted from the front. 'You don't have to do anything you don't feel comfortable with. Besides, you'll have to work hard to make Rahvan canter!' he added.

At this, Kaye relaxed and began to enjoy the view around them. Erkan pointed out the extinct volcano, Ercihas, in the distance, which was one of the volcanoes responsible for forming the unique landscape of Cappadokia. The river was only about twenty metres wide but ran fast. The clear water swirling around hidden rocks underneath, formed eddies and white ripples as it proceeded downstream.

'When you come in the summer,' Erkan said hopefully, 'You'll be able to take the horses into the water and they will swim across.'

'Not sure if I fancy that,' Kaye thought to herself, cringing as Jane replied,

'I'd love to!'

They continued along the path until Erkan decided to cut across a ploughed field in the direction of a small hamlet. The soil was deep and the horses walked with difficulty over the ruts, occasionally stumbling as the piled up soil gave way under foot. Kaye's sense of security was shattered as Rahvan stopped dead in the middle of the field. She kicked him on but he refused to take another step.

'Help!' she yelled. Erkan turned in his saddle and growled at the lazy horse. This had absolutely no effect on Rahvan.

'Kick him harder!' he shouted. 'You can't stay there.'

Kaye kicked, jumped around in her saddle and finally let rip,

'Come on you stupid little shit…..MOVE!'

Surpsrisingly, Rahvan pricked up his ears and started to walk forward.

Erkan roared with laughter, 'Wow! That's some voice you have. I'm glad I'm not a pupil in your class. I think you scared Rahvan half to death! Now you know how to keep him going.'

On hearing the clatter of hooves on the lane that ran through the hamlet, a scruffy dog of indeterminate breed yapped at an iron gate. Khan walked past, head held high, not dignifying the small village dog with even a glance. A group of small children ran out of a small mud built house as they passed.

'*Merhaba*!' they shouted, waving their grubby hands, 'Engleesh?'

'*Merhaba*!' Kaye replied. 'Yes English.'

'*Şeker! Şeker*!' a cheeky girl shouted, asking for sweets.

'*Şeker yok*,' Kaye answered, looking apologetic and making a mental note that next time she must put some sweets in her pocket. '*Görüsürüz!*' she added, waving goodbye.

'They're asking for candy because it's Şeker Bayram,' Erkan informed his group. 'It's traditional to give kids candy at this time.'

'Oh yes, I forgot,' Jane sighed. 'Maybe we should buy some sweets to keep in our pockets to give any children we see.'

'Good idea, said Kaye, ' but any sweets in my pocket will not be there for long!'

When Kaye had helped unsaddle Rahvan she met her friends in Erkan's office. As soon as she picked up her bag she could hear the beep of her mobile phone and knew that there was a text message waiting for her. She opened it to find four messages from Vedat. He had obviously been trying to reach her for the past hour. She replied quickly, explaining that she had been out riding and had left her phone in the office for safe keeping.

[I was worried about you, Kaye. You didn't reply to my messages.]

[I'm sorry. Don't worry. I'm fine.]

[I hope you are enjoying yourself. Do you like Cappadokia?]

[Yes, it's a magical place. We must come together. There are some lovely places to stay here.]

Vedat had never been to Cappadokia, although was familiar with some of the place names as his agent employed many of his seasonal workers from the area. Most of Vedat's two hundred and fifty regular cotton pickers were from a small village nearby.

[We'll see. I need to go now. I've been invited to two weddings, one at five and one at seven. We'll talk later. Kisses xxx]

[*OK. Have fun. Kisses xxx.]*

The next day, despite being saddle sore, Kaye agreed to return to the ranch with Jane for another ride. This time it was just the two of them as Julia had opted to go with some of the others to the town of Ürgüp. They were not being picked up for another hour so they decided to walk down into the town and do some window shopping. There were several carpet shops but one in particular drew their attention. It was a two storey traditional stone building and held an imposing corner position. Finding the entrance was not easy but spying a low doorway at the side, they held aside a curtain and went into the darkness beyond. Carpets of every hue were piled along the walls and they bent down to enter another small corridor, again squeezing between carpets stacked from floor to ceiling along both walls. Just as they were thinking it was like a labyrinth, they stepped up into a huge open hall where two men were folding carpets and throwing them up onto a huge mound against one wall.

'Hello! Welcome!' a voice greeted them. 'My name is Sultan. Would you like to see some of my beautiful carpets?'

'Well, we're not looking to buy, but we'd like to see what you have,' Jane replied.

'Please sit,' Sultan said, gesturing to a seating area at one side of the room. The furniture was traditional in style – a wooden framed couch with padded cushions and a variety of armchairs in different upholstery, forming a circle around a large, round, copper tray on an ornate wooden tripod, which served as a coffee table.

'This an amazing place,' Jane said, admiring the architecture.

'It used to be a caravansaray where traders stopped over as they travelled on the Silk Road,' Sultan informed them. 'This is the main hall where they would eat and drink. The other smaller rooms are where they would have slept. The camels would have been fed and watered out in the courtyard at the back.'

'How many carpets do you have here?' Kaye asked with genuine curiosity.

'About a hundred thousand,' Sultan said proudly.

'I hope you're fully insured,' Kaye added, 'It's one Hell of a fire risk in here!'

Another man entered the room, bringing glasses of apple tea for the guests and began to help his colleague as Sultan barked orders at them about which carpets to release from the piles. One of them tugged at a particular carpet as the other lifted the carpets on top. They then threw the first carpet with panache into the middle of the floor, prompting Sultan to start his spiel about the origins of the carpet, the meaning of the motifs, the quality of the handmade dyes and inviting Jane and Kaye to walk on it to feel the depth of the pile and the quality of the weave.

'It's lovely,' Kaye said with enthusiasm, feeling the need to reward Sultan's efforts.

Before Jane could respond, another carpet was hurled on top of the first one and more cxplanations were given about its provenance. This continued until there were more than twenty carpets scattered across the floor. There were several that the girls liked. They inquired about the cost of particular ones but with the huge choice as the pile increased, they forgot which ones each of them had liked and began to feel overwhelmed by the range of different colours and sizes, and the choice of silk or wool on view. Fortunately, Kaye remembered that they were supposed to be meeting Erkan and after thanking Sultan profusely for his hospitality, they promised they would return later with their friends.

'Phew! I'm exhausted!' Kaye gasped as they came out of the gloomy doorway into the bright sunlight. 'How do you ever choose one carpet over another? After a while they all start to look the same.'

'I think the best thing to do is once you spot a carpet you like, ask them to put it to one side, ask the price, do some bartering and them decide if you really want to buy it or not,' Jane advised.

'That sounds like a good idea. It's such an experience though. We must take the others tonight after we've eaten. I'm sure they'll stay open till quite late.'

Once they were saddled up and ready to go, Erkan suggested they ride to a place called Çavusin. It was in the opposite direction to the previous day's ride so the girls were treated to a different vista, first riding along a narrow lane, across some fields and then out onto an open plain. Today, Rahvan seemed to be behaving himself and Kaye felt relaxed enough to look around more at the scenery and not just at the ground in front of her. Erkan was riding Gigolo who was prancing, eager to have his head and take to the wind. Kaye admired Erkan's horsemanship as, not all fazed by Gigolo's head tossing, snorting and inability to walk in a straight line, he kept a tight rein and continued to point out places of interest and engage the girls in endless chatter.

Ahead of them, the ground became steeper and they climbed a narrow gully between porous rock formations, finally arriving in the centre of Çavusin. To their left they saw tiny holes cut into the steep rock face, where until twenty years ago people had still lived. Erkan explained that the government had forced the cave dwellers to leave as the site was deemed to be unsafe. It seemed incredible that people had lived there until so recently. Kaye and Jane dismounted to stretch their legs and take photographs of the spectacle before them. Gigolo was still prancing, so Erkan stayed in the saddle where he had more control over the lively stallion.

On the way back to the ranch, on the open plain, Jane asked if they could canter.

'How do you feel about that?' Erkan asked Kaye.

'I think I'll be okay,' she answered cheerily, sounding more brave than she felt.

'Okay then. Let's go!'

Without hesitation, Gigolo lurched into a canter, closely followed by Jane on Sevda. Kaye kicked Rahvan and he began to trot. She kicked again urging him to change pace but he stubbornly kept trotting. A cloud of dust rose ahead where Erkan and Jane were fast disappearing into the distance.

'That looks more like a gallop,' Kaye thought to herself, giving a harder kick to Rahvan's belly. Instead of increasing his speed, Rahvan suddenly stopped dead, gave a whinny and refused to move.

'Oh no!' cried Kaye. ' Don't you dare stop now! Come on, get a move on,' she urged, trying not to panic.

By now Erkan and Jane had gone out of sight around a bend in the landscape. Rahvan gave a loud neigh, reared up on his hind legs, spun around and began to trot back the way they had come.

'No you don't!' Kaye shouted, pulling hard on the reins and trying to turn hin round again. Rahvan neighed even louder, now in full panic, thinking that he had been left behind.

Kaye realised that being rough had no effect on her mount, so she softened her voice,

'Come on nice horsey. We need to catch up with the others and then we can go home.' This did not have the desired effect and Rahvan again tried to spin around and when Kaye tugged his head back around to face the right direction, he reared, neighed and turned his head in an attempt to bite Kaye's foot.

'Jaaaannne!' Kaye screamed. She had no idea if Jane could hear her but was at her wit's end. What else could she do? If she tried to fight Rahvan any more she knew she'd end up being thrown to the ground as Rahvan bolted back to the ranch without her.

'Jaaaane! Heeeelp!' she screamed at the top of her lungs. She scoured the way ahead hoping that Jane had heard her. She was just about to burst into tears when she saw dust rising ahead and could make out Erkan at full gallop heading towards her.

'Oh my God! I'm so glad you came,' she wailed. 'This stupid horse thought you'd left him behind and I couldn't get him to follow you.'

'I'm sorry!' Erkan apologised. 'We shouldn't have left you but I thought you were following us until I heard you shout. Are you okay?'

'I'm shaking like a leaf,' Kaye spluttered, taking a tissue out of her pocket to wipe away the tear that was running down her cheek.

'Are you fine to ride on?' Erkan's concern was genuine. He took pride in keeping his riders safe and felt guilty that he had abandoned Kaye.

' I don't know. My legs are shaking so much I can't grip with them.'

'Look, I'll put you on a lead rein and then Rahvan will behave,' Erkan suggested, reaching for a red rope out of his saddle bag and clipping it onto Rahvan's bridle.

'Okay,' Kaye agreed, sniffing into her tissue.

By this time, Jane, too had joined them and the trio slowly and calmly made their way back to the ranch.

'At least Gigolo has used up most of his energy after that long gallop,' Jane commented, trying to lighten the mood.

'Yes, who'd have thought a slow plodder could be so much trouble? Next time I'm going to ride a faster horse so that I don't get left behind,' Kaye said cockily. Those words would come back to haunt her.

Chapter 19

Ankara

January 2002

Kaye was disappointed that she had not seen Vedat in the five months since coming to Ankara. Despite there still being a thousand miles between them, she had thought that they would be able to see each other at least once a month, with him coming to see her or them meeting somewhere mid-way. She knew going to his area was not possible and she had no intention of making his family situation worse. His parents thought that the relationship had ended and Vedat said it was better this way in order to avoid the confrontations and arguments of the past. The only benefits of being in Turkey were that her Turkish had improved and, without the time difference to consider, they could talk at any point during the day or night.

But at last, Vedat was coming to stay for a long weekend and Kaye could not contain her excitement. She wanted to be angry with him for not visiting sooner but that melted away when she heard he had booked flights. She had returned from spending Christmas and New Year with her family in Bakewell and had been shocked at the icy blast that greeted her as she descended the steps from the plane. The temperature was ten degrees below freezing, but, with the wind chill factor, felt much colder. At least a foot of snow lay on the ground and in places, where the fierce wind had blown the powdery snow into drifts, it was deeper still. She had not expected Turkey to have such a harsh winter climate.

On the Friday evening, Vedat's taxi pulled up in the car park in front of Kaye's apartment block and Kaye, who had been waiting impatiently at her window, ran down the stairs to greet him. Skidding on the wet, melted snow inside the doorway, they hugged and clung to each other, with beaming smiles on their faces and giggling nervously. Kaye admired the beautiful, charcoal grey cashmere coat Vedat was wearing and taking his hand, led him up to her flat.

He presented her with the box he had been carrying.

'What is it?' Kaye asked.

'It's *künefe* - a traditional dessert from my area,' Vedat replied.

'Yum!' I can't wait to try it. It's funny that we both come from places where famous desserts are made. I must bring you some Bakewell pudding one day. I think you'll like it.'

Once inside the flat, Vedat kicked off his shoes, flung his coat on a nearby chair and took her in his arms, giving a long sigh and whispering, 'I love you' in Kaye's ear.

Kaye looked into his dark, smouldering eyes as he gently stroked her face. Nothing could compare to the feeling she had when she was in Vedat's arms. She truly believed that they were old souls reuniting again in this life, such was the connection between them. They kissed, savouring the smell of each other, their tongues tentatively touching tips and then exploring deeper. The months of not seeing each other, the pent up passion and longing for sexual release ignited a fire in them both. Unfamiliar with his surroundings, Vedat gestured towards the bedroom on the left, not sure if it was the right room and with a nod, Kaye allowed herself to be guided to her bed. Vedat removed her clothes one by one, kissing each part of naked skin that he revealed, until Kaye was gasping with anticipation. She could feel his hardness pressing against her stomach as he reached around her back to undo her bra. She moaned as he sucked on her nipples and his hand found its way between her legs. When Kaye was completely naked, Vedat quickly undressed himself and lay down on the bed, pulling Kaye on top of him. They rolled over and became a tangle of limbs, eager to touch every part of each other and murmuring words of endearment. Their lovemaking was slow, sensuous and deeply satisfying and afterwards they lay in each other's arms basking in contentment.

They spent most of the next day in bed, only getting up to go to the bathroom or to get food and drink. Kaye had bought Vedat's favourite biscuits and cake, along with lots of fruit, bread, cheese, tomatoes, cucumber and other snacks, predicting that she would not have time to cook. Kaye was eager to try the *künefe* that Vedat had brought. He told her it was best eaten warm so she popped it into the microwave for a minute. She loved the crunchy topping which reminded her of Shredded Wheat and was surprised when she bit into the middle and tasted the melted stringy cheese. Vedat was pleased that Kaye liked it. He loved making her happy.

They listened to music, talked for hours, made love, dozed and not wanting to be apart, accompanied each other to the bathroom as the need arose. Vedat marvelled at how open they were with each other – something he had never experienced before. Kaye laughed at his shocked expression when she told him that she had been brought up in a house where Nora walked around naked and it was common for someone to be on the toilet while another cleaned their teeth at the sink.

As they were sitting propped up on pillows, feeding one another slices of apple dipped in hummus, Vedat turned to Kaye and with a soulful look said,

'I want to have a child with you. Kaye.'

For a second, Kaye hesitated, not sure what to say. 'There's nothing I'd like more than to have your baby, but I told you I can't have children.'

'Why not?'

Her heart sinking, Kaye replied, 'I thought you understood. I told you when we first met that if you wanted children, I was not the right person for you.'

'Yes, you did tell me but I don't understand why not.'

'Well… I explained to you that I had several operations and suffered from endometriosis. There is a lot of damage to my womb and I had one ovary removed so the chances are very slim.'

'But is it possible?'

'Who knows? But there is also the possibility that even if I got pregnant that I couldn't carry the baby to full-term because of the scar tissue on my womb.'

'Could we try?'

'Darling, we haven't used contraception for the last two years and nothing has happened. It's not as though we're not trying.'

'But you're healthy now aren't you? The problems you had are gone so maybe it's possible now. It was a long time ago when you were told that you couldn't have children.'

'That's true. I was only thirty three and it was a dreadful blow. I always thought I'd have kids and I cried for days when they told me.'

'Oh, Kaye, you'd be a wonderful mother. Please let's try.'

'We haven't *not* been trying! she said indignantly. 'I secretly hoped that it would happen but I didn't want to raise my hopes. If you want a baby so much, would you consider adoption?'

'I don't think so. I haven't thought about it.'

'I would be happy to adopt. Is it easy to do in Turkey?'

'Yes, there are lots of unwanted babies here. But Kaye I want *your* baby, with your blood - a mini Kaye! I don't want somebody else's baby.'

'Well, from the little knowledge I have of genetics, the baby would probably have black hair, brown eyes and olive skin – just like you! I'd like a mini Vedat. He'd be so cute!'

'What about fertility treatment?'

'I don't know. There's still the risk of my womb rupturing even if I could get pregnant.'

‘How could we find out?’

‘Some of the girls here have been to a gynaecologist who they say is very good. I could go to see her and see what she thinks. It costs a lot of money, though.’

‘Don’t worry about the money. I can handle that.’

‘Okay then. Shall I make an appointment to see the gynaecologist?’

‘Yeess! I also think this could be a way for us to be together. My father would never allow a child of mine to be brought up without a father. It could be the answer to our prayers!’

‘Please don’t get your hopes up, Vedat. It still might be hopeless.’

‘Okay. But at least if we’ve tried, we’ll know. If we don’t try, we’ll always wonder and might regret that we didn’t investigate further.’

That conversation brought them even closer together. They slept entwined, snuggled in the middle of Kaye’s king-sized bed, dreaming of creating their own family and living happily ever after.

On Sunday evening, the Turkish television news channels announced that all Ankara schools would be closed the next day because of the heavy snow that had fallen throughout the day and the prediction for more that night. A buzz soon spread around the campus, with teachers waiting to hear officially from John Da Souza whether or not there would be school the next day. Kaye received the call from John and as the representative for her building, ran around the block, knocking on doors, shouting, ‘It’s a Snow Day tomorrow!’

The beauty of knowing the night before, was that everyone could have a lie in and it was gone ten o'clock before either Kaye or Vedat woke up. Kaye got out of bed and went to the window to see how much snow had fallen during the night. The ground was covered in at least three feet of snow and the trees were laden, dropping small piles of snow as their branches bent under the weight. Behind the apartment blocks, the children of Özkent staff members, some of whom had never seen snow before, were busily building snowmen, throwing snowballs and rolling around making snow angels. Vedat joined Kaye at the window and smiling said, 'That could be our child one day.' Kaye smiled back but she was not getting her hopes up yet. She knew the fertility treatment road was long and full of pot holes.

Chapter 20

Karabulut,

September 1987

He had been back home for six months. He missed the camaraderie of the military and surprisingly, missed the routine and being told what to do. With no clear aim as to what to do with his life, he spent hours wandering around his father's fields, thinking. He felt extremely lonely. His family could not understand why he was so miserable and dissatisfied with marriage and the match they had made for him.

His return home had been met with much happiness. His mother cried when she saw how much weight he had lost and immediately went to the kitchen to prepare his favourite meal of fresh chicken, rice, *güveç* and yogurt. Many of his large extended family came to visit and were eager to hear stories about his experiences in the army and they sat down in the salon, drinking tea, waiting for him to tell them. He found he had no appetite for idle chatter but knew it would be very rude if he refused. He told them about his job as the General's driver, the friends he had made and they were interested to hear about life in Cyprus. His wife was making sure their guests were given refreshments, so he had not had the opportunity to speak to her alone.

Her eyes had lit up when she saw him and she had coyly kissed his cheeks and hugged him upon his return. He could see she had made a special effort with her dress and wore many of the gold bangles she was given for their marriage.

After making polite conversation for several hours, he excused himself and went to his room, which meant he was able to have some time to himself. He resented that this room was not his alone now, but one shared with his wife. He changed his clothes and lay on the bed. An urge to cry overwhelmed him and he let the tears flow down his cheeks. He loved his parents, brother and sister and had a few close friends, but no one understood him. He could not talk openly about how he felt or what troubled him. The intense feelings of loneliness were unbearable. It felt good to be home, but he wished he was still single and able to make his own decisions about his career and life.

His parents put no pressure on him to do anything, recognising that he need some rest and they were hoping it would not be long until there was the patter of the tiny feet of grandchildren. He needed to spend time with his wife and grow to love her. He had not had any intimate dealings with women whilst being in the army, so at least enjoyed the physical release of sex, and after listening to the stories of his fellow soldiers, experimented with new positions. His wife was compliant but was very conservative and he knew she had no yearning for the racier side of sex that he craved.

He found comfort in going to his refuge in the craggy outcrop, often with a bottle of vodka secreted about his person. He sat on the overhanging ledge, where he had dreamed of flying years ago, and looked back on his idyllic childhood and laughed at the innocent dreams he had then. Despite knowing the traditions and culture he had grown up in, he had somehow thought that the world was changing and that life for him would be different. Most families had televisions and were aware of a different world than their own. Children were growing up with videos and CDs and sang the popular music from Europe and the United States. Young men and women were beginning to wear the fashions heralded by westerners and as many young men went away to work in the Turkish tourist resorts during the summer season, they came back with new ideas and ambitions far outreaching the closed, insular communities they came from.

Now a man, he knew he should shoulder his responsibilities and make a life for himself and his wife. His family had a good standard of living and despite his father's lack of business acumen, the farm supported them well. If he put his mind to it, he knew he could make a place for himself in the family business but his heart just was not it in. He longed to get away to some far off land and live a simple life, with no pressure, no expectations and no restraints but lacked the drive to do it.

Chapter 21

Ankara

February 2002

Kaye's birthday was two days before Valentine's Day so Vedat decided to visit her for a long weekend. They counted down the days as their excitement mounted at being together again. Knowing that he was soon to arrive, Kaye had not told Vedat about the results of her fertility test, feeling that it was better to tell him face to face rather than on the telephone.

'*Hoşgeldiniz*!' Kaye greeted Vedat as she flung her arms around him, barely giving him time to get through the door to her flat.

'*Hoş bulduk*!' Vedat responded in reply to her welcome. 'Ahh! I've missed you, *canım*!'

'I've missed you too *canım*,' Kaye gushed, using the now familiar term of endearment. 'The kettle's boiled. I'm sure you're ready for a cup of tea.'

'Yes, I am, but first let me kiss you. Mmm, you smell so good I could eat you.'

'Ha! Ha! That would take some doing. There's more meat on me than even you could manage!'

'I love your body, Kaye, especially your *popo*.'

Kaye tried to accept the compliment gracefully but found it hard to believe that anyone in their right mind could love her big bottom. Before he could utter any more embarrassing comments about her body, Kaye kissed Vedat's lips to distract him. They kissed passionately until Kaye felt dizzy and had to break away.

'I'll make your tea,' she whispered in his ear and went to the kitchen.

Vedat took off his coat and went to the bathroom to wash his hands. He then crept up to Kaye as she was stirring the required two sugar lumps into his tea, nuzzling her neck and wrapping his arms around her. She luxuriated in his embrace before handing him the glass of tea and ushering him into the lounge.

After inquiring about each other's families and catching up on their daily lives, Kaye eventually told Vedat that she had been to see the gynaecologist for the results of the fertility tests she had done. She remembered the pitying look on Doctor Halime's face as she entered her office and knew straight away that the news was not going to be positive.

'I'm sorry, Kaye but the tests reveal that none of your eggs are viable and you are no longer producing the necessary hormones to make using donor eggs possible.' She had looked at Kaye with such sadness in her eyes that Kaye had smiled and felt the need to reassure her.

'It's fine. Really! I didn't expect there to be any change in my condition. It was just to satisfy my partner and to know for sure that there is no hope of us having a baby.'

'You're very brave,' Doctor Halime sympathised.

'I've had years to accept it,' Kaye responded. 'Thank you for all your help.'

Vedat listened carefully to her account, helping her with some of the Turkish vocabulary, as she struggled with the unfamiliar words and smiling as she giggled at the fact that the gynaecologist's name was an anagram of the Turkish word for pregnant.

'So that's it – no baby for us,' Kaye confirmed.

'This makes me very sad, Kaye.'

'Me too, but there's nothing we can do about it. Anyway, for all we know, you might not be able to father children anyway.'

Vedat looked shocked. 'Of course I can father children!' he said indignantly.

'How do you know?' Kaye asked.

'I just know.'

'Are there any little Vedats running around that I don't know about?' she teased.

'No.'

'Are you sure?'

'Yes I'm sure.'

Kaye had an unsettling feeling in the pit of her stomach. She hoped he was telling the truth.

The next day, after showering and using a clean towel to pray on, Vedat wanted to take Kaye shopping. He wanted to buy her something for her birthday but wanted her to choose it as he was unused to buying gifts for women. Kaye knew she would like a piece of jewellery so they decided to go a shopping mall on the main road into the city. She knew there was a jewellers in the mall, having admired some of their pieces on previous shopping trips.

They stopped outside Kaye's chosen venue, looking at the vast array of gold and silver in the window display. Kaye's eyes set upon a beautiful diamond solitaire ring with a modern setting.

'I love that ring!' she exclaimed, pointing it out to Vedat.

'Let's go inside and you can try it on.'

'It might be too expensive,' Kaye hesitated.

'Come on. We'll see.'

Vedat asked the salesman politely if they could look at the ring in the middle of the window display. The salesman quickly unlocked the glass door and, asking them if this was the correct tray, proceeded to take the ring from its pink satin cushion and slip it onto Kaye's finger. Unconsciously, she had slipped off her friendship ring and offered the ring finger on her left hand. As she showed Vedat the ring, she realised what she had done.

'Perhaps I shouldn't try it on that finger,' she suggested, noticing how snuggly the ring fitted her finger.

'Why not?' Vedat asked.

'Because that is the finger you wear an engagement or wedding ring on.'

'Does it matter?'

Kaye's heart sank. She was not planning to push Vedat into anything but the fact that he did not take the hint or use the opportunity to give her the ring as an engagement ring was disappointing. ‘No it doesn’t matter to me,’ she shrugged.

Negotiating a good price was second nature to Vedat and they left the shop with Kaye wearing her new present and Vedat pleased that Kaye had found such delight in his gift.

‘Thank you! It’s beautiful and I love it,’ Kaye said smiling and giving Vedat a gentle squeeze. She knew he would be uncomfortable if she gave him a big hug in public.

‘You’re welcome, *canım*. I want you to be happy always.’

Chapter 22

Bakewell

June 2003

The school year had drawn to a close. In the middle of the school's end of year ceremony, Kaye received a call on her mobile phone from Nora to say that Frank had collapsed and was in hospital. Her parents had arrived home from a holiday in Turkey the day before and Frank had said he was very tired and gone straight to bed. The next morning as he tried to get up he had fallen on the floor and Nora, being of much smaller build, had not been able to lift him. She could tell by his face that he was seriously unwell and had called for an ambulance, thinking it was another heart attack. Kaye had noticed on their recent stay with her that Frank had lost weight and was in pain but Frank had shrugged it off saying he had been to the doctor and it was just a trapped nerve in his back. Walking was uncomfortable for him and he had used a stick but Kaye had hired a car so her father had been able to do a lot of sight-seeing from the comfort the front seat, including a long weekend stay in Cappadokia, which Kaye had been eager to show them and where Frank had been fascinated by the cave houses and hotels.

By the time Kaye arrived at the hospital, doctors had already done tests and confirmed that Frank had cancer and he was being transferred to a specialist unit in Sheffield. The pain in his back was caused by several tumours on his spine but they needed to do more extensive tests to see if it had spread.

A nurse showed Kaye the way into the unit and told her that Frank was in the end cubicle. Having seen Frank looking ill following his heart attack in no way prepared Kaye for the deterioration she saw in her father that day. It was unbelievable that she had only seen him two days before, but he was barely recognisable. Smiling bravely, Kaye hugged Frank gently, not wanting to hurt his fragile body. He had always been such a big, strong, solid man and now she could feel bones where brawny muscles used to be. Frank, too, was trying to be brave,

'It's not good news, pet. It's cancer and it doesn't look good.'

'Have you seen the doctor today?' Kaye asked, sitting in a high-backed leather chair at Frank's bedside.

'Yes, I've seen two or three different ones who have all taken blood and examined me thoroughly. I'll know more tomorrow.'

The next day, Kaye and Nora were joined by Donna who had flown in from Canada and Jan, who was now six months pregnant, to meet Frank's consultant. They gathered around Frank's bedside to hear his prognosis.

'Good afternoon, Frank! These must be your daughters. Pleased to meet you all. I'm sorry that we have to meet in such circumstances. How are you feeling, Frank?'

'Not so bad. The painkillers you gave me this morning have taken the edge off the pain in my back.'

'That's good. Now, I now you're eager for me to tell you about the results of the tests.... I'm afraid it's not good news. The cancer has spread and the tumours on your spine are secondary tumours, along with masses in your lung, liver and brain.'

Their eyes filling with tears, the whole Rogan family was reeling with shock and Nora passed the box of tissues from the top of Frank's bedside locker to her daughters, and to Frank. Kaye wiped her eyes and asked,

'Is there anything you can do?'

'Well, we could try radiotherapy by there is no guarantee of success. It's up to Frank.'

'I've got nothing to lose,' Frank said stoically.' How long do you think I've got?'

Jan groaned and burst into sobs and Nora loudly blew her nose as the doctor continued.

'It may be weeks, three months at the most. I'm sorry.'

'Thank you for being so honest,' Frank said, his voice breaking with emotion.

'I'll let you digest the news and I'll be back later if you have any questions' said the consultant and went to exchange pleasantries with a man in the next cubicle.

None of the Knowles family knew what to say. They sat with tears trickling down their cheeks, feeling at a loss of how to deal with what was happening. It was Nora who spoke first,

'Oh Frank! What are we going to do?' she wailed.

Frank sighed and said, 'I suppose I'd better try the radiotherapy.'

Kaye could tell by the look on Donna's face that she, too, thought this a waste of time, but neither of them voiced their opinions. Donna worked as medical secretary in a private oncology hospital and was fully aware of the treatments available and saw on a daily basis the hopeless cases of people desperate to undergo any kind of torture if it would give them an extra few months of life.

'If that's what you want, then that's what we'll tell the consultant when he returns', said Nora. 'Let's think positive! You'll be out of here in no time and back at home digging the garden and pottering about in your shed before you know it.'

None of the others commented, wanting to hope Nora was right but deep in their hearts facing the reality that it might never be.

The radiotherapy treatments had little effect on the tumours and a week later Frank's condition had worsened considerably. Despite Nora's pleas that she wanted to take Frank home, Kaye had firmly quashed this and had pointed out the practicalities of looking after someone who was now bedridden, incontinent and in need of intensive nursing. Nora was in denial about the severity of her husband's state and it was left to Kaye to make decisions about Frank's care. Frank had complained that he could not sleep because of all the noise from the other patients, whose screams and groans of pain, cries for help and prayers to die deeply disturbed him. He admitted to one night joining in with them with attitude of 'if you can't beat 'em join 'em'.

The family asked if he could be moved to a small cottage hospital in Bakewell, near to where Nora lived, in order to provide Frank with a calmer environment, to cut down travelling time and to allow friends and neighbours to visit if they wished.

After an emotional visit with Frank, Donna returned home to Canada. She had used up all of her compassionate leave and needed to go back to work. She had given Kaye strict instructions to call her when the time came as she wanted to be there to say goodbye to her father. Jan visited every other day, but the family were concerned about how the stress of the situation was affecting her. The last thing they needed now was for her to lose the baby. Kaye was now officially on holiday for the long summer break she had from school, so was installed back in her old bedroom at the family home, her house having been rented out to a tenant.

Now that Frank was only a ten minute car ride away, she and Nora spent every afternoon and evening at Frank's bedside. He was on morphine and drifted in and out of consciousness. He hated not being allowed out of bed to go to the toilet and the indignity of wearing incontinence pads but he was too under the influence of the opiate to fight. Neighbours and friends were shocked at his appearance. The skeletal face, unfocused eyes and fragile body bore no resemblance to the Frank they had known. Everyone sat telling him their news and talked about the weather and their gardens, knowing that at one time this would have interested Frank, but no one was sure now whether he cared or even heard them. Occasionally, a smile would play on his lips, one eyebrow would rise slightly or his eyes would flicker open for a few seconds in response to what was being said.

Kaye was full of admiration for the nursing staff who treated Frank with tender care and spoke to him with respect. One of the night nurses, Marianne, was a rare individual who seemed to glow with love. It was she who took Kaye aside and told her that Frank had little time left. She said the signs were there – the shuddering and jolting of his body as major organs began to fail, his not being able to eat or drink and longer periods of unconsciousness. Kaye had been preparing herself for this moment and could not bear the thought of her father dying alone. She was adamant that she would stay the night at Frank's bedside. Nora was still in denial and looked drained. The stress of the last few weeks had taken its toll and she looked frail and old, so Kaye urged Donna, who had flown in that day, to take her mother home to sleep and she would call if the time came.

The evening passed uneventfully and in the early hours of the morning, Marianne urged Kaye to go to the Visitor's Room to lie down for a while. Before she did, Kaye opened the French windows in Frank's private room and sat on the balcony running around the back of the hospital where patients who were well enough sat to enjoy the sun during the day. She lit a cigarette and inhaled deeply, gazing at the stars and the bright half-moon. The light scent of the perfumed roses in the beds underneath the balcony wafted in the gentle breeze. She sent Vedat a few texts to update him on the situation even though he would be asleep. She had been overwhelmed by the sensitivity he had shown in his messages and phone calls during the past three weeks. He had lost many family members in recent years to bloody feuds, illness and fatal accidents. He seemed to find the right words to comfort Kaye and she gave thanks that she had found a man who loved her so unconditionally.

During the next night of vigil at Frank's bedside, Kaye began to reflect on her relationship with her father. As she fondly remembered family holidays when she was young and times they had spent together, she told Frank. His breathing was now very shallow but from the slight changes in his expression as she spoke, she knew he was listening. She asked Marianne if she could have some A4 paper, feeling the impulse to write these memories down. She wept as she remembered the laughter, the family landmarks and the funny incidents, tears falling onto the paper, making wet splodges and blurring the words. As she wrote she had been unconsciously listening to Frank's breathing and when it stopped, she panicked and pressed the red button by his bed. Marianne came quickly, stroking Frank's forehead and lifting his wrist to feel for a pulse. Then, with a shudder, Frank's breathing resumed.

'Oh, God!' sighed Kaye. 'I thought he'd gone.'

'That might happen a few times,' Marianne said quietly. 'He's fighting, Kaye. He doesn't want to leave you.'

For selfish reasons, Kaye did not want Frank to go either, but she knew he was suffering greatly and wanted his pain to stop. She had always been an advocate of euthanasia and now had seen at first hand, that dying could be a horrid, humiliating and excruciating affair.

'Give him permission to go, Kaye,' Marianne suggested, 'And tell him everything will be fine.'

Kaye took a deep breath, needing every ounce of self-control not to burst into sobs, and holding Frank's hand with one hand and stroking his hair with the other, said,

'Dad, you can go now. We'll be fine. I'll look after Mum, Donna and Jan and Vedat will look after me. I love you, Dad.'

Marianne nodded as Frank visibly relaxed and his breathing slowed. 'I'll call your mother.'

While Marianne was out of the room making the call, Frank stopped breathing. Kaye held her own breath for what seemed an eternity and when she heard the rasping sound of Frank's chest followed by a gasp of breath, she gulped for air. She continued to talk to him, stroking the back of his hand and occasionally kissing the waxy skin on his forehead. Her thoughts went out to her mother who was struggling to accept the situation and she hoped that Nora and Donna would get there in time. It was only when Marianne whispered, 'He's gone,' that Kaye realised the rattling sound of her father's breathing had ceased.

The funeral was six days later and held at the local crematorium. Frank's wishes were that his ashes be scattered under a white rose in their garden. Hundreds of friends, neighbours and family gathered at the small church to pay their respects to a much-loved, popular man. Kaye had rewritten the notes she had made in the hospital as a eulogy for her father. She had wanted to read it herself but on the day, feeling the unshed tears and raw emotion about to burst forth, had asked the vicar to read it.

'During the last two weeks I have had a lot of time to think about my Dad, what a special man he was and the times we spent together.

As a little girl, I was always a Daddy's girl and my fondest childhood memories are those I spent with him. Before taking your child to work was fashionable, Dad used to take me to work with him in the school holidays. We'd get up at six or even earlier depending on how far away he was working, have a breakfast of fried potatoes and tomato ketchup and get in the work's van to pick up the men. He would find me little jobs to do on the building site or let me sit in his office, thinking I was doing something useful. He always explained his current project, showing me the plans and drawings and patiently answering my questions. That's the kind of man my Dad was.

We spent every evening together, me and my Dad, while Mum was at work at the telephone exchange working the evening shift and in later years when Donna and Jan were asleep in bed. We both loved westerns and our favourite programme was 'The High Chaparral'. He'd send me to the corner shop for a packet of fags and something for myself and we'd settle down in front of the fire. On nights when there was nothing to our liking on the television he'd test me on my times tables or the longest rivers, or the highest mountains and capital cities. He was a good listener and I could tell him anything. He had great ambitions for me and only wanted the best for me. That's the kind of man my Dad was.

Dad believed in justice and would go out of his way to help family members in distress, neighbours needing a helping hand and even people he didn't know very well. I can't remember the number of times Dad was there to bail me out of sticky situations. He was a firm believer in 'give as good as you get' and instilled this in me from a tender age. I never had a problem with bullies or was afraid to stick up for myself. At Infants School when I threw a boy's cap over the school coal-house door and the Headmistress threatened me with suspension; Dad understood how this boy had been intimidating me and supported my action by ripping the coal-house door off its hinges to retrieve the cap. I don't think the headmistress ever got over the shock! You didn't mess with my Dad. That's the kind of man my Dad was.

Nothing was ever too much trouble for Dad. No matter where I wanted to go or what time of day or night, he'd be there. As a teenager, my friends used to marvel that Frank's taxi service could always be relied upon to fetch us from a night out in Sheffield or Manchester in the early hours of the morning. That's the kind of man my Dad was.

Everyone here will be able to think of numerous times when Frank has 'done a little job' for them: mending a leaking roof, re-decorating a bathroom, building an extension or tiling a kitchen. He prided himself on being strong physically and had boundless energy, but underneath he was a sweet, sensitive man, a real softie, a gentle giant, with a genuine sense of fun who loved people and particularly children. The family always came first with him and he adored us all. That's the kind of man my Dad was.

There are so many things that Dad taught me, from changing a ballcock, to oiling my bike chain, teaching me how to drive and how to make the best Yorkshire puddings. He gave me endless DIY tips and pearls of wisdom along the way. He shaped me and made me the person I am today. I adored him – as did we all. That's the kind of man my Dad was.

He touched all of our lives in unforgettable ways and I'm proud that he was my Dad.'

Chapter 23

Cappadokia

August 2003

‘Good morning, my darling,’ Vedat whispered in Kaye’s ear as he leant over her sleeping body.

‘Mmm?’ Kaye responded, coming round from a deep, satisfying sleep. She tried to turn over to face him but was pinned to the bed by Vedat’s weight, so wriggled onto her back, opening her drowsy eyes. She smiled, gazing into his soft, doey eyes. She was about to reach for the glass of water from the bedside table when her lips were clamped in a hungry kiss.

‘Agghh! I need water!’ she mumbled, pushing Vedat off.

He took this as a sign for a bit of rough and tumble and used his weight to prevent her from moving. His lips hovered over Kaye’s as she fought to get free.

‘Please, Vedat, I need water,’ she pleaded, hoping that a few glugs would refresh her stale mouth.

Vedat handed her the glass and she sipped slowly, then turned over, wrapping her arms around Vedat and returned his kiss. She could feel his excitement pushing between her legs and eagerly gave in to a passionate love-making session.

On Kaye's return from Bakewell, Vedat had suggested they go away together for a couple of weeks. He had never been to Cappadokia and after hearing Kaye's reports of her frequent visits there, he was curious about seeing it for himself. He knew Kaye and her family had suffered a great shock at Frank's passing and wanted to distract Kaye from her grief for a while. He flew to Ankara, where Kaye met him at the airport in the car she had hired for the next two weeks. They spent the night at Kaye's flat, before making an early start the next morning for Göreme.

They booked into a sumptuous suite in a cave hotel overlooking the village. It had spectacular views of the surrounding countryside and Kaye was delighted that Vedat, too, found the eerie landscape as magical as she did. She pointed out particular structures and a woman hanging out washing in the distance. It was strange to think that people were carrying out normal every day chores in such a bizarre place.

Their suite was on two levels, with a huge double bedroom and hamam style bathroom on the ground floor. The sturdy wooden bed covered with a fluffy duvet and pillows was topped with a beautiful, handmade bedspread, embroidered with brightly coloured flowers. In a more western environment it would have seemed gaudy but here it added to the authentic feel of the room. Embroidered felt shapes, decorated with beads and shells hung on the walls, along with wall lights which gave a golden hue to the room. Kilims of differing sizes and colours were strewn on the stone floor. A wardrobe had been built into an alcove on one wall. Its dark mahogany door, matching the bedside tables and the stained wooden window frames. The whole of the upper level was designed as a cosy, restful sitting room. All of the décor was in traditional Anatolian style, with patterned carpets and kilims in shades of dark blue and rich red covering the wooden floor and low seating arranged around two walls of the sitting room, was plump with stuffed cushions covered in thick brocade. Local artefacts were carefully placed around the room: a large ornately engraved silver and copper tray on wooden legs, a huge metal Turkish coffee pot stood on the floor, a leather footstool shaped like an old saddle, a baby's woven cradle nailed to the wall, a decorative string of woven wool with tufts of horse hair and coloured wool interspersed along its length ran around the top of the wall and naïve paintings of local scenes, daubed in oils and framed in antique gold. Kaye was intrigued to see that as well as these authentic pieces, the suite was equipped with a CD player and selection of CDs, tea making facilities, a flat screen television and a small library of books. The owners had certainly made every effort to make their visitors' stay as comfortable as possible.

The couple shared a love of music and liked recommending artists and songs that they thought the other would enjoy. While Vedat's repertoire consisted wholly of Turkish and Kurdish music, Kaye's was a broad range of popular and classical music from a range of eras and countries. Vedat had been moved to tears when Kaye had sung Oleta Adam's 'Get Here' to him one night, responding to the relevance of the lyrics, which she translated into Turkish for him. The sentiment of a woman, separated by miles from her lover and pleading with him to get to her by any means, seemed so apt for their situation that this track became their special song.

Since her first visit to Cappdokia, Kaye had spent at least one weekend per month in Goreme. She and Jane went away most weekends to Istanbul, the Black Sea coast, the historic towns of Safran Bolu and Amasia and Eğirdir Lake, all of which were close enough to Ankara to make a weekend stay worthwhile. Their favourite place, though, was Cappadokia. Riding at Erkan's ranch and exploring the area on horseback allowed the stresses of the previous work week to melt away. Time seemed to stand still and they returned to Ankara relaxed and ready to face the week ahead. They had made many friends in Göreme and were now recognised by many of the locals.

Kaye was keen for Vedat to visit the ranch that day. So far, they had driven to Avanos and walked around the town, stopping at Çavusin on the way. They had been to a small French restaurant in Uchisar for dinner and had visited the shops and restaurants in Göreme frequented by Kaye and Jane.

Vedat immediately hit it off with Erkan. They had much in common with their farming backgrounds, although Vedat had never been involved with livestock. Erkan proudly showed his new friend around the ranch, with Kaye trailing behind, patting and nuzzling the horses she now knew by name. Rahvan had now been retired and she usually rode an Akhal Teke mare called Akhal, who was a sweet natured, well trained horse, that Kaye felt confident riding. She helped one of the grooms saddle him up and lead him out to the menage. Erkan chose a slightly larger horse for Vedat, to accommodate his larger frame and gave him a leg up. He gave Vedat a few basic instructions about changing direction and using the reins to halt. Despite, the fact that he had never ridden a horse before, Vedat confidently kicked his mount and followed Kaye around the sandy enclosure. After a few circuits, Kaye shouted, 'How do you feel?'

'I'm fine, thanks,' Vedat responded.

'Do you want to go a bit faster?'

'Yes!'

Kaye urged Akhal on and without much encouragement, Vedat's horse gathered himself into a trot.

'Try and get in the rhythm and use your legs to push yourself up and down like this,' Kaye said, demonstrating a rising trot. She turned round in the saddle, to see Vedat bouncing up and down and clinging on to the pommel on the saddle for dear life.

'Ooof! This is too hard. I'll just sit,' he panted.

'Okay. Just do what feels natural, but please don't fall off!' Kaye knew that Vedat was accident prone and prayed that they would not end up with any injuries today. He had refused to wear a hard hat, confirming Kaye's opinion that all Turkish men think that they turn into cowboys on the back of a horse. Stetsons seemed acceptable but helmets were definitely not considered to be macho enough.

Erkan suggested that they all went on a ride across his land and onto the open countryside. Kaye wondered whether this was wise, bearing in mind Vedat's inexperience, but as Erkan was going to accompany them, she relented.

The searing August heat rose from the land and strong sun beat down on them as they plodded over the dry, dusty ground. The horses picked their way over the deep ruts, which puthered into dust like smashed sandcastles as the horses trod on them. Erkan and Vedat rode side by side, with Kaye bringing up the rear and as ever, Khan trotting behind. The two men chatted amiably, while Kaye enjoyed the scenery and relaxed into Akhal's lilting gait. The faded green hills which rose behind the town of Avanos, undulated before them under a cerulean blue, cloudless sky. Heat haze lay hovering over the arid, parched land. She had treated herself to some new black jodhpurs and had had a pair of knee length leather riding boots made by a local artisan in Ankara. They fitted her perfectly and made the whole riding experience more comfortable. She wondered how Vedat was fairing in his jeans and trainers. He would be totally unprepared for the soreness he would undoubtedly feel the next day.

With Vedat, looking at ease, Erkan eventually suggested that they use the flatter and more even ground to trot. 'Shorten your reins and kick the horse with your heels,' he instructed, doing the same and proceeding to trot. 'That's it! Good, good! Try to relax your shoulders and keep your eyes straight ahead.'

'You're doing really well!' Kaye shouted, watching Vedat from behind. 'You're a natural!'

A small, yapping tan and white dog suddenly appeared from behind a ramshackle hut, a shepherds' hut, pelting towards them, barking furiously, as though to warn them off. Erkan growled at it but the dog came alongside them, not in the least intimidated by Khan's fierce protective stance. Erkan urged his horse into a canter, beckoning the others to follow. Kaye was nervous about Vedat's inability to go faster but was immediately distracted by Akhal's change into his extended trot, an extra gait which characterised his breed, which required a certain seat, rather than a rising trot. As she fell into the bouncing step, she saw the small dog disappear beneath Akhal, trying to escape Khan's menacing jaws. She screamed involuntarily, as she felt a bump underneath her and heard a loud yelp. As she began to turn around to see what had happened to the dog, Akhal lurched into a canter, causing her to lose her balance and cling onto the saddle for support. She wildly tried to regain her balance, screaming at the top of her voice, 'Help! Erkan stop! I think I've trampled the dog.' But Erkan and Vedat were racing ahead, shirt tails flapping behind them, oblivious to Kaye's predicament. A cloud of dust followed in their wake, making Kaye cough. Akhal was trained as a trekking horse and continued to canter after his master.

'Erkaaaan! Please stop!' she shrieked as loudly as she could muster. '*Imdaaat*!' she yelled, hoping that the Turkish plea for help would work.

Vedat heard Kaye's voice and shouted ahead to Erkan, who turned around to see what had happened. He reined his horse to a shuddering halt and spun it around to retrace his steps, galloping back to where Kaye had managed to stop.

'What's the matter?' he asked.

'That dog got under Akhal's feet and I think I've killed it,' Kaye puffed. 'He trod on it. Oh God! Is it dead?' Her legs had gone to jelly and not daring to turn around fearing what she might see, she slumped into the saddle and hid her face in Akhal's mane.

Erkan laughed. 'It looks fine to me,' he added, pointing to where the dog was trotting into the distance with its tail between its legs.

'Oh, I'm so relieved! I felt this crunch and it gave this enormous yelp, then Akhal started cantering and I couldn't stop!' she garbled. I was shouting for ages before you heard me.'

'Are you okay?' Vedat asked, joining them, looking concerned.

'Yes, but I thought I'd killed that dog. It ran under Akhal's legs. Anyway, it doesn't seem to be hurt. It's run off.'

Vedat smiled at Kaye's explanation. 'You were worried about me falling off and you nearly did!' he teased.

'Well, Smarty Pants, there's still time yet. We're still a long way from the ranch. Race you back!'

Kaye relished their time together and wished it could be a permanent arrangement. Intense conversations were interspersed with tender moments and times when they giggled like children at each other's antics. Kaye would have much preferred to wake up next to Vedat every morning and be able to go about their daily routines, sharing a normal life, than their current snatched days away. She knew that Vedat made every effort to make his visits and their holidays as special as possible. No expense was spared and he always insisted on paying for everything. But no matter how wonderful and romantic these times were, Kaye looked at friends' relationships and wondered why she could not enjoy a relationship like them. She was often the only single woman in social groups and suffered her friends calling

Vedat 'the invisible man' as they rarely saw him. She longed to be able to take him to school events, friends' weddings and at every social gathering wished he were there with her. She was sure that Vedat loved her and he, too, was frustrated about their not being together but every conversation regarding their future plans came up with a stale mate and concluded with them both feeling depressed. Kaye had signed a new two year contract at Özkent. She had hoped that by the time her first two year contract was up she and Vedat would be married, but as things stood, they were no farther forward that they had been two years ago. However, they both maintained the hope that one day they would be together and share the life they both dreamed of.

Vedat often asked about what life would be like for them in England but mistook Kaye's reluctance and realistic view for them to move there as her not wanting him to go there. She was more optimistic about life in Turkey as at least they both spoke the language and were familiar with the culture. However, Vedat had a huge extended family and many of the places Kaye suggested as possibilities, were rejected by Vedat because he had relatives living there. Kaye was willing to move to Vedat's village but he had been adamant that she would not enjoy life there and would find it difficult to adjust to a life without independence or relative freedom.

Sometimes Kaye had fantasies about living in a Kurdish village: imagining making friends with the local women and learning how to make regional dishes and crafts from them. She knew there was no pre-school education in the area and thought that opening a crèche or pre-school would really benefit the community. With Vedat's financial backing and her early years' teaching experience, she considered this to be a viable option. She also thought that a mother/toddler centre might be a good idea. Women could bring their children to play, listen to stories and engage in group activities, while the women could socialise and have some time together, knowing their children were being well looked after by someone else. Kaye had a clear image of what the centre would look like and what resources she would need. The only hurdle she could see was that she would have to learn Kurdish as the children did not learn Turkish until they went to school. During one of their discussions, Kaye had told Vedat about her ideas. He had not rejected them outright but had not been enthusiastic either. In time, Kaye would discover that if she were Vedat's wife she would not be allowed to do any such thing.

Chapter 24

Karabulut,

March 1994

He was exhausted! For the last few months he had been working tirelessly campaigning for his cousin who was standing for election in the general election. He had not wanted to stand as a parliamentary candidate himself but had spent hours rallying, speaking at public gatherings and garnering support privately. Following the October 1991 National Assembly elections he and a group of Kurdish politicians had organised themselves as a separate parliamentary party, the Welfare Party, and now they had just won nineteen percent of the total vote, coming third behind the True Path party headed by the President Süleyman Demirel and Prime Minister Tansu Çiller and the main opposition party, the Motherland Party. Both the government and the Kurdistan Workers' Party (PKK) were fervently against his party. The government considered the party members to be political activists and to be working against the state, while the PKK saw the party as a rival as it tried to adopt Kurdish leadership. This result had shown that the Kurds in the South East of Turkey wanted change.

After a celebratory meal at the famous Recep Usta restaurant in Diyabakir, he had come home to sleep. The rest of the family had retired to bed hours ago so he was alone in the living room, slouched on the sofa having a last cigarette. He wondered whether his father had stayed up to hear the result of the election. He knew the old man would be delighted with the support the party had received, as it strived to balance Islamic principles with economic and political agendas. Although the conflict had been going on for over ten years now, the Aga had been shocked by the increased level of terror and political violence in the last two years. He had witnessed too much bloodshed and lost hundreds of family members to this fight for supremacy of the region. The PKK's use of extortion, indiscriminate shootings, bombings, arson and assassination were frequent occurrences. Only two months ago, the family had been rocked by the deaths of a cousin, his wife and two children during a PKK raid on their village near Mardin. His cousin had been the village guard and been shot in the head for attempting to protect his family. Whilst attacks by the PKK on villages was not uncommon, the fact that innocent women and children had been killed in cold blood had horrified the family.

He was suddenly roused from reflecting on the night's success, by a loud rapping at the door. Who on Earth could be visiting in the early hours of the morning? Quickly heaving himself off the sofa, he ran to the door, not wanting the noise to wake the rest of his family. He opened the door to find his friend, Ismail, breathing hard and leaning against the doorframe.

'You've got to come quick! They've arrested most of the party candidates, including your cousin, and other officials when they were leaving the restaurant. It's a good job you left early as you would have been arrested too!' Ismail panted. 'Get your jacket. We have to go to find lawyers and try to get them released.'

'Okay. Just let me get a few things,' he said, returning to the sofa to pick up his cigarettes, his wallet and his jacket from where he had thrown it over a chair. 'Do we know where they've taken them?' he asked.

'Probably to the main police station in Diyarbakır,' Işmail replied. 'That's where we'll go first. Mujdat has gone to get the lawyers and will meet us there.'

It took hours for the lawyers to get the politicians released. Those officials who had not stood for election had been allowed to go after just a couple of hours, but getting the newly elected party members out on bail had been a harder nut to crack. It was now obvious that the result had caused panic with the Turkish Government and they were dealing with it in the only way they knew how – imprisonment.

'You must be shattered!' his wife said sympathetically, ushering her husband to a nearby chair when he finally arrived home that afternoon. 'I'll make you some tea and then you should try to get some sleep,' she added as she bustled round the kitchen, putting water on to boil. 'I'll make sure the children don't wake you when they come home from school. The babies are sleeping and I'll get your mother to take them for a walk when they wake up.

He smiled weakly at the mention of his children. They were his pride and joy and everything he did was to protect them and make sure they had the best life possible. He was now the father of four sons, ranging in age from seven years to just one month old. They were living in troubled times and he felt it his duty to work for peace and take every measure to ensure their safety. Their large extended family made sure that no one went anywhere alone and all of the menfolk were armed. Women rarely ventured from home so were not at as much risk as children going to school and men going about their business.

'I thought that you had taken him home,' he shouted at Ismail down the phone.

'I did!' Işmail said indignantly. 'But apparently, a few minutes after he went inside his house, there was a knock at the door and when his wife opened it, armed police barged in and took him away.'

'*Tanrım Aman*!' he cried. 'What do the others say? What shall we do?'

'The lawyers have been told and they said they'd deal with it,' Işmail reported.

'I'm going to tell my father. Perhaps he can do something or at least contact someone who can,' he responded. 'I'll call you back in an hour. Meanwhile take someone to sit with my cousin's wife, she must not be alone at a time like this.'

'Baba, is there anything you can do to help our cousin?' he asked his father after putting down the phone. He knew that the Ağa had numerous influential friends and acquaintances both locally and also in Ankara and Istanbul.

'I'll call a few people and see what I can do', his father answered, his brow furrowed with a worried frown.

An hour later, he called Ismail to give him an update on the situation. 'No one seems to know where my cousin is,' he stated. 'My father has spoken to the Police Chief who says they released him on bail to his lawyers just after lunchtime this afternoon and he should be at home.'

'Well, that's true. They did. But where is he now?' Ismail said, his voice rising in indignation.

'I have no idea. We'll just have to play the waiting game and see what happens.'

They did not have to wait long. The following day, a dead body was discovered lying by the side of a main road just outside Karabulut. It was his cousin.

Chapter 25

Ankara

May 2004

'Did you like today's story? Kaye asked the sixteen four and five year olds sitting on the carpet in front of her.

'Yeeess!' they chorused.

'I like it when Daisy Duck finds her Mummy,' a bright little girl called Ipek answered, followed by Sinan's eager comment, 'I like it when the monster fish comes!'

'Weren't you scared?' Kaye teased.

'Noooo!' they all replied.

'Now, let's see who's sitting beautifully, ready to put their coats on. It's nearly time to go home.'

Kaye loved her job and she often thought what a good decision it had been to come here. She had fallen in love with the children, mostly Turkish, with the odd foreign child in the mix. They were the sweetest children she had ever taught. At this time of year, after nine months of teaching, their understanding of English was good and they had gained confidence in their abilities to speak enough for them to have basic conversation about what they liked. Her own love of reading inspired her to instil a love of books into the children she taught and she had enjoyed spending a large part of the pre-school budget for the last three years on purchasing a wide selection of fiction and non-fiction books for the classroom reading corners.

She had made a huge difference to the school's Early Year's programme. The pre-school building had been extended and now had twice the number of classes. The addition of a new adventure playground outside and bikes, pedal cars, scooters, a play house and balls, skipping ropes and Space Hoppers for the playground meant that the children had plenty of choice for outside play.

Kaye had overseen the writing of a new broader curriculum, guiding the teachers to adopt a more academic approach and was pleased that they now used the many available opportunities in the local vicinity to enhance their programme. They took the children to the local supermarket, a bakery, a toy museum, a science museum, Ankara Zoo, the Botanical Gardens, the fire station and welcomed the local traffic police who brought along their panda car and police motorbikes for the children to sit in and ride on. The wailing of the police siren always announced their visit and the children looked forward to the event with great excitement. She thought it a shame that there was no working farm for them to visit but soon realised that most of the Turkish children went to relative's farms on a regular basis and had a sound knowledge of farm animals and farm produce.

Despite parental fears, she had built sessions of horse-riding, ice-skating and swimming into the curriculum. She knew that Turkish parents could be overprotective of their offspring and Kaye had fought long and hard to get them to accept the merits of these activities. All of these visits were made easy by the fact that the pre-school had access to its own minibus and driver and with most of the parents being wealthy, there was no problem with them paying for admission fees.

The one thing that was a thorn in her side was entrance testing. Kaye didn't agree with testing four year olds but as it was part of her job, she had no choice but to do it. Özkent had a good reputation and applications rained in from prospective parents. There were five times as many as places available. Over the years, Kaye had been offered, but had graciously declined, expensive gifts, tickets to the opera, holidays on yachts, jewellery and meals at fancy restaurants in exchange for children being accepted into the school. Parents knew places were limited and would stop at nothing to be able to say that their child attended Özkent International School.

The worst part of the whole process was discussing the results with the school's owner, Professor Adnan Deliduman. Kaye always went prepared for their meeting armed with the results and the application forms for each child. Knowing the families' connections was vital. Adnan *Bey* always brought along a myriad of Post-It notes, scraps of paper with names and telephone numbers on and lists of phone calls he had received and in a random fashion, told Kaye who she should accept. On her first such meeting, Kaye had been overwhelmed by the presence of this important man and had been staggered at his insistence on admitting children who she felt were unsuitable but were the sons and daughters or grandchildren of influential politicians, academics and businessmen. She had listened carefully to his reasons, but felt that if she had any principals or sense of fairness it was only right that she should point out that her results were based on professional judgements. What was the point of going to all the hassle of screening the children if her hard work was ignored? Adnan *Bey* had soon come to trust her assessments and listened to her predictions of the problems they would encounter in admitting certain children who, in her opinion, would struggle with the programme. However, each year there were always a few children who Adnan *Bey* would insist upon taking and Kaye, understanding that nepotism was still rife in Turkey, had no choice but to obey.

Kaye's success in the pre-school had not gone unnoticed and she was asked by John Da Souza to apply for the vacant position of Principal in the Elementary School. The school was growing and there were now over three hundred pupils and more than fifty teachers. Judy Allen was planning to return to the UK at the end of the summer term to spend more time with her ageing parents, neither of whom were in good health.

'I really admire what you've done with the pre-school. It's the jewel in our crown! And those are not my words. Noreen Butler said that after our recent accreditation visit by the European Council of Schools. She was very impressed and coming from a skilled Early Years professional, that's some praise.'

'Thank you!' Kaye said humbly, fidgeting in her seat. She was not good at taking compliments but was learning to accept them graciously.

'There's a lot to be done in the Elementary school. My goal is for us to get Primary Years' Programme accreditation within the next four years, so that will be your main goal. It will mean a radical change of teaching approach for some teachers and you'll have to work hard on training them and implementing a new curriculum. You have valuable experience in that area which will be a huge asset. This new position would take you out of the classroom into a purely administrative position. How do you feel about that?'

'Of course, I'll miss having the classroom contact with the children but to be honest, I'm no spring chicken and would probably like a more sedentary job.' Kaye sighed. This was the first time she had admitted to anyone that the physical demands of teaching little ones was beginning to take its toll. Recently, she had felt extremely tired after the school day and had been suffering joint pain in her feet, hands and knees. Whilst she felt lucky that the workload at the school was very light in comparison to what she had faced in England, the thought of doing such a physical job for the next fifteen or twenty years terrified her.

'You'd still be responsible for the pre-school too, so would get lots of opportunities to go up there,' John added. He then proceeded to go through the job description, outlining what the job would entail. 'Are you going to apply then?'

'Yes, I think so. Are there any other applicants?'

'I'm sure there will be but I'd be surprised of any of them have your knowledge or experience. I'm happy you're going to apply. Good luck!'

Chapter 26

'Congratulations!' John cheered, down the phone. 'I know I said it earlier after your interview when we told you that the position was yours, but I wanted to tell you again how pleased I am that you accepted the job.

'Thank you, John!' Kaye gushed. 'I thought that my recent health problems might prevent me from getting it.'

'No. As a valued member of the school's management team, we have no concerns about your ability to do it. And besides, life happens and we deal with it. You're a lot better now and after the summer break, you'll be totally ready for action.'

'I hope you're right,' Kaye giggled. 'I'm looking forward it. However, the pre-school teachers are not happy and think I'm abandoning them.'

'They'll be fine. They'll miss you being there all the time and are worried about the change. Don't let their sadness spoil your success. I hope you've got a good bottle of wine to open to celebrate. Come and see me tomorrow and we'll go through the teacher applications to find your classroom replacement and talk more about your new role.'

Kaye put down her phone and smiled. She had never wanted to be a head teacher or even deputy head, preferring to be in the classroom with the children. She couldn't quite believe that she was about to begin a new chapter in her teaching career, never having planned or desired it. But she believed in fate and maybe this was what was best for her. It was pleasing to know that she was making progress in one area of her life. Even if her love life was still a cause of much frustration and disappointment and her health had deteriorated, she was finding success in her career. In light of her recent short stay in hospital, things were turning out rather unexpectedly.

Kaye had never felt so tired! This was not the exhaustion that all teachers feel at the end of a school year but a debilitating fatigue that rendered her useless. She woke up feeling tired and could happily have slept for days on end. The joint pains were also getting worse and she started each day assessing which joint hurt the most and how she was going to manage to get ready for school. Some days were a struggle to fasten her bra, such was the pain in her hands and fingers. After taking a few days off work and feeling no better, she decided to go to the local Health Centre and consult her friend Kemal. She had got to know him as one of the pre-school parents and, as an orthopaedic surgeon, was the perfect person to help her.

'I think it might be rheumatoid arthritis, Kaye,' Kemal stated, after giving her a thorough examination.

'No way! That's an awful disease,' she blurted, imagining gnarled, bent fingers and wrist in splints. 'I haven't got that!' Kaye said indignantly. 'I just need some anti-inflammatories and I'll be as right as rain,' she added hopefully.

'We need to do some blood tests and I think you should be in hospital for a few days to rest and we need to try and get all this swelling down in your joints.'

'Hospital?' Kaye exclaimed with horror. 'Can't I just rest at home?'

'You could. But if you're in hospital I can monitor you and do all the tests you need. You will be treated like a queen and don't need to worry about getting meals or having to do anything. I'd also like our rheumatologist to have a look at you while you're there.'

Kaye slumped down in her seat. The thought of being looked after for a few days was very appealing. 'I've wondered whether I have chronic fatigue syndrome,' she whispered, feeling deflated. 'I looked on the internet and I have all the symptoms. You get joint pain with that too.'

'Yes it could be, but we won't know for sure until we see the blood work. I'm going to write you a sick note for a week and make a phone call to the hospital to arrange a room for you. You've got private health insurance, right?'

'Yes I do. That's part of the teachers' package at Özkent,' Kaye said weakly. 'When will I go to the hospital?' she asked.

'I just need to finish up here. I'll only be five minutes. Then I'll take you home to get your things and then I'll take you to the Umut Hospital.

While Kemal was making a phone call, Kaye quickly sent Vedat a text message to tell him what was happening.

[Oh no! Kaye are you OK? I'm so worried about you.]

[I'm fine really. I just need to have some tests and to rest for a few days.]

[I know you've been tired but I didn't think you were ill.]

[*I'm sure it's nothing to worry about. I'll be better soon. Sorry canım but I've got to go now. We'll talk later xxx.]*

[OK my darling. I'm sending you hugs and kisses. *Geçmiş olsun*!]

Kaye smiled at the message. It was a phrase used commonly in Turkish as a wish for something to pass and was used as a get well sentiment as well as for any other misfortune or sad event. She stood as Kemal left his office and walked with him to his car, trying not to show how difficult walking had become.

'Hi *canım*! How are you?' Meltem asked a few hours later, seeing Kaye all tucked up in bed surrounded by ice packs.

'I'm fine thanks,' Kaye said chirpily. 'Can you believe this room? It's like a five star hotel suite.'

'Yes it's nice,' Meltem replied, looking around at the beautiful suite with its own bathroom. It was tastefully decorated in shades of green and had a television and modern paintings mounted on the wall to give it a homely feel.

'There's even a sofa bed for visitors to sleep on!' Kaye enthused. 'Not that I want anyone staying here with me,' she quickly added. She knew that it was usual for Turkish families to camp out in hospital rooms with their sick relatives and had no desire for anyone to do that for her. When she was ill, she was the type to retreat into her own cave and recover quietly without any fuss.

'Do you need anything?' Meltem inquired, settling into a soft green armchair by Kaye's bed.

'No, I'm fine. I think I'm going to be spending a lot of time asleep – that's if I've not got frostbite from all this ice!'

'What's that for?' Meltem asked.

'Apparently, it will reduce the swelling in my joints. I've already had loads of blood taken and they insist on my being on this saline drip.'

'They always put everyone on a drip. Don't worry about it.'

'Listen, Meltem. I need you to do me a favour. Only a few people know I'm here. I don't want to be inundated with visitors. I know what you Turks are like! Can you please tell people I don't want anyone to come and see me? I'm only here for a few days and the whole point is for me to rest. How can I do that if there is a constant stream of people coming in and out?'

'Okay. I'll pass the word around. I hope you don't mind me being here!' Meltem teased.

'Of course I don't!' Kaye responded.

Meltem, though Turkish, had spent many years abroad studying and performing as a solo violinist in her youth. She spoke perfect English and was married to a Canadian. She was more internationally minded and open than many of the foreigners Kaye had met whilst in Turkey. The two women had much in common – their love of music, interest in all things spiritual and a fondness for a glass of wine. Meltem would often drop in to see Kaye after a long day of rehearsals or concerts, dressed in her pyjamas, carrying a bottle of wine in one hand and a packet of cigarettes in the other and accompanied by her beloved Chihuahua, Pepsi. She was fascinated by Kaye's relationship with Vedat and they talked for hours about what was happening and what Kaye should do. Kaye valued Meltem's opinions and used her as a sounding board before she broached certain subjects with Vedat. Encouraged by Meltem, Kaye now led Özkent A Capella, a staff choir formed initially to sing a tribute at the annual Teachers' Day dinner, but which had expanded to include members mainly from the ex-pat community from across Ankara. Meeting weekly to rehearse, the group had a growing reputation and sang at venues and events around the city.

'I'd better go,' Meltem suggested. 'You need to sleep. Is there anything you'd like me to bring tomorrow? It's Saturday, so after my private lessons in the morning, I'll pop in to see you.'

'No thanks. Look I'll be fine. Don't feel that you have to visit tomorrow. I know you have a concert tomorrow evening. I'll understand if you don't come.'

'*Aşk olsun*!' Meltem admonished. 'I'll be here about twelve.' She stood up, leaned over Kaye and gently kissing her cheek, whispered, 'Goodnight *canım.'*

[Did you sleep well? I hope you are comfortable. I'm thinking of you and sending you hugs and kisses.]

Kaye read Vedat's message, trying to hide her phone from the cleaner mopping the already sparkling floor. Phones were not allowed in the hospital rooms.

[*Yes I slept really well, although nurses kept coming in all through the night to check my blood pressure. I've just had breakfast and the rheumatologist is coming soon. How are you?]*

[Of course I'm worried about you. My darling, please, please, please look after yourself. I love you so very much and I want you to be OK. How long will you be in hospital?]

[*Only a few days. It depends on how long my health insurance company will agree to.]*

[You are the most beautiful woman on Earth and very special to me. Oh! How I wish I could be there with you.]

[*You can! There's a sofa bed in my room for you to sleep on. Come!]* Kaye's heart began to race at the thought of seeing Vedat, although she was not sure she wanted him to see her in this state.

[I don't know, Kaye. What would I tell my family?]

[*Tell them you have to go to Ankara as an old friend is in hospital. That's the truth.]*

[They'd ask questions about which friend and as they have met all of my friends, it could get complicated.]

[*Well, it's up to you. Think about it. I've got to go now - a nurse has come to change to drip. Talk soon xxx.]*

Following detailed questioning and an examination by the rheumatologist and a brief visit from Meltem, who had brought her some chocolate and biscuits, Kaye had fallen into a deep sleep. She was roused from a vivid dream where Vedat was massaging her bottom by someone bumping the bed. Thinking it was a nurse, she shifted position as far as the ice packs down each side of her would allow and opened her eyes. Looking at her intently were a group of seven or eight people she instantly recognised as parents of her current class. She quickly tried to sit up and holding back the groan that was about to erupt from within, she croaked,

'Oh, hello! I wasn't expecting visitors.'

'Hi, Miss Kaye!' one of the fathers' gushed. 'We thought we'd come and see how you are. Is there anything we can do for you?'

Inwardly groaning, Kaye said politely, 'I'm fine thanks. I don't need anything.' Muttering under her breath, she added, 'Except for you to leave me alone.' What were they doing here? The message about not visiting her had successfully been conveyed to the staff at the school, but obviously no one had thought to mention it to the parents. She was suddenly aware of two beady eyes staring at her from amongst the group. Surely, that wasn't Alp! Who would bring a child to see their sick teacher in hospital? The poor boy was clinging onto his mother's coat, looking in horror at the woman lying in front of him. She knew he was having difficulty recognising her without her make-up on and her hair stuck flat to her head.

'Hi Alp!' she said as cheerfully as she could muster. 'Don't worry! I'll be fine. I just need to rest for a while.' She hoped that her words comforted him but he still clung to his mother, not uttering a word and showing her his usual dazzling smile.

'As you know, my wife and I are both doctors,' another parent began, lifting her notes off the hook on the bottom of the bed. 'And we are ready to help you. What do they think is wrong with you?'

Kaye was shocked that without permission, he was perusing her medical notes. How dare he? It was one thing coming to visit unannounced but this was totally unacceptable. She could hardly grab them off him and she didn't want to seem rude but this was an invasion of her privacy. 'As you can see,' she said, putting on her formal teacher's voice, 'my blood results show there is inflammation, which is why my joints are swollen and why I'm surrounded by ice. I've come here to rest for a few days and will hopefully be back to normal in a few days.' She had emphasised the word 'rest', hoping they would get the hint that she had not appreciated being disturbed.

'My friend is a rheumatologist and would be glad to advise you. I'll give you her phone number,' another parent proffered, taking a pen from his pocket and scribbling down a number on the back of a business card. 'I'll give you my card too,' he added, prompting much shuffling as other parents dug in pockets or handbags to retrieve their cards too.

Kaye thanked them, taking the cards and putting them on her bedside cabinet. How was she going to get rid of them? She yawned widely, hoping that this would be their cue to leave. 'Thank you so much for coming!' she lied. 'I think I need to rest now.'

'We understand,' Alp's mother said tenderly. 'We'll go now. Take care and let us know if you need anything,' she added, shepherding the rest of the group out of door, as they each offered similar sentiments to Kaye.

'Thank God for that!' Kaye sighed, as the door closed behind them. Snuggling back down into the nest of pillows with relief, her irritation subsided and she reminded herself that she was in a foreign country and should be grateful that anyone cared about her enough to visit her. She knew they meant well. It was just another cultural difference she would have to become accustomed to.

Chapter 27

Feeling more comfortable physically having been prescribed anti-inflammatory and painkilling medication, Kaye was struggling with her mental state. The rheumatologist had been hesitant to make a firm diagnosis. There were a large number of possibilities in auto-immune disease and further tests were needed to eliminate certain ones, which Kaye found worrying. However, this was nothing compared to the disappointment and anger that she felt owing to Vedat's absence. He had not come to see her while she had been in hospital or since she had returned home. What did that say about their relationship? All the sweet, loving messages in the world, could not compensate for his lack of compassion and inability to be by her side in a time of need. She was beginning to doubt his sincerity and wonder whether he was as invested in their future as she was. She had even considered that the emotional strain of their relationship could be the root cause of her illness.

For the last month she had not initiated any text conversations with him and only replied to his texts in a perfunctory manner. Something inside her had died. She no longer had hope. Too many times he had ignored her for weeks on end, driving her almost to insanity. Her head told her to forget about Vedat and move on with her life. She was tired of listening to his litany of endless problems and the plans that never materialised. However, in her heart she felt that now she had found true love, everything would work out in the end, wouldn't it? It would be a huge waste of the time and energy she had spent on their relationship if she were to walk away now. Silently, she railed against fate. How could it be so cruel? What the Hell was the point of it all?

Kaye had a tendency to over analyse everything Vedat did and said. The bouts of not talking had become more frequent. She knew this was partly because he was desperately trying to find a way out of his financial woes but was he beginning to lose interest in her? She knew he still loved her but was torn between being with her and his sense of responsibility to his family and community. Kaye acknowledged that it would be a huge leap of faith for him to leave everything behind, but wasn't she worth it? When Vedat was with her everything seemed so easy and he seemed so happy but as soon as he returned home it all became so hard. Her friends had all lost faith in him and thought he was a lost cause, saying he lived in fantasy world. But how could he have continued in this relationship like this for so long if his heart wasn't in it?

Another school year was coming to a close and her frustration that things were no further forward prompted her to put pen to paper and write him a letter.

Dear Vedat,

I have decided to write to you to express how I am feeling. There is too much to say in text messages and I am unable to express myself fully in Turkish in a phone conversation. This way, I can think carefully about what I write and you, too, will have time to think how to reply.

I am devastated that you didn't come to see me while I was in hospital. How sick do I have to be to get some attention? You didn't even send flowers! If your mother, father or anyone in your family were ill you would drop everything to be with them. How do you think this makes me feel? You say I am the most important person in your life but I now know I am not. You think I am strong and independent and use this as an excuse that I can cope with whatever life throws at me on my own. I can.... but being in a relationship means that you share, love, give, take and support each other. I feel totally alone in this relationship with you.

For the last six weeks, I have withdrawn from you but you haven't even noticed! I have loved you since the first moment we met and will always love you but I want a partner to share every moment of my life, to give me emotional and physical support and to be there for me every single day. I want to care for them, wake up each morning next to them and go to bed with them beside me. I want to be loved and give love in return. I have tried to teach you what a loving relationship should be about. Sometimes you are unaware of how much you hurt me. My being in hospital showed me that you cannot be there for me. I deserve more than this. It was embarrassing trying to explain your absence.

Whenever I complain about your situation, you always quote figures about how much you have to make each year. It means nothing to me. I am not interested in money. There are more important things in life. Money seems to be your main motivation. In this we are not compatible. Your pride, honour and self-respect are all tied up with how successful you are in money terms. What a shame! You have said so many times that money does not lead to happiness and you would prefer a simpler life, but I wonder, could you really live without your money?

You said you are addicted to honour, pride and self -respect. What are you trying to prove? To whom? Is your self -esteem so low that you are not happy being yourself and who you really want to be? I have said before that you need to decide what your priorities in life are and what you want from life. If you can't envisage a life with me then please be honest and tell me. I can't go on like this and put my life on hold indefinitely.

This is in no way a criticism of you or your life, just a statement of facts. Nor is it an ultimatum. I just have to tell you how I feel before I withdraw completely from our relationship and hurt you. It is time to be completely honest with each other. Five years is a long time. I feel that we are moving backwards instead of forwards.

I don't doubt that you love me and if things were different you would marry me but the reality is that there are more important things in your life. I deserve to be number one in someone's life and not pushed to the end of the queue for your attention. You are the most important thing in my life.

I have been tempted many times to turn up on your doorstep and confront your father but have not done so out of respect for your wishes and your relationship with your family. I still think that if you were brave enough to acknowledge our relationship, your family would eventually come round. But you are not willing to take the risk, whereas I would risk everything for us to be together. Maybe to you I have nothing at stake but I gave up my life in England to be closer to you.

I love Turkey and with or without you my future is here. I will never return to the UK. I would love my future to be with you, but the reality is that we could wait another ten years for something to change. I am not willing to continue like this. I just can't. It has taken all my strength of character to endure the last five years. If I could see some tangible proof of an improvement, it would give me hope. I told you last year that if I saw you more often, that would be enough, but I have only seen you once this year. I know it is hard for you too but only you can make the situation more tolerable.

I know what I have written will upset you but I have reached a crossroads. Something has to change.

Love always,

Kaye xxx

Chapter 28

Turunç

August 2004

After sending the letter to Vedat, Kaye had waited an agonising five days for his reply. She half expected him to call an end to their relationship, saying he couldn't make the changes she wanted and prepared herself mentally for such a situation. No matter how hurt and upset she may be, she was resilient and knew that she would be able to overcome the heartbreak.

Vedat had been surprised to receive something from her in the post and even more shocked to discover its contents. He had no idea she was so unhappy and had immediately called her to talk on the phone. He had apologised profusely for not visiting her in hospital and agreed it was remiss of him. He had promised her that things would improve and in an effort to make it up to her, had said that he wanted to take her away for a long luxurious holiday this summer. They had agreed dates and he had told her to find somewhere suitable, book flights and that he would pay for everything.

Kaye had already been to Ölü Deniz for two weeks with Anna, followed by three weeks in Bakewell with her mother. Nora was coping well since Frank's death but was glad of Kaye's company as she loved going out to eat and the frequent shopping trips Kaye arranged to stock up on toiletries, clothes and shoes.

Spending time with Vedat was the highlight of her long summer break from school and she had bought them both new clothes. She now kept a wardrobe of clothes for Vedat at her flat so that he didn't need to bring clothes with him.

Sitting in the First Class lounge at Ankara's Esenboğa airport, Kaye was buzzing with excitement. She and Vedat were on their way to Dalaman airport and then on to Turunc, a small village on the eastern side of the Bozburun Peninsula. Neither of them had been there before and Kaye had been eager to go somewhere new. Nora had sent Kaye a cutting from the back pages of the Daily Express showing a beautiful photograph of a luxury hotel with an infinity pool overlooking the turquoise sea and Kaye had immediately been smitten.

They arrived at the hotel well after midnight after a tiring two hour journey from Dalaman airport in an uncomfortable minibus driven by the manager of the hotel. He and Vedat chatted amiably during the ride and when Vedat stated that he was very hungry, he stopped at a restaurant in Marmaris and made sure that his guests were satisfied.

The hotel was built into a hillside overlooking the sea and a series of terraces, dotted with wooden chalet style bungalows spread out before them.

'Oh, God! There are so many steps!' Kaye gasped, dragging herself up another steep flight of stone steps. Her knees were still a little stiff and she became tired easily. 'Trust our bungalow to be right at the top!'

The manager opened an ornate wooden door, switched on the lights and showed them around their accomodation. A large open plan living room was tastefully decorated in a rustic style with solid pine furniture, cream linen curtains and splashes of cobalt blue made the space look fresh and modern. Their bedroom was done in similar style, with the focal point being a large four poster bed, draped in mosquito netting. A beautiful ensuite bathroom, again in cream and blue, led off the bedroom and Kaye was delighted to see fluffy towels, towelling robes and slippers and a huge array of travel sized toiletries arranged in a basket on the long marble slab between his and hers sinks.

'This is gorgeous!' she gushed. 'Do you like it?' she asked Vedat.

'Yes, it's very nice.'

The manager bade them good night and Vedat plonked himself down on the bed with a sigh. 'Oooff! I'm exhausted! I didn't realised the drive would be so long.'

'Me neither,' Kaye added. 'But we're here now. Would you like some tea?'

'Yes I would.'

'I brought some tea bags with me. I wasn't sure whether there'd be any here,' Kaye said, grabbing their case and opening it to find a small box of teabags and a small Tupperware container full of sugar lumps. She left Vedat on the bed and went to the kitchen area to boil the kettle.

'Here you are. I've put sugar in it but haven't stirred it.'

Vedat sat up and heaved himself onto his side to take the tea. His foot caught in the mosquito netting draped over the bed and as he pulled it free there was a loud ripping sound. A large swathe of netting hung down from the wooden frame, leaving a huge hole where Vedat's foot had stuck through it.

'Vedaaat! You're so clumsy! Kaye shrieked. 'Come and drink your tea in the living room, while I see if I can fix the drape.' She stood on the bed, wobbling precariously on the soft mattress and tried to hang the netting to hide the hole. She had already heard the whine of a mosquito and the thought of sleeping without the protection of the net sent shivers through her.

Vedat was sitting on the settee, looking sheepish and holding his glass of tea carefully, when she went to join him. 'This sofa is as hard as rock,' Vedat complained, banging the foam pad with his hand.

'It's because it doubles as a sofa bed,' Kaye said. 'They're never very comfy. I can't be bothered unpacking our case but I'm going to have a shower before we go to bed. The cubicle is really big so we could have a shower together.'

'Mmm! Let's go!' Vedat said eagerly.

Having taken a steamy, passionate shower, Kaye and Vedat got into bed. They both usually slept on the right hand side but when they were together, the decision about which side to sleep was always dictated by which side was closer to the toilet. Kaye didn't want to disturb Vedat during her nightly visits to the bathroom. They snuggled close, Kaye ensuring that the mosquito net was spread evenly around the perimeter of the bed. Despite being tired, Vedat's unsatisfied longing for Kaye's body prompted him to begin caressing and kissing her. She moaned in delight and responded by reaching for his hardness. It wasn't long before Vedat positioned himself on top of her and entered her fiercely.

'I've missed you sooo much, Kaye. My heart will burst love for you. This feels sooo good!'

'Me too, my darling. Aagghh!'

Their sweet nothings were interupted by a splintering crash as the mattress dropped to the ground and the pair lay in a twisted lump of limbs, sheet and pillows in the middle of the wooden bed frame.

'We've broken the bed!' Vedat giggled, trying to sit up and assess the situation.

'I don't believe it! Kaye too giggled. 'Can you get up?'

'I'm trying! Help me!' Vedat spluttered as he pushed himself onto his arms and swung his leg over the bed frame, finally standing up next to the bed. He helped Kaye off the bed and they both lifted the mattress up to see the damage below. Three of the wooden slats forming the base for the bed were completely snapped and the couple knew that there was no way of repairing them.

'What shall we do?' Kaye asked, still laughing.

'We'll have to sleep on the sofa bed in the living room. There's no way we can sleep here.'

So, they hauled the sheets and pillows from the bedroom and Kaye made up the sofa bed. Gingerly, they lay down, snuggled together and settled down for the rest of the night.

'What are you doing?' Vedat shouted crabbily minutes later.

'This room is full of mosquitoes! They're buzzing in my ear and I already have two bites on my arm. I'll have to find the mossie spray in the case or I'll be eaten alive.'

'Aggh! Don't spray that stuff on me!' Vedat coughed as Kaye liberally sprayed herself and the whole room.

'You don't want to get bitten do you?'

'They don't bite me,'Vedat replied. 'When they've got sweet, juicy English blood to suck, they're not interested in mine.'

'Very funny!' Kaye said sarcastically, swiping Vedat with a pillow. 'After all this messing about, the sun is rising. We'll have to get up for breakfast in a couple of hours.'

There was a deep groan from the other side of the bed.

'Good morning!' Kaye said pleasantly to to the two couples who were seated on the table next to where Kaye was putting down her plate of croissants. They were obviously English, pale skinned and recently arrived. They smiled but did not answer her. Vedat joined her, carrying a plate full of tomatoes, cucumber, cheese, olives, fresh bread and a hard boiled egg. He said good morning to their neighbours too, but got a frosty response.

'What's wrong with them? Miserable sods!' Kaye whispered.

'They're making me feel uncomfortable, as though I don't deserve to be here,' Vedat said back, not making any effort to whisper as he knew they probably couldn't understand Turkish. 'They probably think I'm a terrorist or someone you've just picked up.'

'Don't be silly. Of course you deserve to be here! You've paid just the same as they have.' It still surprised her that Vedat was so ill at ease with foreigners and embarrassed by his self-perceived lack of finesse. Despite the fact that he came from a small village, his courteous behaviour and polite manners had impressed Kaye.

Over the course of the next hour as Kaye and Vedat leisurely ate their breakfast, enjoying the stunning view of the sea below them, more Brits sat down to eat. They chatted amongst each other but blatently ignored Kaye and Vedat.

'I don't like these people,' Vedat announced. 'I don't like this place. It's too remote.There's not even a shop to buy cigarettes. I want to go somewhere else.'

'But we've paid a deposit here. Where do you want to go?'

'I don't know but I don't want to stay here.'

'I'm sorry. I thought this place would be idyllic. I was wrong. If we're going to leave, we need a plan. This hotel is miles from anywhere and we don't have a car. How are we going to get down to the village?'

'Look, it's not your fault. You go and pay for the room,' Vedat suggested, handing Kaye a handful of Turkish lira, 'and I'll go and find a way out of here. I'll meet you back at the room in ten minutes. Okay?'

'Okay'. Kaye replied, getting up from her chair and making her way to the hotel reception. She was tempted to lie about the reason they were leaving but decided to explain politely that her partner didn't like it here. The manager accepted her apology and only charged her for one night. Feeling light with relief, Kaye would have skipped back to their room if the steps hadn't been so steep.

'Quick, get our things together, we've got a lift in two minutes,' Vedat urged.

' What are we going to do about the bed?'

'Leave it! By the time they discover it, we'll be well away from here.'

Kaye pulled the door closed behind them, leaving the key on the outside of the door, as instructed by the hotel manager. Vedat lugged their case down the many steps and shouted to a grubby looking man standing next to a tractor. He lazily flicked the butt of his cigarette into a nearby bush and gestured to the trailer at the back of the tractor.

'Here's our lift. He's the gardener,' Vedat announced proudly.

'You must be joking!' Kaye giggled.

'It's either getting in the back of this trailer or walking for miles down the hill.'

'Okay, then. Help me get up.'

As they chugged down the hill, jostled by every bump and rut in the road, their mood became one of hilarity and they laughed out loud as they left the hotel behind.

'This is as far as I go,' the gardener announced, pulling into a sandy layby. 'The sea is through those trees. There's probably someone with a boat who will take you to where you want to go. Or the village is that way,' he continued, pointing right, 'There are taxis there.'

Kaye hoisted herself off the trailer, while Vedat lifted the case, jumped down and, handing over a generous tip, thanked the gardener for his trouble.

'What do you think? Boat or taxi?' Vedat asked.

'Well, it depends on where we want to go. I've no idea where we are.'

'There's a small café through those trees. It's so hot. Let's sit down, have a drink and then we'll make a decision,' Vedat decided, leading Kaye between the trees and seating himself at the nearest table. He ordered a Coke for each of them and, lighting up a cigarette, told the waiter about their situation.

'You could go to Marmaris. It's around that headland and my uncle could take you in his boat,' the waiter suggested. 'Or you could go across to Gocek and Fethiye. There are other small villages you could go to on the *dolmuş*,' he added, 'But the hotels and pensions are probably fully booked there as it's high season.'

'Which is nearer?' Kaye wondered, wanting to get to their destination as quickly as possible. The sweltering heat was draining every ounce of energy she had. All she wanted to do was laze by a pool with Vedat at her side.

'Let's go to Marmaris!' Vedat exclaimed at learning that Marmaris was the closer option.

'I don't know,' Kaye hesitated, remembering the miserable time she had spent there four years ago. 'I have such unhappy memories of Marmaris, I'm not sure I want to go back.'

'All the more reason to go back!' Vedat enthused. 'We'll stay somewhere different.... a luxurious hotel.... and we'll create some new wonderful memories to blank out the old ones.'

'Okay then,' Kaye agreed. 'Tell the waiter to find his uncle.'

Salty spray splashed their faces and a cool breeze whipped Kaye's hair into a straggly tangled mess, as they were buffetted by the waves lapping at the small boat. Kaye had imagined an altogether larger craft and had a moment of panic when she was led to the battered, pale blue rowing boat, fitted with a small outboard motor, which was bobbing on the edge of the sea. 'We're never going to fit in that!' she cried, turning to Vedat, who was also looking a little worried. Neither of them was slim and with the added weight of their heavy suitcase and the stocky, overweight uncle, it seemed unlikely that the boat would carry them all.

'*Problem yok*!' the waiter reassured them. 'Don't worry! My uncle built this boat himself and takes people to Marmaris every day.'

Kaye frantically looked around for an alternative boat and was horrified to discover there was none. It was this boat or none at all. The waiter threw their case to his uncle who wedged it at the front of the vessel and then gave both Kaye and Vedat a hand as they paddled in the shallow water and heaved themselves over the side of the boat and sat down opposite each other on the narrow slats of painted blue wood that served as seats. They smiled at each other across the boat and started to giggle as their knees banged together. The engine roared into life and gathered speed as they left the shore behind them and headed out into open water.

Both Kaye and Vedat sat admiring the beautiful scenery; the pine forested mountains rising high above the cliffs in the distance, the spectacular coastline, dotted with sandy bays and craggy inlets, the expensive yachts, whose passengers waved as they passed them and the cloudless blue sky above them. They were lost in their own reveries and enjoying every precious minute. When they were together, they always seemed to have unexpected adventures and Kaye hoped that this holiday would be full of happy, joyous times, which they would remember forever.

Chapter 29

Ankara

January 2005

'Damn! Bugger! Blast!' Kaye yelled as she stomped around her living room, phone in one hand, cigarette in the other. She could feel tears welling up in her eyes and she was aware that she was smoking herself into a fog. She had been texting Vedat and frantically trying to keep up with his torrent of texts, hurrying to translate a long text before the next one pinged and before she had chance to work out her reply. They were in the middle of a heated argument, each raging with pent up emotion and blaming each other for not supporting the other. Vedat had then accused Kaye of being distant and ignoring him while she had been visiting Nora for Christmas. Kaye was outraged. She had made every effort to text Vedat every evening, despite being kept busy with frequent shopping trips, household jobs which Nora saved up for her, family visits and other business she had to attend to while she was in the UK.

[*Don't you dare say that I have ignored you for the last 2 weeks! I have sent you messages every night. It's not my fault that some of the messages have been delayed or the signal goes weak. I told you that one night the battery on my phone died.*]

[When you are in England, you don't want to talk to me. I think you have another man there.]

[*Oh, don't be so ridiculous! Why am I living in Turkey if I have a man in England?]*

[I don't know. In fact I don't know anything anymore. You make me so confused. I love you so much it's like you are in my blood. I never knew I could feel like this. But always I am in the wrong. I have no joy in life, my life is meaningless.]

Kaye hated it went Vedat became maudlin. This was becoming more recurrent and she wondered if it was an attention seeking tactic. He had recently talked a lot about his father and she had sensed a great tension between them. Since his stroke, the relationship between the Ağa and his elder son had been strained. Vedat now referred to his father, not in his former adoring fashion, but in uncomplimentary terms, such as 'the cockerel' or 'the one called Ibrahim *Bey*'. Sometimes, Vedat talked about leaving this world and Kaye wondered if he had some psychological illness. As soon as life threw a curveball at him he talked about giving up. She knew his emotional intelligence was not high and spent hours coaching him on positive thinking and seeing the best in a situation. She was surprised that in his moments of despair his faith didn't seem to give him strength. He went to Friday prayers every week, to the mosque most evenings and prayed at home after his morning shower. Kaye respected the fact that his religion was important to him and that he didn't try to convert her or preach to her.

[*Vedat, please don't talk like that. Of course your life is not meaningless. Look at all the people you employ and take care of! And what about me? What would I do without you?]*

[Sometimes I think it is good I met you and sometimes I think the complete opposite.]

[Well, thank you! It's normal for people to think this, especially in a relationship as complicated as ours. Long distance relationships are HARD, which is why I don't understand why we don't see each other more often. If we tried to see each other once a month, it would take off some of the strain.]

[You're right but I can't get away from here so easily. There is always business to attend to or crops to harvest or plant. I wish I was free like you. You have a wonderful life but mine is full of responsibility and duty.]

Before Kaye could add more, another text from Vedat pinged.

[Let me tell you something. Generally, I am really successful, decisive and know what I am doing but when it comes to us, I am totally indecisive, unsuccessful and am bewildered about what to do. You don't deserve this and deserve much better. I only give you sadness, upset, frustration, hopelessness and stress.]

[When you are sad, I feel terrible and tell myself I don't deserve you. I am a barrier to your happiness. Why are you wasting your time on a stupid person like me?]

[*Because I love you.]* Kaye replied simply. Then sent another text asking if he was at home.

[No. I haven't been home all day. I wanted to talk to you. Now that I have I feel calmer. Thanks for putting up with me.]

[*You're welcome canim.]*

The next morning, while Kaye was having her mid-morning break, she sent Vedat a message to see if he was alright. By the time she arrived home late in the afternoon, there had still been no reply. 'He's probably busy,' she thought and proceeded to throw off her school clothes and grab the fleecy sweat shirt and jogging bottoms from the chair in her bedroom. It was minus eight degrees outside and a foot of dirty snow lay frozen in piles by the sides of the road, but luckily the central heating in her flat was turned up full and all of the rooms were toasty.

Later that night, she sensed that something was not right. She and Vedat had a kind of telepathic bond. They often said exactly the same thing at the same time and picked up on each other's moods. It was weird that after him criticising her for not being very communicative, he was now not responding to her message. She sent another one, asking again if he was okay. No reply.

For two days, she continued to send texts at regular intervals, begging him to reply and telling him how childish it was not to respond. Nothing. What a selfish, immature bastard he was! Her nerves were frayed and anger simmered until she felt fit to explode. How was she going to sleep when she was so agitated? He was right – what was she doing with such a man?

Kaye felt immediately guilty, when finally a text came the next morning from Vedat to say that he had collapsed and was in hospital with a serious heart condition.

[I have arrhythmia and have been here for 2 days. My heart rate is very erratic and they say if it doesn't regulate soon, I will have either a heart attack or possibly a stroke. My heart could suddenly stop beating and I could die.]

[*What? Oh my God! How did this happen?]* Kaye texted frantically.

[I don't know. I felt very weak and my heart was racing so my mother insisted that I come to the hospital. I've had loads of tests and am under observation. My mother, father and all my relatives are very scared and they're all here in the hospital.]

[*Do you feel any better now?]*

[My head feels like it will explode and I keep passing out. I haven't told my parents how bad it is and I'm not supposed to have my phone switched on but I knew you'd be worried too.]

[*Of course I've been worried but I thought you were just busy. I had a bad feeling though last night that something could be wrong.]*

[If it's my time to die so be it. I believe in fate. If anything happens to me you are my lawful wife. OK? Forever I am your Vedat and only yours. You are my everything, *karıgım*.]

A lump came to Kaye's throat. The word '*karıgım*' meant 'my darling wife'. It was the first time he had used the endearment with her. She always dreaded that something terrible should happen to Vedat and that because no one there had her phone number she would never know. She had mentioned several times that she thought someone should have her number in case of an emergency but Vedat didn't trust anyone enough to give it to them. If anything happened to her she knew that Ebru or Meltem would be able to contact him.

[*How long will you be in hospital for?*]

[I don't know. They say the next 24 hours are critical. If I'm still here then, I should be OK.]

[*Oh my God! I can't believe it! Is there anything I can do? Do you want me to come?*]

[No, there's nothing you can do. I would love to see you but you know what happens when I do. I don't think my heart can stand it! And can you imagine what my family would say? The stress of that alone would finish me!]

[*Do you think it happened because you were upset the other day?*]

[I don't know. My father has heart problems and my mother has high blood pressure so maybe it's a hereditary thing. My mother thinks it's the Evil Eye and someone wants to harm me!]

[*I'm sending you all my love. I wish I could be there to hug you too.*]

[I know you do. Don't worry about me. I need to rest now. Love you xxxx]

[How can I not worry about you? Think positive! You'll be fine. Love you too xxx]

Kaye immediately called her friend, Ebru. Increasingly, most of her friends were now Turks. All but one of the original group she started Özkent with had moved to pastures new and were now spread across the globe or back in their home countries. Kaye found the end of each year, when people said farewell very unsettling, even though she had no intention of leaving herself. The Turkish teachers were the stability in the school, rarely leaving, except for maternity leave and now that her Turkish allowed her to participate easily in conversations, she was swept into a circle of Turkish women who loved the fact that she had assimilated into Turkish life so well. Kaye had also become hesitant to invest the time getting to know the foreign teachers who would inevitably move on after their two year contracts.

Ebru was the Head of Art and although they had worked on various school committees together and collaborated on the school's Art Show, it was only after sitting next to each other at a posh diplomatic dinner arranged by one of the parents, where they got hideously drunk on the freely flowing champagne and laughed uproariously together that they decided they must get to know each other better and arranged to go out for a drink the following Friday to the Bistro on Özkent campus.

This was to be a memorable occasion for both of them, as they talked about their lives and experiences. Discovering that they had so much in common, in their love of the creative arts, both having been avid potters at different points in their lives, was a delight to them both. Ebru was fascinated by Kaye's relationship with Vedat and was shocked that Kaye had a secret man. She was amazed that Kaye had kept her relationship out of the prying eyes of the rest of the Özkent staff. The campus was like a goldfish bowl where everyone knew each other's business. Ebru's grandfather was Kurdish and so she was not surprised by the cultural difficulties Kaye was facing with Vedat. She was curious how the two had met and listened carefully to Kaye's brief summary of their relationship so far.

In sharing her own story of an unsuccessful relationship, Ebru mentioned that she believed in fate and this led their conversation onto spiritual matters. A common fascination with fortune tellers and tarot card readings forged the bond between them and they spent the remainder of the night exchanging views on reincarnation and past life regression.

Over the last six months, they had spent many hours enjoying each other's company and had become close friends.

'I'm sure he'll be okay,' Ebru soothed, after hearing about Vedat's admission to hospital. 'You know he can be a bit of a drama queen. Turkish men don't deal well with illness and of course his mother will be wailing at his bedside, bemoaning the fact that her precious son is dying!' she added with a giggle.

'I just feel so helpless!' Kaye sighed. 'My natural instinct would be to go straight away but I know it would cause a huge problem with his family – not a good idea in his present state. I don't care what they'd say or do to me, but the stress would be unbearable for Vedat. I thought things would get easier but there always seems to be some trauma for us to deal with. I feel like we're going through the twelve labours of Hercules or paying for some huge karmic debt in a past life. I'm a strong person but how much more can I put up with?'

'Yes, you're right,' Ebru acknowledged. 'You are both being tested. I'll send you both some healing energy.' Ebru offered. She was a Reiki Master and was always sending or receiving energy for the good of the Universe.

'Thanks. Do you need his permission? 'He'd freak if he thought someone was interfering with his ethereal body!'

'I'll just do it anyway. It's just like other people pray. He'll never know.'

Chapter 30

Batman

March 2005

'This is the last call for Turkish Airlines Flight TK2683 to Batman. Passengers should proceed to gate number 108.'

Picking up her handbag, Kaye joined the queue waiting at the gate to board the plane. Normally a relaxed and confident traveller, today, her nerves were strung to breaking point and she was firmly outside her comfort zone. She had been disturbed to see well-dressed men handing in pistols and boxes of bullets at the x-ray machine on arrival at the airport and had watched as they were asked to sign for them. Kaye heaved a sigh of relief as she read the sign that said no guns were to be allowed on board. Then, sitting at the gate, she was aware that not only was she the only woman on the flight, but also the only foreigner. Feeling very self-conscious, she avoided giving anyone direct eye contact.

Kaye settled herself into her allotted seat and prayed that the seats next to her would remain empty. She surreptitiously kept an eye on the stream of expensively suited men taking their seats, hoping that none of them had smuggled a weapon on board and making sure not to give any of them more than a sweeping glance. She knew it didn't take much for a lingering look to be interpreted as interest and to be followed by an intense stare and develop into full-on flirting. She was glad that she had not worn anything revealing and had made sure her ample bosom was not on display.

No one came to sit in the empty seats next to Kaye and she breathed a sigh of relief. Gazing out of the window, seeing the early morning sun sparkling on the wings of parked planes, she began to unwind. She was so looking forward to seeing Vedat now that he had recovered from his heart scare and was excited about her first visit to the south east of Turkey. The political situation had much improved with the election of a new pro-Islamic party and terrorist activities were now less frequent. Vedat had assured her she would be safe and they had agreed to stay in Batman where Vedat was less likely to bump into friends or family.

Coming in to land, Kaye observed the military hardware and bunkers dotting the airfield. She knew the airport was small but had not realised that it was a military base too. The plane touched down and as it taxied along the runway, she noticed two army jeeps coming up alongside.

'Ladies and gentlemen, please do not leave you seats until the 'No Smoking' signs have been switched off and please have your ID cards ready,' the cabin chief announced.

The plane came to a halt and instead of everyone jumping out of their seats to retrieve baggage from the overhead bins, as was usual behaviour, they sat quietly in their seats. The doors opened and two soldiers carrying Kalashnikovs entered the plane.

'Oh my God! There's a terrorist on the flight!' Kaye immediately thought, her heart pounding as she watched the soldiers proceed down the aisle, stopping every so often to check ID cards. As the only foreigner and the only blonde on the plane, she stuck out like a sore thumb. She tried to look as relaxed as possible when she was asked for her passport and smiled politely at the taller of the two soldiers as he compared her face to the photograph in her passport. A sigh of relief slipped out when he handed the document back to her and continued down the plane. She had never been in such close proximity to a gun and hideous images of maimed bodies and indiscriminate firing flashed in her head as she fought to remain calm.

Walking down the aircraft steps onto the runway, she noticed that one of the soldiers was at the bottom of the aircraft steps and seemed to be asking questions to individual passengers, while the other was standing next to a battered old bus. Some of her fellow passengers were lined up in front of a row of hand luggage and suitcases. Those with just attaché cases were getting on the waiting bus. One by one, the men stepped forward to point out which piece of baggage was theirs. This was then loaded onto a truck. Feeling like she was in a firing line, Kaye pointed out her small case and re-joined the line, wondering what would happen if there was a case that no one claimed? This was unreal! Why hadn't Vedat warned her that things here would be different? This was like being on a film set, acting out the role of a secret agent trying to look normal when really a sniper was about to pick one of them off after he had been identified pointing to his bag.

Finally, after a short bus ride to the terminal building and waiting for her case to arrive on the squeaky carousel, she pushed her way through the throng of men crowded in front of the terminal entrance to see if she could see Vedat. He wasn't there. She moved to the edge of the pavement and looked up and down the road. Still no sign. Feeling alarmed, she was just about to reach for her mobile phone, when she spotted a shiny, black Mercedes coming very slowly towards her. With its dark, smoked windows it was impossible to see inside. The car stopped right I front of her and the door was pushed open.

'Vedat! I'm so pleased to see you!' Kaye spluttered. 'What a journey I've had!' she exclaimed as he put her case in the boot. Most of the men on the flight had guns!'

'That's normal here,' Vedat commented. 'I told you - life here is very different than in Ankara.'

'Anyway, I'm here now. How are you?'

Vedat grinned broadly. He loved Kaye's exuberance and was thrilled that she had come. 'I'm fine now that you're here,' he said, clasping her hand and stroking it tenderly. 'I want to kiss you but I can't here.' Public displays of affection were frowned upon and when the woman involved was a foreigner, it was assumed that she was a prostitute.

'So where are we going?' Kaye asked with interest.

'Shall we drive around a little, so that you can see the area? We don't need to go to the hotel yet.' Vedat suggested.

'That sounds great! Are you going to take me to your home?' Kaye teased.

'Nooo!' Vedat replied firmly. 'That would be a very bad idea.'

'Could we at least go past your home or your fields? If I stay in the car, no one would be any the wiser that I was here,' Kaye suggested.

'Kaye, everyone knows my car and it's far too risky. Are you hungry?' he said, quickly changing the subject.

'Not really. I had a sandwich on the flight.' Kaye replied, disappointed to have come all this way and then not to be able to see anything related to Vedat.

'Okay then. We'll find somewhere nice for lunch later.'

They spent the next two hours, driving leisurely from Batman to Mardin. Kaye had been fascinated to see the nodding donkeys on the outskirts of Batman, where oil was being drilled. Although on a small scale, it was her first time seeing oilfields and she took photos from the car window. Vedat kept up a steady stream of chatter, pointing out various crops growing in the fields and places of interest. They were following the course of the Tigris River and Vedat pulled up on a grassy verge for them to admire the view. Below them was a gorge and in the distance Kaye could see the minaret of a mosque in a small village built into the side of the gorge.

'This is Hasankeyf,' Vedat explained. 'If you look closely, you can see windows and doors in those rocks. People still live there I think.'

'Yes, it reminds me a bit of Cappadokia,' Kaye commented, taking in the spectacular view. 'It's just like a picture from the children's Bible that I had when I was a child. It feels like a place that time forgot.'

'Well, they haven't forgotten it, because there are plans to flood this whole area to make a new dam.'

'Oh no! That would be awful!' Kaye cried, genuinely horrified. 'I'd better take some photos in case I never get to see it again.'

They decided to go into the village to have a closer look around. Vedat parked the car in a side street and they got out to walk through the narrow cobbled streets. Vendors standing at rickety wooden stalls were selling the usual array of textiles, copper pans, dried fruits, silver jewellery and trinkets. They were invited to enter a small café and after the host had enthused about the wonderful views from his veranda, they were persuaded to sit down and have a drink.

It was a beautiful spring day and Kaye soon became too warm in her jacket. She was dressed for Ankara temperatures and here it was much milder. Trees were already sprouting new buds and the clear, blue sky was almost cloudless, with the odd cotton wool wisp of cloud strewn across it. She put her jacket around the back of her chair and then took out her camera. After taking a few shots of the landscape, she got a close up of Vedat looking into the distance. She was so happy to be with him and wanted a souvenir of their time together. The waiter was willing to oblige when she asked him to take a snap of both of them, asking them to stand with a view of the river as a backdrop.

On smelling the meaty aroma coming from the kitchen, Vedat asked to see a menu. He was hungry. The waiter said they had a very limited menu which included *köfte,* lamb chops and fish from the river. Kaye inquired about the fish and despite not being familiar with the Turkish word for it, plumped for it anyway as she was not fond of meat. It turned out to be catfish. Kaye recognised it when it came to the table and saw its whiskers.

Refreshed after their cooling drinks and light meal, they decided to venture further up the road to where there was a palace built into the rock. It soon became too steep and rugged for Kaye to continue. Her knees were not up to steep and uneven walking, so they turned round and made their way back down. As they drove over the bridge to join the main Mardin road, Kaye looked down to watch a couple of young boys paddling in the river trying to catch fish with a piece of fishing line and a hook and giggling as they splashed each other. It was a scene that warmed her heart and she hoped that this idyllic landscape would not be spoilt in favour of modern development.

As they neared Mardin the landscape changed dramatically. There were no trees or greenery and the soil and rock changed to a lighter, sandy colour. She knew Mardin was famous for its ornately decorated buildings made from this honey-coloured stone.

They drove straight into the heart of the old town, weaving their way up through the narrow cobbled streets, avoiding laden-down donkeys clopping along and men pushing handcarts piled high with fruit, vegetables, grain and huge sacks of rice. Every now and again she caught a glimpse up a side street where washing was hanging out on lines strung from window balconies and children played in the dirt. Compared to Ankara, it was like being in a different exotic country. On passing the famous post office with its lace work stone carving around the windows and doors, Vedat told Kaye to look right. 'That's Syria over there,' he said.

Kaye looked at the flat expanse of land, hoping to see signs of habitation but there were none. 'It must be a long way away,' she stated, 'I can't see any buildings.'

'No, it's about twenty kilometres away,' Vedat continued. 'The nearest village is further away than that. The land you see is farm land. There are many Syrians living here in Mardin and Arabic is spoken here more than Turkish.'

After a leisurely drive, the two lovers ate dinner at their hotel in the middle of Batman, before settling down to chat and relax in their room. Vedat had recently bought a new mobile phone which had a camera and video facility. He showed Kaye, saying, 'I've got something to show you.'

'Mmm! Nice phone. When did you get that?' Kaye asked.

'I bought it so that I could show you something,' Vedat replied, opening the phone and tapping the keys. 'I've started to build a new house. I've taken some photos so that you can see it,' he added proudly.

'Wow! You never said anything about building a house!' Kaye asked, intrigued, looking closely at the picture of the foundations of a building. 'It looks big. Who's it for?'

'Well it might be for us,' Vedat said hesitantly. 'What do you think?'

'I'm stunned! You're building a house for us? Where is it?'

'In my village on land my family owns next to my parents' house. I began to think about it last year when you sent me that upsetting letter. You told me I had to do something and now I am! I don't want to lose you, Kaye.'

Kaye's mind was whirring with questions. 'I can't believe you started to build it without asking me first!'

'I thought it would be a nice surprise,' Vedat said, his voice lower and with a hint of disappointment.'

'It's certainly a surprise!' Kaye responded. 'I had no idea this is what you were thinking. Do you really think I could live there?'

'That's up to you. It will be a huge change for you but I will treat you like a queen and be your slave. You will want for nothing.'

Kaye giggled at the thought of her waltzing around a beautiful house ordering Vedat around and him bowing and scuttling around obeying her every wish. Of course she knew he didn't mean it literally but it was an amusing daydream. 'When will it be finished?' she asked, her brain going into overdrive as she thought about when she would have to give her notice in at school.

'It should be finished by June and then we'll have to think about furnishings. I've already ordered a jacuzzi!' Vedat mentioned. 'And of course there'll be a pool.'

'A pool!' Kaye shrieked. 'I've always wanted a pool! How big will it be?'

'I'm hiring a master craftsman to make the pool. He's done the pools in lots of luxurious hotels and he will install a special system where the water is pumped from underground in a continuous flow. There will be no need to use chemicals as the water will be renewed constantly. I'm planning to have a changing room and sound system as well as a large decked area for chairs, tables and sun loungers. You'll love it!'

Vedat went on to tell Kaye about the proposed dimensions of the house and his plans for the interior. The house would be in the traditional style of the area with the ground floor being used as a huge storage depot for vehicles and machinery and the upper floors used as the living quarters. Kaye became more excited the more she heard.

'If the house will be ready after the summer, I should give my notice in now to give them time to find a replacement for me.' Kaye said seriously.

'No, don't do anything yet.'

'But I can't just leave!' Kaye said adamantly. 'If I'm not going to return for next academic year, I should have told them in January. It's already late.'

'Look, Kaye, when we decide you're leaving, you will tell them one month before. It doesn't matter if they don't want to give you a reference or are upset. You won't be working ever again as I will take care of you. Just walk away!'

Kaye listened carefully to what he had said but was uneasy about leaving without proper notice. Vedat had never been an employee so didn't really understand the world of work. However, she knew enough about the way things worked in Turkey and decided she would do nothing until everything was certain and the house was fully ready for habitation.

Their lovemaking that night was particularly tender. Kaye was filled with hope that finally they had a plan and the waiting to be together might be coming to an end. She fell asleep in Vedat's arms, smiling and ridiculously happy.

Chapter 31

Karabulut,

October 1995

He had made a decision. It was no longer safe for his brother, Yusuf, to stay in Karabulut. Teenage boys were being targeted by the PKK and the school playgrounds were the main arena for recruitment to the terrorist organisation. Despite being a sensible, level-headed boy, he knew that it would not be long before the threats towards his brother for not succumbing to the enticements and taunting would be carried out. For his safety he needed to get away.

He had arranged for Yusuf to go and stay with relatives in Istanbul, well away from harm and where he would be able to continue his schooling in a relatively safe environment. His mother sobbed as she packed his clothes and belongings into three huge suitcases, ready for his departure later that day. He knew his mother's heart was breaking and had sat her down to talk to her and make her see that this decision was for the best. His father, though upset at having to send his younger son away, was more pragmatic and agreed that Yusuf could no longer stay in the village.

Three years ago, schools in their area had been forced to close as teachers became PKK targets and last year fourteen teachers had been killed. Many families had made the gut-wrenching decision to move west to Istanbul, Ankara and Izmir to avoid the violence. Earlier this year, whole villages had been burnt and the inhabitants forced to flee and seek refuge in the nearby cities of Diyarbakır and Batman. The population of these cities had doubled in the last six months. Living conditions were poor as people crammed into accommodation with thirty or forty other family members or lived in nylon tents on waste ground.

The human abuses were shocking on both sides as the Turkish government retaliated for PKK attacks. Innocent people were caught in the middle. He had been sickened by the atrocities his friends and family had endured. The Turkish military had recently forcibly deported more than one hundred and fifty thousand Kurds from eight hundred and fifty villages in the south east in an effort to diffuse the situation from the area. Many of the houses in depopulated villages were destroyed, and at times the belongings of the displaced, including farm animals and implements, were wrecked along with their homes. There were no measures to provide food, temporary housing and medical care for these people and no adequate compensation for destroyed homes and property.

This not only brought terrible disruption to families but changed the issue from a regional one to a national one. It was only because he was the Ağa and had important connections with influential people that his village had not suffered like others in the surrounding area. He was well-respected and known for his strong Muslim views. He lived his life by the Koran and to some of the younger generation appeared to be traditional verging on radical. Yet, he was respected as a fair and generous man, always willing to listen to problems and lend a helping hand, not just financially to his community. A strong adversary and not one to be crossed, he held sway with many powerful people all around the country. He was not willing for either of his sons to be sacrificed in this senseless conflict. He trusted that his elder son, who had done his National Service could look after himself, but his younger son was only just entering adulthood and needed family protection.

Chapter 32

Dalyan

September 2005

Following a recent check-up, it was discovered that three of Ibrahim *Bey*'s arteries were clogged and, needing immediate surgery to unblock them, he had been flown to Ankara where the best heart surgeon in Turkey practised.

Expecting news that his father's heart surgery had been a success, Kaye had been shocked to hear that Ibrahim *Bey* had died on the operating table. She felt sorry for Vedat and sent messages of condolence and sympathy, but couldn't help the feeling of lightness and hope that bubbled up inside her. Now that his father was no longer the main obstacle to their relationship, maybe things would improve and they would find a way to be together.

Having booked the flights and hotel for their holiday before his father's death, Kaye decided that, even though Vedat was in mourning and unable to join her, she needed some time alone to relax and reflect on everything. There had been so much heartbreak, frustration, upset and disappointment over the last six years that she felt emotionally drained. Her illness was now under control with a cocktail of drugs but she still suffered from fatigue and the stress of their relationship was taking its toll. Planning to spend much of her time by the pool reading, meditating and trying to find some clarity on her relationship with Vedat, she had brought a stack of reading material with her, including some self-help books.

Dalyan was proving to be the perfect place for Kaye to unwind. Acting upon Meltem's recommendation, she was relishing the prospect of exploring somewhere new and being somewhere which allowed her to be anonymous. The town nestled along a meandering river, with ancient Lycian tombs dug into the craggy hills facing it. Surprisingly green, despite the long hot summers, Kaye immediately sensed that there was something magical and soothing about the place. Upon arrival, it was as though her body had heaved a huge sigh of relief. Pleased that the resort where she was staying was at the far end of the town in serene, peaceful surroundings where the only sounds were the gentle lapping of water and the occasional crowing of a cockerel, she knew it was only a fifteen minute stroll to the hustle and bustle of the main street where hundreds of foreign tourists filled the numerous bars and restaurants, if she craved human interaction.

As she lazed on her sun lounger, watching the armada of tourist boats ferrying people to the beach and remembering past holidays where they had shared wonderful times on such excursions, Kaye's thoughts inevitably turned to Vedat. He had told her at the end of last year that he was a different person now to the one he was before he met her.

'I used to love life and was confident in everything I did. Now I have no enjoyment of life and my self-confidence has gone. I know I have everything in life and people think I'm lucky but I am miserable.

I'm making a mess of my life. I don't seem to be able to make anyone happy, especially you. I feel weak. The only time I'm happy is with you. Sometimes I hate myself and I think that you would be better off without me. You could find someone better and be happy. If it wasn't for you I wouldn't be able to bear this life. You are the only comfort I have. I adore you Kaye.'

When she looked into his eyes, it was clear how much he loved her and she felt that the excitement and joy he felt when he was with her was genuine. But was love enough? She had always thought it was, but now she was not so sure. She had found someone she absolutely adored and who was perfect for her in many ways but his family and cultural traditions were a major obstacle and proving difficult to overcome. In the early days she had been filled with hope but as the years passed, the hope faded and was replaced by uncertainty and disillusionment.

Throughout his life, Vedat had been used to having everything he wanted and had adopted a casual attitude to money. He spent lavishly on entertaining his friends, family and business acquaintances and regularly treated himself to new clothes and shoes. He had good relationships with the bank managers of various banks where he had accounts and they readily agree to loan him funds when he required large amounts to buy new tractors or land. Now, through his own negligence and a series of unfortunate events he found himself in a huge amount of debt. The previous year, cotton prices had slumped dramatically as cotton from China flooded the market. He had barely sold his cotton, let alone made the usual profit from it. This meant that he missed payments on loans he had taken from the bank several years earlier. When the bank manager had called him in to the office to discuss matters, Vedat had been shocked to see how much debt he had amassed. He had also been the guarantor for a large amount one of his cousins had taken out to found a new business. The venture had failed, his cousin had lost everything so Vedat would now have to find the money to pay back the bank for that too. If he had known his fiscal situation was to become so dire, he would never have begun to build his new house, which, nearing completion with mounting payments for fittings, interior decorations and landscaping of the grounds, was adding to his debts.

For the last six months he had been in negotiations with an old family friend in Ankara who had decided to sell a large portion of land he owned near where Vedat lived. Kaye thought that buying more land when he was in such debt was financial suicide, but Vedat had insisted that if he bought the land for a good price, he could farm it and the profit from the crops would help to pay off his debts. Vedat had come to Ankara several times to negotiate terms with the man and Kaye had been pleased that she had been able to see more of him.

Feeling more relaxed after a week at the hotel, Kaye decided to have a change in her daily routine of sitting by the pool and join other guests at the hotel on a boat trip to Iztuzu Beach. This was the closest beach to Dalyan and was famous as a nesting ground for the endangered Loggerhead turtles. After breakfast, she waited on the hotel's jetty for the boat to arrive. Soon, a blue and white painted boat with a canvas canopy puttered to a halt in front of the group. The captain helped them on board and Kaye sat on wooden bench seat around the perimeter of the boat's interior. With everyone seated, the captain started the engine and reversed away from the jetty, joining the procession of other similar boats around the bend in the river towards the sea. The journey took them through reed beds, where it was said the film 'The African Queen' was filmed although Kaye knew this to be a myth, having read about it in her guidebook. She had been to Egypt and noted the similarity to travelling along the River Nile, surrounded on both sides by tall reeds. Now and again, the captain pointed out different birds: cormorants, ibis and herons, and told them to look out for turtles. Enjoying the hot sun on her back and gentle breeze from the water as the boat chugged along, Kaye amused herself by taking photos of the stunning scenery and chatting to the other passengers.

She was looking forward to taking in the sea air and swimming in the sea. Vedat teased her about being a mermaid as she loved water and took every opportunity to swim. As the reed beds opened up into a wide delta, she caught her first glimpse of the sea in the distance. Boats were moored up along a jetty and a string of people were making their way to the beach along a wooden walkway across a sandy embankment.

Finding an empty sunbed under a straw parasol, Kaye placed her beach bag by its side, stripped off her sundress and made her way to the water's edge, narrowly avoiding the steel tripod stuck in the sand which marked the site of a turtle's nest. The sand was blisteringly hot underfoot and she was glad she had kept her flip flops on. She kicked them off at the edge of the beach and walked into the clear turquoise sea. Instead of the cooling water she had anticipated, it was like walking into a warm bath. Her toes sunk into the fine sand as she waded deeper, but it took some time before the water was deep enough for her to be able to swim. Plunging down underwater, she relished the feel of the water caressing her body and enveloping her. She swam until the people on the beach became a blur of brightly coloured dots. Vedat worried when she swam so far out but she was a strong swimmer and had no fear. Even this far out, she could still see the sandy bottom of the ocean way down below. She loved the feeling of weightlessness and bobbed around, looking at the entire five kilometre length of the beach. As an environmentally protected area, it was totally unspoilt and had none of the usual speed boats, inflatable bananas, parascending paraphernalia or other water sports so common at other resorts. There were just a few wooden huts, painted green to blend in with the environment, which housed toilets, changing rooms and a small restaurant.

Kaye's phone pinged as she sat on her sunbed munching on a chicken *döner* kebab. She saw it was from Vedat. He was worried about her. She typed a short response saying she was fine.

[Are you really fine or you just don't want me to worry?]

[I'm really fine. I love it here. How about you?]

[For days now thousands of people have been queueing down the road to pay their respects to my father. They come and pray with my mother and of course I have to provide tea, cold drinks and snacks for everyone. It's exhausting! My mother has also insisted that we give money to the poor in my father's name so I'm arranging that too.]

[It must be a very difficult time for you. You need to look after yourself too.]

[For 40 days we will be in mourning so after the people have stopped coming I will be able to rest and take stock.]

Knowing it was probably indelicate to ask, Kaye couldn't help herself, *[Will this improve things for us?]*

[It's too early to say.]

They exchanged farewells and Kaye took another bite of her kebab, reflecting on the death of her own father and the contrast between the ways their families had dealt with the loss. To Vedat, cremation was abhorrent and he had been shocked when Kaye told him of their funeral arrangements for Frank. Explaining that they were following Frank's wishes, Kaye had enlightened Vedat on how British people choose whether to be buried or cremated according to their personal preferences. There was no judgement involved. Kaye had similarly felt alarmed to learn that Vedat's father, according to Muslim belief, had been buried within twenty four hours of his death. She tried to imagine how that would feel. There would be no time to grieve before the body was put in the ground and knowing that it was not the custom for women to attend the graveside, she shuddered at the thought of Vedat's poor mother sitting at home, weeping at the loss of her husband and not being able to say goodbye as he was laid to rest. Then, having to cope with the never ending parade of well-wishers paying their respects for days on end and having no private time to mourn. This prompted her fear that if something dreadful happened to Vedat, he would be dead and buried before she knew about it. Not being able to kiss him goodbye was an unbearable thought.

Telling herself not to be so morbid, Kaye lapsed into a daydream of how she and Vedat would now be able to live in the new house and begin their life together. There was nothing stopping them now was there?

Chapter 33

Ankara

January 2006

Kaye had returned from spending Christmas the UK in time to be with Vedat for the New Year. They had a quiet but enjoyable time together, although Kaye had thought Vedat was not his usual happy self. There seemed to be something on his mind but when she asked, he had shaken his head and said he was fine. She noticed that there were more grey strands in his hair and that new fine lines had begun around his eyes. He had joked that he was becoming an old man and felt tired. When he had left, Kaye noted that he had not waved at her from the taxi as it pulled away as he normally did. She hoped this was not a sign of something brewing. She had grown used to Vedat's frequent bouts of silence and not wanting to communicate, but this time her disquiet was worse. She knew there was something he was not telling her.

A week later, when she had not heard from Vedat, Kaye's sense of unease had grown to fever pitch and she knew she had to do something. Meltem had recently talked of a fantastic psychic she had visited and who had been spookily accurate about certain events in Meltem's life. Kaye decided that she needed some guidance and asked Meltem to take her to meet the psychic at a café on the other side of the city. She was becoming frustrated about her relationship with Vedat. Would they ever be able to get married? How long would she have to wait? Now that his father had died, what was stopping them being together? Hopefully, some of these questions would be answered today.

As they entered the café and were directed by a waiter to a table in the far corner, Meltem said.

'Kaye, please don't blame me if she tells you something you don't want to hear.'

'Of course I won't!' Kaye assured her friend. 'If there's something bad, I'd rather know about it. Anyway, I asked you to bring me here. You didn't drag me here against my will. Make sure you listen carefully in case I don't catch the all of the Turkish.'

Kaye insisted that Meltem sit at the table too, in case there was anything she was unable to translate. They sat opposite a small, wizened old Turkish lady, wearing a mismatched bobbly jumper and cardigan with traditional baggy *şalvar* trousers, who sat with her dirty, bare feet tucked underneath her. She poked a wisp of greying hair under her headscarf and began stroking a large glass bowl, like a fish bowl, filled two-thirds full of water. She welcomed them with a prayer-like gesture and immediately began speaking, gazing at the water and swirling it around. It took Kaye a few seconds to realise that the woman's words were aimed at her and she focussed intently on what was being said.

'You have been waiting a long time for this man to marry you,' she spoke softly as the water settled. Kaye nodded in agreement at Meltem.

'There is no marriage in the stars for you and this man ……He has at least four children.' Meltem squeezed Kaye's hand but did not speak as the woman continued. 'He makes every excuse not to be with you…… Your stars are not in harmony…… I am not telling you to finish with him or stay with him but you are waiting unnecessarily.' She swirled the water again and looked into the bowl, frowning,

'He is managing two women at the same time…… It is never, never in your destiny to be with this man….. He has lied to you…… Your illness is clear……. He doesn't reply to your calls and you are depressed……. I am a hundred percent sure this man is married.'

Kaye sat motionless, hardly daring to breathe in case she missed something the woman said. She hoped Meltem was paying attention to every detail so that they could discuss everything afterwards. Her heart was in her mouth as the woman spoke again,

'He is just satisfying his ego with you…….If you write to Allah or pray to him he will accept your prayers…… Between the two of you there is no wedding contract.' She took a deep breath and sighed, 'Someone in his family has put a curse on him…… They know there is a foreign woman in his life and they have bound him to them and their home…… He is managing his home and you on the side…… You keep saying if only his family would accept me, everything would be fine………It will never happen.'

The water stilled and the woman took a sip of water from a glass next to her. She looked deep into Kaye's eyes and asked if she had any questions.

Kaye was too stunned to think of anything and looked at Meltem.

'Are you absolutely sure he's married with children?' Meltem asked.

'I am. Not ninety-nine percent but a hundred percent sure. There are at least four children, maybe more.'

The whole reading had taken less than ten minutes and Kaye had heard enough. The woman's sympathetic, pitying look was too much to bear and she handed the woman money and thanked her, before rising from her seat and walking towards the door.

'Oh, God, what are you going to do? Meltem asked with panic in her voice.

'I'm not going to do anything. I just need to think.'

'But everything she said was true - your illness, you waiting for him, him not replying to your calls, the excuses. There's no reason why the other stuff isn't true as well.'

'You're right. I just need time to get my head around it. If he is married, I'll kill the bastard!'

The next day, still hearing no word from Vedat, Kaye went to the pre-school during her break time and asked Feyza, her secretary, who she trusted implicitly, to do her a favour. She needed concrete proof that Vedat was married and the only way she could think of to do this was to call the Public Registration Office in Diyarbakır, where births, marriages, deaths and changes of residence are recorded. Feyza got the number from Directory Enquiries and dialled it. She asked to speak to someone about an inquiry and was instantly put through to a helpful man who asked for the details of the man she was looking for. She gave Vedat's name, date of birth, parent's names and where he lived and waited for a response.

'Yes, I've found him. The details you gave me are correct.'

'I'd like to know if he's married.'

'Do you want to marry him?' the man asked.

'No, I'm ringing on behalf of a friend. Is he married?' Feyza was jotting everything down on a scrap of paper so Kaye could see.

'Yes, he's married.'

'Does he have children?

'Yes.'

'How many?'

'Lots.'

'How many is lots?'

'Six.'

'Thank you. You've been very helpful. Good day.' Feyza closed her mobile phone and looked at Kaye. 'Well, your fortune teller was right. Now you have definite proof. I'm so sorry, Kaye. I don't know what to say.'

'There's nothing you can say. I don't know what to say. Last night as I was going over what the woman had said, everything fell into place. I can believe he's married. It explains why it was always so hard for him to get away. I thought the problem was his father, but now I know it was his wife!'

Thanking Feyza, Kaye said that she had better go back to her office and do some work. She wandered down the hill and was just about to set foot in the elementary school building when a surge of emotion hit her and she realised she was going to break down. Children were going to their lessons and she did not want any of them to witness her losing control. She turned on her heels and made her way across the playground, not knowing where to go or what to do. Taking her mobile phone from the pocket, she decided to call Ebru, who was in her office nearby.

'Ebru, it's Kaye, I'm outside. Can you come?'

On seeing Kaye. Ebru immediately knew something was dreadfully wrong. Kaye's face was grey and her hands were shaking as she paced about. 'What's wrong? Are you okay?'

'No. Can we go somewhere to talk?'

'Let's go to my office.'

'No. I can't be in school.'

'Shall we go to your apartment?' Ebru suggested and taking Kaye's arm led her across the playground, out of the school gate and up the hill. Halfway up the hill Kaye gave a scream so loud that Ebru jumped away.

'Kaye, what is it? What's happened?'

'The bastard's married with six kids!' Kaye shrieked.

'Ssssh! People will hear. Calm down. Wait until you get inside you apartment before you start shouting.'

But Kaye couldn't wait. She cursed, she swore and she threatened Vedat with every hideous torture imaginable until she could find no more words and broke down sobbing.

'Let me call school and say we're dealing with an issue in the Pre-School,' Ebru suggested, as they entered Kaye's flat. 'You need to take some deep breaths. I'll get you some water,' she added, taking control of the situation.

'I need brandy!' Kaye yelled and went to find the bottle she kept under the sink.

Sipping the warm, soothing alcohol, Kaye told Ebru of the last two days' events, as Ebru listened, shocked at what she was hearing.

'I can't believe it!' she spluttered. 'I mean I can believe he's married, but to keep you in the dark for all these years and all the misery he's caused you, when he knew he already had a family. That's disgraceful! What are you going to do?'

'I'm going to confront him. In fact I'm sending him a text right now.'

[Give my love to your wife and kids.]

A few minutes later, a reply came.

[OK I will.]

'He's not even denying it!' Kaye shrieked, showing Ebru the message.

'Perhaps he thinks you're joking,' Ebru suggested.

[Why aren't you denying it?] Kaye wrote.

[Is this a tactic, a game or do you know something?]

[I know everything. I know you're married with 6 kids.]

[I don't know what to say. There's no point in saying anything – I know I've lost you now.]

[Why didn't you tell me? Why did you lie?]

[Many times I wanted to tell you but I wasn't brave enough. I was terrified of losing you. You told me that you would never have a relationship with a married man when we first met.]

A torrent of rambling texts came so fast that Kaye couldn't respond. She kept reading.

[You have changed my life so much. I never knew what it was to love. You have shown me what true love is and have made me so happy. I have seen a different life with you. I wish I didn't love you so much. If love is a crime, then I'm guilty.]

[After we met, I told my wife and children all about you but the fear of you ending our relationship prevented me from being honest with you. Sometimes I wanted to finish with you for your sake, not mine. I knew that when you found out, it would be the end.]

[I am not a liar. I just hid this one thing – for love.]

[I have behaved like your husband and have been totally faithful to you. I never slept with my wife after we met. We have separate bedrooms and there were no more children. In my heart I have never been married. My father married me off when I was 15 years old. I had no choice. I was promised to this girl in the cradle. I had a wonderful childhood but you can't imagine my life after this.]

[I know you will be shocked but I am so relieved to be able to tell you this. Kaye, believe me, apart from this I have been truthful with you. I know you will doubt everything now but I'm begging you, please don't leave me.]

[I once told you that there were things you didn't know about me but you said you could read me like a book so I shut up. When you asked me how many bedrooms the new house would have and I said 6, you said we wouldn't need so many. I nearly told you then but my courage deserted me.]

[My conscience has been very troubled by this for all these years. I want you to know this. Please don't ask me questions. You know what you need to know. My heart is breaking at the thought of losing you. I am crying.]

Kaye didn't know what to think. She was still furious. She felt humiliated, stupid, gullible and very hurt. How had she been so blind? She needed to digest everything and talk it through with her friends. How was she ever going to get over this?

Chapter 34

Ankara

February 2006

During the last month, Kaye had gone through a gamut of emotions. Initially, she had felt physically sick, not being able to eat and chain smoking until she began to develop a smokers' cough. She felt so stupid. She spent sleepless nights mulling over the events of the last six years, searching for clues. Why hadn't she seen them? Now it seemed so obvious that Vedat was married. She'd fallen for the oldest trick in the book. How could she ever trust her instincts again? She prided herself on being a good judge of character. She had been so wrong about him. Her friends had been aghast that he could have done this to her but differed in their advice. Her close friends in England had told her outright that she should have nothing further to do with him but her Turkish friends had been a lot more sympathetic towards him.

'Can you imagine what it must have been like for him, being married off at such a young age? Ebru had asked. 'He had everything to look forward to, hopes and dreams like we all did, but they were all snatched away. What must it have been like to be married at fifteen and still at school?'

'But surely he would have known he was promised to that girl?' Kaye questioned.

'Not necessarily. They could have arranged the whole thing without him knowing and he was suddenly told he was getting married. He probably never met the girl before he was engaged.'

'I feel so guilty about his wife and kids. That poor woman! Fancy him telling her all about me when we met! She must have been through Hell these last seven years, wondering if he was going to leave her. I feel like writing to her to explain that I didn't know he was married and how sorry I am that she has suffered.'

'She probably can't read and to be honest, she probably hates you so much that whatever you say won't change her feelings towards you.'

'I'm not bothered about that. I just feel I want her to know that I'd never try to steal someone else's husband.'

'I know you don't want to hear this, Kaye, but I feel sorry for him. He loves you so much that he put himself through all this torture so he wouldn't lose you. That's true love. It's a wonder he's not a basket case with the mental strain he's been under. And now that he's tasted what life could be like with you, it must be hard for him to maintain any kind of relationship with his wife. I can understand why he keeps talking about leaving.'

'I can't feel sorry for him, Ebru! I think true love means you put the other person first. He didn't do that. He was only thinking of himself. He's lied and put me through years of frustration and heartache for nothing! All this talk of marrying me one day was crap.

He's already married. I worked out that he's been married for twenty-three years!'

'Well, technically he could take you as his second wife. It wouldn't be legal but he would treat you like his wife in every other way.'

'You must be joking. I'm not being anyone's wife Number Two!' Kaye exclaimed.

'Have you heard from him?' Ebru asked tentatively.

'No and I don't want to.'

'Well, you will hear from him – be sure about that. You both need some time to let things sink in and you will probably have questions for him at some point, Kaye.'

Then, the anger came. She couldn't sit still and had the urge to break things. One night she had felt so violent that she had thrown cushions against the wall, had pounded them with her fists and screwed them as small as she could, in an effort to rid herself of the aggression she felt. She really wanted to hear plates smashing against the wall but knew that she couldn't risk causing a commotion that her neighbours could hear and being the talk of the campus for losing her cool.

Thank God, she had a demanding job and never had a spare minute to think about her personal life while she was at school. Her days were a constant round of meetings, observing teachers, meeting disgruntled parents, dealing with petty discipline issues with children and fitting in time to catch up with her emails and processing applications from teachers and prospective parents.

Once the anger began to dissipate, Kaye started to yearn for Vedat. She missed talking to him, especially late at night before she went to sleep. She wrestled with her conscience, torn between her love for him and the guilt of being the cause of so much heartache for his wife and children. What had been the point of this relationship with Vedat? Was it bringing her to Turkey? If so, there was no need for their relationship to continue for so long. She would have stayed here even if she was no longer with him. She tried to remember things that he had said that now could not possibly be true. He had once told her of an argument with his father and had thrown, 'If I can't marry this English woman I will never marry and you will never have grandsons,' back at the Ağa when he firmly stood his ground and refused to listen to Vedat's pleas. Did he really say that? Or was it just to make Kaye feel that he was trying to do something? It didn't make sense. The Ağa already had grandsons. How many of these stories or reported incidents were true? Kaye doubted everything he had ever told her. Was the new house that was now finished and he had shown her on Google Earth really his? Was all the land that he had taken photos of on his phone and shown her really his? At least she knew his name and parents' names were true because she had seen them on his identity card. She knew Vedat was unsure about his true birthday and the one on his card was not necessarily right and was an estimate by his father when he started school. But wait! She had seen '*bekar*' on his identity card, showing that he was single. Why didn't it say '*evli*' for married? The picture on the card was definitely Vedat. Was it a fake card?

Questions and memories jumbled in her mind. She went over every holiday they had spent together, in depth conversations they had had and memories he had shared about his life, searching for answers. Would there ever be the happy ending? She doubted it now. How could Vedat bear to leave his family? And if he did, what sort of relationship would she have with them, if any? The rollercoaster of emotions was sucking the energy out of her and sometimes she wished she could sleep forever and not wake up.

[Happy birthday, Kaye! I wish you health and happiness on your special day. You deserve every good thing in life. With all my love, Vedat.]

Kaye looked at the message, unsure whether to reply or not. It meant a lot to her that Vedat had remembered her birthday and sent her a text.

[Thanks.] She wrote simply, not knowing what else to say.

[How are you?]

[I'm just fantastic.] Kaye replied sarcastically.

[I can imagine. Look, Kaye, I want to talk to you face to face but am so embarrassed I'm not ready to see you yet. I know you're very angry and you would kill me if I came now. I also need to find the courage to face you.]

[I don't know if I can ever see you again.]

[I understand. I will never put pressure on you. It's your decision alone whether you love me or not and whether you want to continue this relationship or not. I am so embarrassed, ashamed and guilty that

I have no right to make any demands on you. I'll do whatever you want.]

[Finally, you're deciding not to be selfish. Ha!]

[Don't forget that I love you, Kaye. To live with this guilt is eating me up day and night. I miss you.]

[You deserve to suffer. I have to be somewhere.]

Kaye knew that once Vedat started to talk of love, she would soften and she was in no mood for hearing sentiment. Her friends were arranging a night out and although it was hours away, she didn't want to spend any more time talking to Vedat. She was going to pamper herself in preparation for a fun night out. She badly need to let off some steam, drink copious amounts to anaesthetise her pain and laughter was the best distraction she knew.

Chapter 35

Karabulut

June 2006

'You shouldn't be looking at my phone,' Vedat said calmly. 'If you're upset it's your own fault.' He had come back from the bathroom to find his wife looking at a picture of Kaye. It was one she had sent him last year.

'She's beautiful,' his wife stated, wiping a tear from her cheek. 'I use to think that she was a passing fancy and you would get over her, but I see she's still in your life. She must love you very much if she still waits for you.'

'She does.'

'If you want to be with her, why don't you go?' she asked, her voice breaking with emotion.

'It's not that simple. I can't go anywhere while I have these debts hanging over me. That's my priority at the moment.' After a pause, he inquired, 'Do you want me to go?'

'No, but I can't stand to see you so unhappy. If she will make you happy, then you should go to her.'

'We'll see.'

Sometimes he thought about getting a suitcase, leaving everything in Karabulut behind and going where no one would find him. It would be just him and Kaye, starting a new life together. But then, something would happen: illness in the family, death in the family, a financial crisis or a crucial business deal, that made leaving impossible. He had left once but he had paid dearly for that. The guilt he felt about his father's stroke and the subsequent damage it had done to their relationship had been a daily reminder of what was at stake. On his death bed, his father had made him promise that he would never leave the family. He had promised.

Vedat had told all his family about his love for Kaye and all of them except three of his cousins were against it. They said it was not appropriate for them to have a foreigner and a non-Muslim in their family. He could only imagine what they would have said of they had known she was older than him and that she couldn't have children. It angered him that they had married him off once and seen how unhappy he had been. He had done his best to support them all and give them a good standard of living. Wasn't it time that they thought of him for a change? Didn't he deserve to be happy? He never dreamed it was possible to feel like this and Kaye was the only thing he wanted in life. She was his world. Despite the difficulties, the love he felt for Kaye was so deep and special that he could leave everything behind for her, couldn't he? Sometimes he felt so alone, hopeless and weak. Kaye was the only comfort he had.

Last year, he had been approached by the local government officials to stand as the Mayor of Diyarbakır in the coming year's elections. He was flattered that they wanted him and seriously considered the proposal. Before he met Kaye, being the Mayor of

Diyarbakır was something he aspired to and was a long term goal. However, presently he didn't have the funds to mount a campaign and more importantly, it would put Kaye at risk. As a public figure, every miniscule part of his life and history would be investigated and would be up for public consumption. Even though Kaye didn't live in this area, the fact that she was in Ankara and worked at Özkent, made her an easy target for newspaper journalists and paparazzi.

Some years earlier, one of his uncles had stood for office and every event he attended was recorded and reported by the media. Unbeknown to him, a prostitute had been hired by a rival and was present at most events. Eventually, the newspapers pointed this out, prompted by a hint from the rival, and made a huge scandal of the fact this his 'mistress' came to all events with him. The woman had cleverly planted herself at Vedat uncle's side during photo opportunities and was snapped holding his arm on a couple of occasions. His uncle's political career ended in ruins after the media broke the story and his denials fell on deaf ears. He had never met the woman! Vedat couldn't risk his family bring subjected to any embarrassment as that would surely bring about the end of their relationship.

In March, he had finally plucked up the courage to go and see Kaye in Ankara. He didn't tell her he was going. He knew that particular weekend she would be at home and just turned up on the Friday night. Her face was a picture! They had been talking more and though she hadn't forgiven him for deceiving her, she had been willing to listen to his explanations. She had bombarded him with questions about things he had said and done in the past, trying to prove beyond doubt that he was a liar. When she had asked about the new house, he had admitted shamefacedly that his family had moved into it. There was nothing to be gained from pretence now. Kaye had been curious about his children and asked him numerous questions about them. He had sent her some photos of them on his phone and told her a little about them: who looked like him and who didn't, their characters, what they were doing and what their ambitions were. He had made sure to tell her that he loved all of them very much. She had also asked about the identity card he had used in Marmaris. It was not a fake one as she suspected, but an old one. The government had recently updated all identity cards and he had shown her his new one, stating that he was married.

The relief he felt at no longer having to hide anything was immense. A huge weight had been lifted from his shoulders and now that there was still hope that they could find a way forward, he was thrilled. His fear that he would lose her if she knew he was married had been unfounded, but he knew it was only because after all they had shared in past years that the bond between them was strong. If she had found out years earlier, the outcome would have been very different. He knew now that to keep Kaye he had to make amends and needed to come up with a solid plan for their future.

On the Saturday morning, after a late breakfast and deciding it was too wet outside to go out, they sprawled on Kaye's sofa, one at each end, their legs intertwined in the middle and weighed up the options of Kaye moving to Karabulut or them both moving to somewhere new. When facing a big decision, Kaye often wrote down a list of pros and cons and taking an notebook from her coffee table, she explained to Vedat what she was about to do.

'We'll have a separate page for life in Karabulut and another page for somewhere else, then we'll make lists of the positive and negative points about each place.'

'Let's start with Karabulut,' Vedat suggested. 'I think that will be easier because I know about life there.'

'Okay. What are the pros of me coming to live in Karabulut?' Kaye asked, pen at the ready to write down the list.

'We already have a house or you could choose to live in one of my apartments. They're huge and you could make it your own. It will also mean that you have your own space and won't be crowded by the family….. I have a successful career there…… We will be part of a larger family. …..You wouldn't have to work which would be better for your health. …….We would have a good standard of living. …….I wouldn't be losing anything by staying there.'

'Now the cons,' Kaye prompted, shifting her position to get more comfortable.

'Would my family and friends accept you? ……You would lose your independence…... Would you be bored? Life for a woman there is not what you're used to. You would not be able to go out alone.'

Kaye stopped writing. 'Why couldn't I go out on my own?' she inquired indignantly, with a puzzled expression on her face.

'It's just not right for a woman to go anywhere alone. Where would you need to go anyway? There is no need to go shopping for food as either I would buy it or I would give an order to the supermarket and they would bring it to the house.'

'What if I wanted to go for a manicure, get a haircut or buy some clothes?'

'I would take you to the beauty salon or they could come to the house. I could take you shopping from time to time.'

'But if I was at home all the time, I wouldn't get to see anyone!'

'Family and friends would visit and you could go to other ladies' homes if they invite you. You'll have to learn Kurdish too as most women don't speak Turkish well.'

'Oh, great! Well, I'll have plenty of time for a new project because I'm not allowed out and no one will come to see me. Will my family and friends be allowed to come and visit?'

'Of course they will but they'll have to bear in mind that there will be no alcohol in my home and they will have to dress in a conservative manner.'

'I can't imagine many of them would want to come then,' Kaye stated glumly.

'Would I be able to go to Mum's for Christmas?'

'Not on your own.'

'But that's ridiculous. I've been going everywhere on my own for the last twenty odd years! What's the difference?'

'You haven't been my wife before. That's the difference.'

'Well, if I'm not allowed to go on my own, you'll have to come with me. Spending Christmas with my family will be a real experience for you!'

'Kaye, I've told you many times before that life in Karabulut would be hard for you. It's a totally different way of life than you're used to.'

'Yes, I can see that now. Let's move onto the pros of living somewhere new.'

'My family would be very upset that I've left,' Vedat began.

'That's not a pro. Think of the positive things,' Kaye encouraged.

'We would be together, just us……I can't think of anything else,' he said, looking defeated. 'What do you think?'

'I think it would be fun starting a new life in a new place. It would be an adventure!'

'Yes, I'm sure it would but what would we do every day? If we're not working, how would we fill our days? Won't we be bored?'

'Are you saying I'm boring?' Kaye teased, laughing to break the tense mood that threatened to encroach on their conversation. 'There'll be lots to do, furnishing our new home. You could grow fruit and vegetables in our garden and we could cook together. I can always find things to occupy myself.'

'It might take us a long time to find a house.'

'True. We could always rent somewhere first until we find our dream home. Maybe we will decide to buy land and build our own house,' she added eagerly. It had always been one of Kaye's dreams to design and build a house to her own specifications.

'Let me add some pros to the list………Not having to deal with your family………Living a life that I'm used to…………Being on the coast in a better climate……..Having a less demanding job or not working at all……….. Living in a place that family and friends would want to visit…….. If I needed to work, I won't have a work visa unless we are legally married and that's going to take years. Actually that's a con,' she realised, crossing out what she had written and starting a new column under the title, 'Cons'. She turned to Vedat, sensing that his thoughts had already turned to a long list of negatives.

'I will feel guilty about leaving my family……..I will miss them…… I would lose my honour……...How will they manage the farm after I've gone?……Everything is unknown…….It's full of risks…...We wouldn't have jobs……I've never worked for anyone else…….What sort of work could we do?........If one of my parents became ill would I be able to go back to see them?............ If one of them died could I go back for the funeral?...... Would my children still speak to me?'

As she jotted everything down, Kaye was also thinking about each of the points Vedat made. She didn't have the answers and this clarified what an enormous decision it would be for Vedat to leave Karabulut. 'The list of cons for living somewhere new is the longest,' she concluded.

Later that day, after they had been out for a delicious meal at a traditional Turkish restaurant in the city, their attention returned to the topic of their future.

'I think you'll hate living in Karabulut, Kaye,' Vedat declared, 'And if you're not happy, I won't be happy either. Living somewhere else is the best option. I hope to pay off my debts by the end of next year. Then any money I make after that will be for us. How much money do you think we will need?'

'I have no idea.' Kaye said honestly. 'We will need a house, a car and then enough money to live on for the rest of our lives. It depends on whether we work or not. If we had some kind of business, we wouldn't need so much at first,' she added.

'I want us to have a good standard of living. I'm not used to doing without.'

'Well, I've never been poor either. I've always had enough money to do what I want, but I'm careful with my money and only spend what I have. I'd never go into debt.'

'I want a quiet, modest, happy life with the one I love. That's all.' Vedat stated, making Kaye smile.

'What sort of business could we have?' Vedat asked, genuinely interested on Kaye's opinions.

'It depends where we live, but we both have experience of managing things. Whatever business we have, we will employ people who have the skills and we just manage the business to make sure it's profitable.'

'I've always wanted a hotel,' Vedat admitted. 'A beautiful, luxurious hotel where the rich and famous stay.'

'You'd have to sell alcohol. How would you feel about that?'

'I'm not sure. Not selling alcohol would limit the number of guests.'

'True. Styling the interior and bedrooms appeals to me. I'd love that, but having a hotel is a lot of work. Maybe we should think smaller to begin with.' Kaye suggested.

Following his visit, Vedat spent hours thinking about where they could go. He knew that Kaye wanted to live by the coast, in a villa by the sea. They were both small town country people and city life was not for them. There were places he would not go as he had family there. His uncle was the Chief of Police in Antalya and he had relatives around Izmir too. Bodrum, Fethiye, Marmaris and the Aegean area were all possibilities. He had mentioned to Kaye that a piece of land was for sale on Bozça Island, off the North West coast. He had heard a group of friends talking about it and joined their conversation to learn more. It was a sizeable piece of land right on the beach, with building permission for two large villas. There was also a small vineyard, olive groves and a fruit orchard as part of the deal. The price was reasonable too but he knew he could bargain and get the price down. As yet, the island was unspoilt but was ripe for development as the rich and famous from Istanbul were just discovering its charms. It had been the location for two very successful films and people wanted to see it for themselves. Being only a couple of hours drive from Istanbul, it was perfect for a weekend getaway.

Kaye had immediately looked on the internet and found photos and information about the island. 'It's small, only five or six kilometres across and looks quiet,' she told Vedat. 'The houses are very Greek looking as it used to belong to Greece. There's also a huge medieval fortress on the north of the island. The beaches look totally unspoilt. Apparently, it's very windy there, so it will be cool in the summer.'

'Do you think you could live there?' Vedat asked.

'Well, it looks lovely but it depends on where the land for sale is. Are you going to go and see it?'

Yes, probably. I won't buy it without seeing it first.'

'Can I come too?'

'We'll see.'

Chapter 36

Karabulut,

November 2006

How many more traumas could he endure? This year had been a disaster from start to finish and now this. Was Allah punishing him for lying to Kaye?

During an argument about an outstanding debt of four hundred thousand lira, Vedat's uncle had stupidly hit someone on the head with his gun. The gun had gone off wounding the man in the head. The man was severely injured and was fighting for his life in hospital. He was from a very powerful family who had now declared a blood feud between the two families and vowed to carry out a vendetta against Vedat's family. If he died, they would seek revenge with death. Vedat wished his uncle had come to him first as he knew the family well and could have spoken to them. They respected him and he was sure he could have averted this disaster.

Incidents like this were not uncommon among the different clans in his area. Kurds were volatile and disputes over land, water and money could last for years and end in tragedy. In the past, his father had been called upon to act as mediator in these situations, reasoning with both sides and reminding them about what kind of example they were setting. Sometimes, blood money was offered to the aggrieved family to end the feud without loss of life. Vedat knew it was now his duty to try to find a peaceful solution before tit for tat killing began.

Even though he had not been involved in the initial incident, the fact that he had been working on his uncle's behalf to get him released on bail had been seen by the injured man's family as an injustice and made him a prime target. So too, was Yusuf, his brother who was now back at home after completing his university degree. He was doing all he could to keep them both safe and had employed two security guards to be with his brother at all times to protect him. He went everywhere accompanied by at least two of his cousins, who were armed with pistols.

For the last three weeks, he had been so preoccupied with negotiating with the police and lawyers to keep his uncle out of prison that he had not harvested his cotton. There had been terrible floods in the area and now his fields looked like lakes and his crop was in danger of being spoiled. Luckily, the fluffy cotton was still above water but harvesting it was going to be a challenge. Could he expect the two hundred and fifty casual workers he employed to wade through the water to pick the cotton? He would have to do something soon as the weather was about to change. If his cotton got wet, his profit for the year would be decimated, ruining his plans to pay off as much of his debts as he could.

'I need to go to the bank near my office this morning,' Vedat informed his cousin, Muhammed. 'Come and pick me up at ten o'clock.'

A car, carrying Muhammed, his older brother and being driven by another cousin arrived at the designated time. As soon as Vedat was inside, the car sped off into town. They parked the car on a piece of waste ground as near to the bank as possible and with Vedat in the middle, Muhammed by his side and the other cousins at the front and rear, they walked along the pavement towards the bank. A white BMW slowed down alongside them and gunshots rained down on the cousins. Without hesitation, Muhammed shoved Vedat to the ground and threw himself on top of him. People began screaming and running for cover. But as suddenly as it started, it was all over. The car screeched away and in seconds was out of sight.

Vedat was mildly winded from being pushed to the ground so forcibly and was struggling for breath. He tried to rouse himself but the weight of Muhammed on top of him meant he couldn't budge.

'Muhammed, get off!' he gasped. 'Let me get up!'

Muhammed didn't respond. With hearts pounding, the two other cousins were on their feet and dusting themselves off, thankful that they were unharmed. Their immediate fear was for Vedat so they turned to help Muhammed. His brother took Muhammed's arm to help him up but it was a dead weight. Then they saw the gaping hole in the back of his head.

'*Tanrim aman*! They've killed him! The bastards have killed him!' Muhammed's brother screamed, taking his brother in his arms and rocking him like a baby.

Vedat, now relieved of the weight crushing his body, sat up on the pavement and put his head in his hands. This had been meant for him. How could he ever forgive himself? Because of him his twenty-six year old cousin was dead. He had his whole life to live for and now had been snuffed out in an instant. Tears flowed down his cheeks and he began to pray silently.

'Are you hurt, sir?' someone asked him.

He looked up to see the owner of the café they were sitting outside. He shook his head, not finding himself able to utter words. He was fighting the urge to scream and kept swallowing in an attempt to choke the sobs that were threatening to erupt.

'Let's get you inside,' the café owner continued, helping Vedat to his feet and ushering him inside the café.

'No! I can't leave him,' Vedat whispered. 'I must be with him,' he muttered, pushing his way back through the assembled crowd to where Muhammed was being cradled in his brother's arms. 'Have you felt for a pulse? Has anyone called an ambulance?' he asked his cousin.

'An ambulance is on its way,' a bystander announced.

Vedat knelt down and took Muhammed's limp wrist in his hand and felt his neck. There was no pulse. It was too late for an ambulance. He shook his head, kissed his cousin's forehead and whispered, 'I'm so sorry.'

A week later, after the funeral had been held and when he had finally been able to talk about what had happened, Vedat called Kaye to explain why he hadn't been replying to her texts. Kaye found it hard to reconcile the fact that these people who had mobile phones and satellite televisions, drove expensive cars and wore designer clothes still upheld these medieval traditions.

[I didn't want to upset you with the awful situation I find myself in and my terrible life. Do I deserve these things or is it fate? My life has been turned upside down. How many burdens heaped upon me can I endure? Positive things are just a dream for me now and I can't imagine being happy ever again.]

[I know you're having a hard time, Vedat, but you'll get through it. It's just that everything seems to be happening at once – losing your father, your financial problems, the floods, the vendetta and now the killing. You must be strong and take each day as it comes.]

[I feel guilty for getting Muhammed killed and also for making you unhappy. All I ever give you is sadness, upset, frustration, pain and tears. You deserve much more than this. Maybe you should try to find happiness without me. If you are happy then I will be happy for you too.]

Kaye didn't reply. She couldn't find it within herself to say she would never be happy without him. Maybe he was right. It was time to move on. The stresses and strains of Vedat's dramatic life were impacting her too and she was not sure how much more she could take.

[I'm so stressed even my dreams have become nightmares and I wake up in a cold sweat. I'm praying many times a day asking for Allah to help me find a way out of this mess. The family are all pestering me about what I'm going to do but I need time to think. I can't risk any more bloodshed. I have to find a way to solve it peacefully.]

[Take as much time as you need. The other family won't do anything now. They've taken their revenge. Is the man your uncle shot still alive?]

[Yes, but they say he'll never recover properly. He has permanent brain damage. He might as well be dead. Thanks for talking to me Kaye. I need to go now. Bye.]

Kaye closed her phone, relieved that the conversation was over. She spent too much time calming Vedat down and soothing him but rarely got the tender loving care she sometimes needed back from him. She felt he was sucking every ounce of energy out of her and was aware that she needed to conserve as much energy as she could to cope with her illness and work full time.

Chapter 37

Bakewell

January 2008

Snuggled up on the sofa amidst a soft pile of cushions, Kaye was watching tiny flakes of snow float in front of the window land briefly before melting into the sodden grass. Nora had gone to Canada to visit Donna after Christmas, leaving Kaye alone in Bakewell for week before she needed to return to work. With plenty of time to think, Kaye had made a huge decision. She just couldn't face signing a new two year contract at Özkent. The struggle of working full time was starting to affect her state of mind and she knew she was reaching her limit. Anti-depressants had taken the edge off her ragged emotions, numbing her senses and dulling her responses, stifling the unexpected bouts of crying and sudden urges to run away but she knew that this was not a long term solution. Something had to change. An article in a magazine 'When You Take Risks You Truly Start Living' had been the motivation she needed to think how she was going to make a change. The thought of another year of the same meetings, the same issues and the struggle each morning of overcoming the stiffness in her joints, coping to get dressed, dry her hair and get to school on time, drained of energy before she began her work day, made her feel physically sick. She decided that she needed a year off work. She wanted the old Kaye back. She need to recharge her batteries and without the stress of work, hoped to wean herself of some of the heavy drugs she was taking before she suffered any long term side effects.

In the past, Kaye had always known when it was time to move on. After seven years at her last school, she had recognised the need for a change. It was like an itch that she couldn't scratch, a feeling of restlessness and a yearning to declutter. It began with the urge to go through her wardrobes and streamline her clothes, throwing huge amounts into black bin bags for the charity shop. Cupboards came next and when there was nothing left to purge, she was only left with the bigger picture of her life. She never made impulsive decisions and gave herself plenty of time to adjust, explore options and make plans.

Kaye quickly dismissed spending the year in the UK. It would be good to have time to spend with family and friends without being restricted to school holidays, but she also needed time to herself and that would not be possible if she stayed with Nora for the year. Ideally, she would love to stay in Turkey. Perhaps renting somewhere on the coast? A warmer climate might be beneficial for her joints and if she had a pool, she could swim every day which her rheumatologist had recommended. She had sold her house in Greenhill and had money in the bank to fund herself for at least a year.

On returning to Ankara, Kaye talked through her decision with Ebru, who understood how she felt and why she needed a break, but was upset that she would be losing her friend for a while. She advised Kaye to make an appointment to see Professor Adnan Deliduman, who, as the Chair of the Board of Governors at Özkent, would either agree to or refuse her request for a year off and keep her job open.

'Welcome!' Adnan *Bey* enthused, guiding her to a seat in his sumptuous office a week later. 'Would you like some tea?'

'That would be lovely!' Kaye responded, sitting carefully on a beautifully upholstered armchair next to a ornately carved mahogany coffee table. She put her handbag down on the silk Turkish carpet and looked around the room. It was more like a lounge than an office, except for two large desks at the far end near the window, where a personal assistant sat.

'Jale, may we have tea, please?' Adnan *Bey* asked, beckoning his assistant.

'Certainly, sir,' she replied before picking up the phone to order the refreshments.

'So, how can I help you?' Adnan *Bey* continued, taking a seat opposite Kaye.

Kaye didn't feel it necessary to go into details about her illness and kept her request short and to the point. 'I have been having some health issues and would like to take a year off to improve my health.'

'I'm sorry to hear you're not well. How do you plan to spend the year?'

'I'm going to rent a villa on the coast and, honestly, not do much. I need to recharge my batteries.'

'You're not going back to the UK?' Adnan *Bey* asked out of curiosity.

'No. The climate is better here and I'm sure my family and friends will come out for holidays,' Kaye said, taking the cup of tea proffered by a lady bearing a tray full of crockery and biscuits.'

'I'm sure they will. I see no reason for you not to have a year off. How long have you been with us?'

'This is my seventh year.'

'That's a long time for a foreigner. Is there anything else I can do to help?' he asked, taking a sip from his cup of tea.

'I'd like to know if I can still continue with my health insurance while I'm away.'

'I don't think that will be a problem. I'll ask Jale to arrange it for you. What about your flat?'

'I'm not thinking of keeping it. I can't afford to pay two lots of rent. I will be allocated another when I return.'

'Have you talked this through with John? Will he find a replacement for you?'

'Yes, I have. No decision has been made yet. But it seems likely that my Assistant Principal will take over for the year. Hopefully, we'll get PYP authorisation in April so everything will be in place by then and the next year should run smoothly as there will be no need for any major changes.'

'That all seems fine. Well, Kaye, I wish you all the best and hope you come back to us in the best of health,' Adnan *Bey* said, standing up and holding out his hand.

Kaye stood up and shook his hand, thanking him for his support. She bent down to retrieve her bag and was shown to the door.

'He said yes!' Kaye squealed down the phone to Ebru.

'I knew he would. You're a good employee and he doesn't want to lose you.' Ebru gushed. 'Have you decided where you want to go?'

'I've been thinking about Dalyan. I loved it there and it's the perfect place to relax.'

'I've never been but your photos looked lovely.'

'How do you fancy going with me in our March break? We could have a holiday and look at villas too.'

'That's a great idea. Can Matt come too?' Ebru asked, thinking that it would be an ideal opportunity to have some time away with her husband too.

'Of course,' Kaye agreed. She got on well with Matt and the three of them spending a week together would be fun. 'I'll look for somewhere for us to stay. Shall I look for flights too?'

'Matt would probably prefer to drive down. It would be like a road trip! And then we'd have the car there too which will make it easy for us to explore and look at villas.'

'That sounds like a plan, then,' Kaye said excitedly. She was pleased that she wouldn't have to look at villas on her own. 'Thanks, Ebru. See what Matt says and then we'll make definite arrangements.'

That night, when Vedat called, she told him of her plans to take a year off work. She hadn't mentioned it before she had Adnan *Bey*'s permission in case he had refused. Vedat was surprised at this development. This was not something they had discussed, but the more he thought about it, the more it appealed. He was already planning to be with Kaye at the end of this year, so if she was already somewhere suitable, the location part of the problem would be solved.

'What if I don't get enough money together? Would you still want me without any money?' he asked tentatively.

'That's a stupid question! Of course I'll still want you,' Kaye sighed down the phone. I have enough money saved up to last us the year and after that if we run out we'll just have to come back to Özkent….although I'd rather not come back. I'm moving all my stuff with me and letting my flat go so that if I don't come back, I'll already have everything with me.'

'I hope after we've been together a while you don't abandon me.' Vedat said quietly. 'Promise me, Kaye that you'll never leave me.'

'I promise.'

'You'll be my wife, mother, father, brother, sister, friend and confidante all rolled into one. In sickness and in health, for richer, for poorer, in times of trouble and difficulty we will always have each other. It will be our world. One day the sun will shine and the darkness will end. You are half of me. You are in my blood. You are in my soul. You are in my heart. You are my every breath,' he said, wanting her to know how much she meant to him, before adding, 'No one in my family must know where we are.'

'Why not?' Kaye asked, wondering if they would be in danger.

'If they find us, there will be trouble.'

'What kind of trouble?' A mounting sense of disquiet unsettled Kaye.

'My wife's family are very important people. They will make me go back home and then you will not be protected.' Vedat refused to say more, in case Kaye panicked and decided their living together was too much of a risk.

'If you don't have enough money, by the summer, why don't you sell some land?' Kaye suggested.

'Yes, I could do that. I've just sold a small parcel of land to pay off my remaining debt to the bank, but I still have a lot left. One field alone is worth a million dollars.'

'Wow! If you leave and are not planning to ever go back, what's the point of keeping the land? Will your sons continue to farm it?'

'Only one of them has any interest in farming. The others all have other careers in mind. I always wanted to build a dynasty for my children, but if I'm not here, everything will go to dust.'

'Well then, you might as well sell most of it and then we can live comfortably. If you leave them some, then they won't have any financial difficulties either.'

'Yes you're right. I'll have to think about it.'

Chapter 38

Dalyan

March 2008

Kaye, Ebru and Matt were staying in a charming villa owned by a local architect who was an old acquaintance of Meltem's. On their first evening, the architect, who lived next door to their villa, brought round a bottle of wine to welcome them and they felt obliged to ask him to join them. During the ensuing conversation, Kaye mentioned that she was looking for a villa to rent for one year and had several viewings the next day. He asked what she was looking for and then offered to show her another villa that belonged to him. Kaye readily agreed.

They all followed the architect as they went out of the garden and into another gateway along the stone wall. Even though it was dark, Kaye gasped as she saw the beautiful garden with mature fruit trees and rose beds surrounding a softly lit circular pool.

'Wow! This is gorgeous!' she exclaimed.

'Wait until you see the house,' the architect said with pride, guiding them along a crazy paved path to an outside seating area in front of the house. Taking a key out of his pocket, he opened the glass door and led them inside. 'Here is the lounge,' he gestured, welcoming them into the semi-circular room with well-stuffed, patterned cushions placed upon a stone surround, providing integral seating around the open stonework wall at the rear of the room. Pointing to a sunken wooden coffee table, surrounded by similar seating which faced the open fire, he added, 'It's very cosy in winter,' knowing that Kaye would be concerned about heating through the colder months.

'It's so unusual,' Kaye enthused, 'I love the natural feel of the stone and the muted colours you've used,' she continued, touching the open stone work on the back wall and admiring the olive green paint on the other walls.

'The whole villa is designed on a theme of circles and semi-circles,' the architect explained, proceeding up two stone steps to a semi-circular kitchen. 'And has been featured in many magazines over the years.'

'I'm not surprised,' Kaye raved, 'It's stunning!'

'There are three bedrooms, all with ensuite bathrooms,' the architect continued, 'Two are downstairs and one upstairs. Come!' he said, inviting them to follow him along a small corridor, pointing out the built in wardrobes along the length of the corridor and into a large bedroom.'

'A circular bed!' Kaye cried. 'I've never slept in one of those. Did you have to have the sheets made yourself?' she asked, ever practical and immediately thinking that her sheets would not fit.

'Yes, all of the soft furnishings were made to order locally. In fact, everything for the construction was locally sourced too. It was impossible to find anything readymade. There is air conditioning in every room which is very necessary in the summer months,' he added, taking the back down the corridor and into another large bedroom opposite. 'This bedroom has twin beds which is useful for visitors who don't want to sleep together.'

Ebru saw that Kaye's eyes were shining brightly and she was smiling broadly as she wandered around the villa and she knew that Kaye had fallen in love with the villa. As they climbed the steps to the upper bedroom, she whispered to Kaye, 'Can you see yourself living here?'

'Of course I can!' Kaye replied, 'but I'd never be able to afford to rent a place like this. I bet he charges a fortune. I've looked at some of the estate agents' websites and villas like this are a thousand pounds a week to rent. I don't have that kind of money.'

'And this is the third bedroom with its spectacular bathroom,' the architect announced, switching on the lights to both rooms. Again the large double bed was circular and there was a built on wardrobe and wooden bedside tables.

'Oh, wow! Look at this Kaye!' Ebru shouted from the bathroom. 'It's incredible!'

Kaye walked into the circular bathroom and felt like she was entering a space ship. The whole room was round, tiled in highly glazed blue ceramic tiles with shiny chrome fittings and had a sloping smoked glass ceiling.

'You can see the stars and even the Lycian tombs over the river from here. Look, Kaye! They're lit up at night,' Ebru said, standing on tiptoe to see the view.

Kaye stood next to her friend and sighed. This villa was perfect but she knew it was out of her price range so it was no use getting too excited about it. 'Why don't you live here?' she asked the architect.

'I have a modest villa next door and I can make more money from renting this one out in the summer. What do you think, Kaye? Would you like to live here?' he asked hopefully.

'Of course I would. It's perfect. But I am sure I won't be able to afford it.'

'What sort of price are you looking at for the whole year?' he inquired, slowly descending the stairs back to the lounge.

'I've budgeted for a thousand pounds a month. I can't afford more than that.'

'I think we can do that.'

'Are you serious? You would really let me have this villa for a year for that amount?'

'Yes,' he confirmed, smiling and nodding. 'I have a few bookings for the summer but they can stay in one of my other villas.'

'I can't believe it! Ebru, he says I can have this villa for a thousand a month! Kaye squealed, skipping around the room and hugging herself. 'I never imagined I'd find somewhere this beautiful.'

'You haven't even seen it in the daylight, yet,' the architect gushed. 'Tomorrow morning let's come again and then you can make a decision.'

Kaye had already decided that this would be her home for the year, but she didn't want to appear too eager until the deal was signed.

'I'm so happy for you, Kaye,' Ebru said sincerely, wrapping her arms around her friend.

'I'm happy for me too. I'm so excited! Now that I have a lovely villa, everyone will want to come and stay. I can already imagine a house full of visitors enjoying barbeques in the garden and lazing by the pool!'

The next morning, Kaye wolfed down her breakfast eager to go next door to see the villa in the daylight. It had seemed so magical at night, she hoped it was just as wonderful as she remembered. Lying in bed, before finally dropping off to sleep, she had mentally arranged the villa with all her possessions and smiled with relief that everything seemed to be falling onto place.

'It's just as beautiful as I remembered,' Kaye sighed, entering the garden of Cennet Villa. 'Its name, Paradise Villa, says it all. The architect had given Kaye the key and said he would join them later when they had had time to look at the villa at their leisure.

'Even the pool is unique,' Kaye said pointing to the green tiling. 'It looks so natural being green instead of the usual blue. It blends into the garden so well. It'll be lovely sitting here in the summer with the natural shade from the trees. I wonder if there are sun loungers?'

'There must be. He'll be storing them somewhere. Have you seen the quaint little *köşk* in the corner?' Ebru asked, pointing to a shingle covered hexagonal raised platform on which was a round wooden table and chairs. 'This'll be a great place for having lunch on hot days. What do you think, Matt?' she asked, turning to her husband.

'I think the whole thing is great and you're lucky to have found somewhere so suitable. It's not too big and yet you still have room for visitors. Are you still going to go and look at the other villas? Remember you have other appointments today.'

'I think we should still go and look at them and then you can make an informed decision later this afternoon,' Ebru advised sagely.

The three of them dutifully visited a handful of villas in various locations around the town. All of them were similarly priced and had their merits but none of them compared to Cennet Villa, so later that afternoon Kaye sat down with the architect to sign the contract.

Kaye returned to Ankara, confident in her decision, excited at the prospect of her year in Dalyan and ready to begin making preparations for her move.

Chapter 39

Dalyan

July 2008

It had taken Kaye the best part of a week to unpack her belongings and find new homes for them. Gülsema, the local woman who looked after the garden and pool, had helped her put away kitchen equipment, bedding and clothes, leaving Kaye to do the bit she enjoyed most - the interior styling and decoration. She had placed her Turkish carpets in each room and displayed the beautiful ceramics, plates, wall hangings and trinkets that she had either bought for herself over the years or had been presents from parents and children. It was now starting to feel like home.

As she had expected, her friends and family were eager to come and visit. As soon as schools had broken up, Anna had been to stay and now Kaye was preparing for Vedat's imminent arrival. He was coming for three weeks and the last few days of his stay would overlap with Nora's. Kaye was eager that the two of them should get to know each other better and was looking forward to her time with them. With the temperature hitting fifty degrees by mid-afternoon, doing anything physically exerting during the day became punishing.

Even the locals complained about the heat. Kaye was frantically washing and cleaning. She wanted everywhere to look perfect. She wore her swimming costume to do her chores and when she became too sweaty, jumped in the pool to cool off.

'What do you think?' Kaye asked Vedat eagerly as they entered the garden, hoping he would love the villa.

'It's nice. I'm not sure it's my style but if you like it, that's all that matters,' he said, taking Kaye in his arms and hugging her tight.

'But I want you to like it too!' Kaye said pushing him away and taking him inside. 'Look! Isn't it unusual?' she said, taking his hand and leading him through the whole villa and finally ending up in Kaye's bedroom. 'The round bed takes a bit of getting used to, but it's comfy.'

'I don't care what shape the bed is as long as it has you in it,' Vedat whispered, nuzzling her neck. 'I need to take a shower after the journey and then we'll try out the bed,' he said cheekily, pulling off his shirt and walking towards the bathroom.

They spent their days having a late Turkish breakfast of cheese, eggs, tomatoes, olives, cucumber, bread, yogurt and honey in the *köşk,* followed by hours lying on the sunbeds next to each other, reminiscing about past holidays, interspersed with cavorting in the pool, splashing each other, diving between each other's legs and just lying in the cooling water. Kaye had devised an aqua aerobic routine for herself that she did several times a day. She was determined to improve her fitness and, hopefully, lose some weight. She was much more agile in the water than she was normally and enjoyed being able to move freely without joint pain. Vedat was intrigued by her routine and tried to copy her, but his awkwardness soon had them giggling and falling about like school children.

By mid-afternoon, when the sun was at its hottest, they usually had a siesta in the comfort of the air conditioning, before showering and getting ready to go out to eat.

Kaye now had a selection of favourite restaurants and tonight she was taking him to one owned by a family from Diyarbakır. She has discovered it with Ebru and Matt and she and Anna had loved its rustic charm and traditional Turkish food. She had mentioned to the owner that her partner was from near Diyarbakır and he had insisted she bring Vedat when he came.

'You look beautiful,' Vedat complimented Kaye as she came out to join him on the seating area outside the villa.

'Thanks. You look very handsome too,' she responded, admiring his dark wavy hair and his sparkling dark brown eyes. He looked great in jeans and a short-sleeved blue and white checked cotton shirt. She still couldn't believe that this gorgeous man was hers.

'Your skin is like milk chocolate now, not chicken,' Vedat said, smiling at his old joke.

'It's more like toffee,' Kaye stated, liking the colour of her tan against the white and fuchsia pink of her tunic top. 'I don't think I've ever been this brown. Imagine what colour I'll be by the end of the summer!'

They walked hand in hand the short distance to the restaurant. Kaye was elated. It was simple things like this that she longed for during the lonely days when they were apart.

'*Hoşgeldiniz*! Welcome!' the owner greeted them enthusiastically, shaking Vedat's hand and ushering them to a table. He then spoke rapidly in Kurdish, ordering the waiters to bring drinks and engaging Vedat in conversation. Kaye sat, bemused. It was fascinating how Turkish people automatically respected Vedat and seemed to know he was someone important. The owner was a gracious host and welcomed everyone politely to his restaurant, but Vedat was receiving extra special attention. No one else got the hand kissing and grovelling treatment. The first time Ebru had met Vedat on one of his visits to Ankara, she had whispered to Kaye that he had the 'Ağa Walk'. Puzzled, Kaye had no idea what she was talking about. Ebru had explained that ağas have a very exaggerated slow pace, walking very upright and sometimes holding their hands together in front of them. Kaye knew that Vedat always walked slowly but she thought it was just his way. She was surprised to learn that it signified his status.

Vedat took the menu and proceeded to order an array of dishes. Kaye had become accustomed to this over the years. Initially, she had been insulted when he ordered food for them both and had insisted on choosing her own meal, but Vedat's crestfallen face had made her realise that in his culture it was his way of taking care of her and now that he knew what she liked, she was happy to let him take charge. He was used to entertaining his family, friends and business colleagues lavishly and always ordered far too much food but as he always footed the bill, Kaye had no cause for complaint.

'Ouch!' Kaye exclaimed, rubbing her shin. 'I forgot to spray and I've just been bitten by a mossie,' she added, beckoning a waiter and asking for some insect repellent. Seconds later, Kaye stood up, moving away from any tables and liberally dowsed herself with the repellent. 'I'm sure this stuff is toxic but it's better than getting eaten alive.' The mosquitoes in Dalyan were renowned for being ferocious and it was said that the reason the Lycians moved away thousands of years ago was because of them.

The food was delicious and after a couple of vodkas, Kaye was bathed in a warm glow. Electric lanterns strung between the trees and candles on the tables added to the romantic ambience. Even the stray chickens pecking around the tables and the cats ever watchful for dropped scraps, could not spoil her mood. Sighing, Kaye said, 'Wouldn't it be wonderful if we could do this all the time? Spending our days together and going out to eat at night.'

'Yes, my darling, it would. Maybe it will happen soon.'

'Really?'

'Yes. I've had the time of my life this last two weeks. I don't know how I'm going to leave you. I want to stay.'

'Stay!' Kaye cried. 'I want you to stay. Don't go back. Just stay here with me.'

'I'd love to but I need to go back to sort everything out. I need to explain things to my family and get enough money together.'

'I understand. But you really will come back and we'll be together forever?' Kaye asked, hoping that this was the moment she had been waiting so long for.

'Yes, I've been thinking a lot while I've been here. This is the perfect place for us to be together. When I went for a newspaper yesterday I sat and spoke to a couple of people about potential business opportunities here.'

'You didn't say!' Kaye looked perturbed. 'I thought you'd been gone a long time.'

'Farming is on too small a scale here but car rental might be an option, as could buying a pension or small hotel.'

'That sounds great!' Kaye agreed.

'I want you to look for villas to buy. Where you are now is too expensive to buy and I'd prefer somewhere more comfortable.'

Kaye nodded. While she loved Cennet Villa, the seating arrangement in the lounge was too formal and not conducive to lounging about and if there were two of them, they would need a larger sitting area. The circular bed had lost its appeal too. Whichever position was adopted resulted on either arms or legs falling off the edge of the bed.

'We definitely need a pool and I'd like a bigger garden.'

'I think the garden is big enough. Why would you want a bigger one?'

'Well, I was thinking we could have a cow. Then, we could have fresh milk, butter and cheese.'

'A COW!' Kaye spluttered, nearly choking on her drink. 'Are you mad? If you think I'm going to be milking a cow and making butter and cheese every day, you're sadly mistaken!' She couldn't work out if Vedat was joking or not.

'I'm serious. There's nothing like fresh milk, butter and cheese. Perhaps we could have chickens too.'

Kaye burst out laughing. 'Oh Vedat! How are we going to have a cow trampling around the garden? Will it swim in the pool too?' She was now laughing so hard, tears were rolling down her cheeks and other customers were looking to see what was amusing her so much. 'I could cope with a few chickens and I'd love a dog.....but a ccccow!' Her voice rose and Vedat shushed her. 'Oh wait until I tell my Mum this. She'll think it's hysterical.'

Nora had indeed laughed when Kaye related the story to her over a cup of tea. She had arrived with a case loaded with goodies. Kaye squealed as she saw the Cabdury's Dairy Milk, Battenburg cake and malt loaf as well as chocolate Digestives and a pack of magazines from the airport. There seemed to be no end to the array of treats coming out of the case. Nora had bought a stock of Kaye's favourite brands of toiletries too.

'Wow! Thanks Mum. Have you brought any clothes?' Kaye giggled, wondering how Nora had found room to bring so much.

'Yes, but not many. From what you said as long as I have plenty of bikinis and a few clothes for going out, that'll be enough.' Nora replied. 'Anyway, you've got a washing machine so I can always wash things through.'

'True. Are you tired?' Kaye inquired.

'Yes, it's been a long day.'

'There are towels and toiletries in your bathroom. Just shout if you need anything. The air conditioning has been on for a couple of hours in your room so it'll be nice and cool but you might want to switch it off once you're in bed,' she added, conscious that the dry air might trigger one of Nora's asthma attacks.

Kaye and Vedat had spent a few hours during the cooler part of the morning cleaning and tidying. Vedat had offered to do the hoovering, which had amused Kaye. He hadn't trusted himself with dusting as he was clumsy and afraid he might break some of Kaye's valuables.

'If my mother could see me doing this,' Vedat had mumbled, 'she'd never believe it!'

'You're becoming quite the house husband,' Kaye teased. 'You'd better get used to it!' She knew Vedat was trying to impress her and she loved him for it.

With the cushions plumped, the floors sparkling after a thorough mopping and not a speck of dust to be found, Kaye had gone into the garden to cut some of the gorgeous roses and arranged the varying shades of red and pink blooms in two round glass vases: one for the lounge and one for Nora's room.

On his forays into town, Vedat had become friendly with one of the river side restaurant managers, where he usually chose to sit and have a glass of *çay*. Mervan was originally from Mardin, although had spent most of his life in the Marmaris area.

The two men enjoyed each other's company and Vedat, eager to find out more about life in Dalyan, welcomed the opportunity to speak in his mother tongue. Mervan was a wealth of information and being able to speak Dutch, English and German as well as Turkish and Kurdish, provided Vedat with a perspective of what life would be like, not only in Dalyan but also living with a foreign woman. He, too had had a traditional arranged marriage to a Kurdish girl but also had had liaisons with a variety of foreign women. Knowing the Vedat came from a very traditional family, he understood the difficulties that lay ahead and tried to give his new friend the best advice he could.

The following night, Kaye, Vedat and Nora were planning to go to Mervan's restaurant to eat.

'Are you ready, Mum? Kaye shouted from her bedroom, where she was adding the finishing touches to her makeup. Putting on foundation was pointless as within minutes, with sweat trickling down her face, she ended up wiping it off. She carefully applied a coat of sugary pink lipstick and went to join Vedat who was already sitting outside smoking.

'You look nice,' Kaye said as Nora came out onto the sitting area outside the front door.

'Yes. Very beautiful, Nora honey,' Vedat agreed. It had tickled Kaye that Vedat had adopted this affectionate name for her mother. As his English was still very limited, it was his way of forming a relationship with Nora, without having to say much. 'Let's go!' he said, positioning himself in between the two women and taking one of their hands in each of his.

‘It’s a long time since a man had held my hand,’ Nora said, smiling. Thank you, Vedat. This is lovely.’

This gave Kaye a warm fuzzy feeling and she squeezed Vedat’s arm. It was a relief that Nora and Vedat were getting along so well, although she sensed that for Vedat it was a strain.

Chapter 40

Dalyan

September 2008

August had passed in a blur of sunbathing, reading and swimming and Kaye had begun to relax. Not returning to school at the end of the month had felt strange and she had experienced a pang of guilt while lying in her idyll, knowing that others were having to pick up her workload. Until then it had been like a normal school summer holiday but as the end of the month loomed and the usual thoughts of a new school year started to creep in she couldn't help wondering how the new teachers were settling in, whether the new building extension had been completed on time and how they were managing without her. She prided herself on her organisational skills and had done as much as she could to ensure that her secretary, the assistant principal and other members of the elementary school management team knew where everything was. She had even written step by step guides to some of her responsibilities, not wanting anyone to criticise her systems. With a wry smile, she also hoped that they were missing her and maybe they would appreciate her more when she was no longer there.

There were only two months left before Vedat would be here.....for good. She had badly needed a distraction from counting the days until his arrival and was overjoyed when members of her family booked flights to come over for two weeks. The intense heat had now abated and the weather was perfect for sightseeing and sunbathing, without the risk of getting badly sunburnt or being reduced to a dripping puddle of sweat.

'Morning, everyone!' Kaye greeted the group sitting under the shade of the *köşk*. Nora had arrived the previous week, followed by Donna and her friend, Jessie, and last night they had gone to the airport to meet Kerry and her partner, Ben. It was the first time that Ben had met the others and Kaye had worried that as the only man, he might feel uncomfortable but Kerry and assured her that Ben was used to female company and he would be fine. The others had not been together as a group for years and they were all looking forward to spending time together.

'So what are we having for breakfast?' Kaye asked, glad that her guests were feeling at home and had helped themselves. She had made sure that her cupboards and fridge were full of food.

'Jessie made French toast, which is scrummy,' Kerry said, wiping her mouth from the last mouthful of the eggy bread. 'This honey is lovely too,' she continued, 'Is it local?'

'Yes, I bought it from the market, which we should go to today so you can see all the produce. It's a great photo opportunity.'

'I'd love that,' Jessie piped up. 'Shall I make you some French toast?' she added, looking at Kaye, who nodded gratefully.

'Did everyone sleep well?' Kaye asked, taking a seat next to Nora at the table. She had let Kerry and Ben have her bed, while she slept in the other twin bed in Nora's room. Donna and Jessie were happy bunking up in the upstairs bedroom.

'I did, but those cockerels make some noise!' Donna replied.

'I heard the call to prayer but then dropped off again,' Nora commented, sipping her cup of tea.

'If you think the cockerels are noisy, you should have been here when the storks were here!' Kaye said, helping herself to a glass of sour cherry juice. 'They make such a racket, clacking their beaks together. Their nest was just over the wall on the roof of the villa next door, quite near my bedroom. It took me ages to be able to block them out.'

'Where are they now?' Donna asked.

'When their babies were grown by the middle of July, they all flew off. Probably to Africa. I'll show you the nest later. There are so many nests all around the town – on top of mosques and telegraph poles.'

'I would love to have seen them,' Ben said eagerly, getting up from his seat to make way for Jessie as she returned from the kitchen with a fresh pot of tea.

'So, do you want to go to the market?' Kaye asked, mentally planning the day.

'Yes,' they all said enthusiastically.

'We could have lunch by the river and then spend the afternoon by the pool, before we hit the town tonight. How does that sound?' Kaye suggested.

'Sounds great!' Donna said, looking round to see everyone nodding.

Kerry and Ben had never been to Turkey before and were enjoying discovering a different culture. The market was a sensory overload, bustling with tourists bartering over souvenirs and local produce. Stalls were laden with cheap fake designer T-shirts, jeans and handbags of every hue and style and the stall holders were doing their best to attract shoppers with cries of 'Cheaper than Sainsbury's' and 'Genuine fake Armani here!'

Nora, ever on the lookout for a new handbag had spotted a black leather bag with a leopard skin design on it. As soon as she picked it up, the stall holder was upon her, pointing out the workmanship and showing her the quality of the interior material.

'What do you think?' she asked, turning to Kaye with the bag slung over her shoulder.

'Yes it's nice. I didn't know you needed another handbag,' Kaye replied.

'I don't, but I like it. I haven't got an animal print one and it's not too big.'

Turning to the stall holder, Kaye asked for the price in Turkish. She had learnt that speaking in Turkish, showing the vendor that she was not a naïve tourist just off the plane, gave her a better price.

'One hundred and twenty lira,' the stall holder replied.

'That's far too expensive!' Kaye exclaimed. 'No way.'

'Okay, one hundred.'

'Forty,' Kaye countered, calculating how much it would be in English pounds and knowing what Nora would be willing to pay.

'Oooff!' the stall holder sighed, shaking his head. 'It's real leather. Look!' he said taking a lighter from his pocket and waving the flame over the bag. 'Real leather doesn't burn. Eighty lira. That's a special price for you, lady.'

Kaye shook her head and stuck at forty lira. She whispered to Nora to walk away. 'No thank you,' she told the stall holder and putting the bag back on the pile on the stall, started to follow Nora. 'Do you really want it?' she asked Nora.

'Yes I think so.'

'He'll call us back with my price in a minute.'

And sure enough, Kaye heard a voice shouting, 'Okay, lady. Forty lira.'

'Told you,' Kaye said to Nora with a satisfied grin, returning to the stall to hand over the money.

Nora took the brightly coloured plastic bag containing her new purchase and followed Kaye through the crowded market to where the others were admiring some Kashmir wool pashminas.

'These are gorgeous,' Jessie told Kaye, feeling the luxurious silky material and draping the shawl in muted colours of blue over her shoulders. 'They're cheap too. I can't decide on what colour.'

'That one looks great against your skin,' Donna interrupted, admiring a pink and purple patterned pashmina. 'This one would look lovely with my purple dress.'

With the sale completed, the group walked onwards, passing stalls selling homemade butter and cheese, plump green and black olives stored in huge vats, locally produced honey, jams and preserves and baskets full of brightly coloured spices. Ben, an avid cook and lover of curries, bought an interesting selection of different peppers, turmeric, saffron, ground coriander and cumin, before continuing along the row of stalls to the fruit and vegetable part of the market.

'Look at the size of the cauliflowers and cabbages!' he exclaimed. 'I've never seen such big ones.'

'Neither have I,' Kerry agreed. 'It's weird….the cucumbers and bananas are tiny and yet most of the fruit and veg is much larger than we get at home. Just smell those tomatoes!' she added, picking up a ripe red tomato and holding up to her nose. 'Mmm! Delicious.'

Groaning under the weight of their laden bags, the group made their way towards the river and Mervan's restaurant, where they ordered ice cold beers and were pleased to sit down in the sunshine to relax.

Kerry and Ben both celebrated their birthdays while they were with Kaye, which gave Kaye an excuse to do some baking. She outdid herself by making Ben a decorated chocolate cake and Kerry a tower of pastel coloured cupcakes. Both of which were washed down with the Cava and Prosecco that her guests had bought at Duty Free. While alcohol was freely available in supermarkets in Dalyan, Turkish wine making didn't stretch to good sparkling wine.

All too soon, their holidays were coming to an end and they were determined to make the most of it. They began drinking at lunchtime by the pool and had all nodded off in the late afternoon on their sunbeds. Kaye had woken up first and had gone inside to make jugs of cocktails, canapés and nibbles for when they woke up. She had loved having her family to stay and they had created some lasting memories. She would create a photo book to give each of them at Christmas to remind them of a super holiday. They were all delighted that things with Vedat seemed to be looking more positive after her years of patiently waiting and they cooed over the brochures of potential villas from the estate agents that she had shown them. Kaye deserved to be happy.

Carrying the tray of refreshments out to the poolside, Kaye smiled to herself as she remembered Nora's comment about them being pleased to welcome Vedat into the family on a permanent basis. 'The next time I see any of my family, I'll have Vedat by my side,' she thought. Were the years of waiting finally coming to an end?

Chapter 41

Karabulut

October 2008

Now that his debts were all paid off, Vedat could concentrate on the future. He was in the process of selling some land that he hoped would be enough for him to buy a house in Dalyan and have enough left for them to have a buffer before settling upon a business venture. As much as he wanted desperately to be with Kaye, he still had moments of great doubt. He knew he loved her. She meant the world to him but the devastation he would leave behind here was a constant source of worry.

He had decided that he would leave after Kurban Bayram, the Feast of Sacrificing at the end of November. He was planning to talk to his family openly and hoped they wouldn't make too much of a fuss. One of his cousins had recently married a Russian woman, who had gradually been accepted into the family so times were changing and the old traditions and prejudices were being broken down.

His three weeks in Dalyan with Kaye had been wonderful. He could now visualise what life with her would be like. When they were together everything seemed so natural and easy. She was the woman of his dreams, not only in looks, with her violet, blue eyes, blonde hair and curvaceous body, but in personality too. She was funny, intelligent, caring and had been so patient with him. He couldn't understand what a woman like her saw in an ignorant country boy like him. It had nearly broken his heart to leave her there when he walked through the departure gate to catch his flight home. They had both cried and clung to each other, but at least the end was in sight and the waiting would be over.

Once, a haggard old peasant woman had walked straight into his office and held out her hand. He thought that she wanted money and was about to reach into his pocket for some loose change, when she had chastised him, saying that she wanted to look at his right hand. He obediently showed her his hand, which she turned palm side upwards. She traced the lines with a gnarled finger, before telling him that a blue-eyed blonde woman would steal his heart and she would be the love of his life. Vedat had laughed at the ridiculous prophecy, dropping a few *kuruş* into her palm and shooing her away. She shuffled to the open doorway, turning round to say, 'I don't lie. You'll see, sir. She's coming soon.'

Vedat had thought the whole incident comical and had shared it with his friends, laughing at the improbability of him meeting a woman like that. How on Earth, living in Karabulut, was that going to happen? It was at a time when curfews were in place and socialising on any level was difficult, never mind having a fling with a woman. But it seemed the old woman had been right. Kaye had come into his life and he couldn't imagine her ever not being part of it.

Kaye often talked about her belief in reincarnation and was convinced that the reason she felt so at home in Turkey was because she had lived there in a past life. She also believed that she and Vedat had had a past life together and this is why they had experienced the magnetic draw to each other when they first met. Vedat found this hard to digest and spent many hours contemplating the possibility of them knowing each other in a previous existence and struggling with the conflict of his own Muslim beliefs, which did not acknowledge reincarnation. He could not deny the strength of the bond between him and Kaye and even though he felt the overwhelming feeling that she felt like his mother, his embedded religious faith dismissed the idea that he and Kaye were soul mates and had known each other before. Once, while making love a bizarre feeling had swept over him. A feeling that he wanted to swim up inside her, back to the womb, so that he could be totally immersed inside her and feel protected. This was the only time he could feel that Kaye might have been his mother before but then maybe that sensation was nothing to do with reincarnation?

He worried about Kaye not having a religion. Her not being a Muslim was not a concern but a person not having the security of faith made her seem vulnerable. Once, while they were talking about getting married, Kaye had said she would become a Muslim so that their marriage could be blessed by an Imam. She also knew that the religious marriage ceremony was more important to Vedat than the legal, civil ceremony. He would never put pressure on her to convert to Islam, but appreciated her desire to make him happy.

He had shared his plans to leave with only one trusted friend, who had known about the relationship from the beginning. While not in full support of Vedat's decision, he knew how his friend had suffered and wanted him finally to find true happiness. Vedat had not divulged the location of where he would be. He didn't want anyone to be responsible for Kaye being put at risk. He knew what certain members of his extended family were capable of.

Chapter 42

Dalyan

November 2008

The autumn weather had set in with howling winds and occasional torrential rain storms, when thunder and lightning had cut off the electricity supply and a distinct chill in the air made lighting a fire necessary. Kaye had packed away most of her summer clothes to make room for Vedat's winter clothes in the wardrobes and had been cooking his favourite meals and storing them in the freezer, anticipating days when she was unwilling to spend hours sweating at the stove, when she could be in the arms of her beloved.

Vedat had worked hard to harvest his cotton, wheat and lentils in record time before the first rain of the winter came and after spending Kurban Bayram with his family, he would be joining Kaye at the villa. He had suffered a set-back in October when millions of sparrows had eaten the rice which he was about to harvest. He said it was like something from a horror movie as the birds gathered in the bushes and trees around the perimeter of the rice fields and swooped down in a cloud to decimate the crop. Nothing he or his workers did had any effect. They had fired shots into the air from their rifles, but the birds had just moved further down the field away from them.

Vedat was only able to save one third of his rice - a major disappointment as this was the money he was planning to use to purchase a new home for himself and Kaye. He hoped this was not an omen for the future.

As he had instructed, Kaye had collected details of various suitable villas in Dalyan from the internet and from the numerous estate agents in the town. Due to the recession, many foreign home owners had put their houses up for sale and there were some good bargains to be had. Some she had easily been able to dismiss as they did not have the swimming pool that she deemed a necessity or the garden was either too small or overlooked. She had been spoilt by having total privacy at Cennet Villa and was not prepared to have neighbours spying on her as she lay half-naked by the pool. She had been waiting for this for nine years and fantasised about furnishing and styling her favourite of the villas, choosing colour schemes and browsing on the internet for ideas on interior decor. It had been her dream to build a house to her own design and this too might be possible of they found a suitable piece of land to build on. It would depend on how much money Vedat had available.

Vedat's text messages to Kaye had been full of excitement and he reiterated his desire to be with her. He was impatient to leave behind the stress of his current environment, having to deal with his extended family's problems and being at the mercy of everyone's demands. He craved the freedom that a life with Kaye would bring and longed to spend every minute of the rest of his life with the woman he loved.

'I haven't heard from him for the last three days,' Kaye told Kerry, who had telephoned to see how she was. 'He was planning to talk openly to his family about leaving to be with me two days ago. Not knowing what's happening is driving me crazy!'

'Maybe no news is good news,' Kerry said optimistically, trying to calm Kaye's mounting fears. 'He could well be on his way at this very moment and is planning to give you a surprise. Is he flying or driving?'

'He said he was going to come in his car,' visualising him driving the long, twenty hour journey, hoping that he would stop for rest breaks and not be tempted to drive the whole way in one go. 'He must have talked to them by now. I told him it wouldn't be easy and that his children would be very upset.'

'Yes, he must know that but he's still willing to go through with it.'

'Oh, I wish he'd send me a message! I hate it when he does this.'

'Just hang on in there. You've waited this long, what's another day or two?'

'You're right, but I have this uneasy feeling. I don't know whether I'm scared about finally living with someone after being on my own for so long or whether I'm picking up some bad vibes from him.'

'Try not to worry. I'm sure everything will be fine and the next time we speak you'll be deliriously happy. You've both been through so much and deserve to have a happy ending.'

'I hope you're right. Thanks for cheering me up.'

Sitting at the kitchen table, mixing together butter and sugar in preparation for a cake in a desperate attempt to distract herself, Kaye tried to quell the rising sense of panic that threatened to overwhelm her. ‘Please let him come,’ she chanted to herself. ‘Please let him come. We’ve been through enough. Please don’t let all the energy, effort and time we’ve spent be wasted.’ She had been so sure that all the traumas, frustration, loneliness and heartache of the last nine years would, one day, all be worth it. She had trusted her instincts when she first met Vedat and all the way through their relationship. He wouldn’t let her down again would he?

Breaking eggs into a bowl and whisking furiously, doubt began to invade her thoughts. What if he doesn’t come? What if Vedat’s family had threatened to kill her? Had they threatened to harm his children if he left? She had heard of many incidents in the South East of Turkey where family honour had been breached and people had died as a result. Had Vedat lied about his intention to leave? Had he just strung her along because he could not bear the thought of not seeing her again but now he had run out of excuses for them not to be together? There were so many doubts and questions flying around in her head that unwittingly she had added the eggs to the butter and sugar without any flour and was now stirring a curdled mess. Had he had an accident? Was he lying injured by the side of a road somewhere waiting for help? Or dead? A shiver coursed through her body and feeling sick with despair she abandoned the idea of baking and threw the mixture into the bin.

What would she do without him? What about the rest of her life? Switching the kettle on with shaking hands, she took a mug from the cupboard and then jumped in alarm as her phone rang. 'Oh, God, please don't let it be bad news,' she said aloud, picking up the phone but hesitating, not daring to look who was calling. It was Vedat.

'Can you come?' he asked.

'What? Where?' Kaye stuttered, confused, immediately imagining him in desperate need.

'Can you open the gate?' Vedat repeated.

'Which gate?' she asked, not understanding.

'Your gate!' he laughed.

'You mean you're here?

'Yes. I'm here. Hurry up I'm getting soaked.'

Kaye threw down her phone, yanked open the door and ran, being careful not to lose her footing on the wet, mossy paving, to the gate. She paused, for fear that Vedat would not be standing on the other side, but on hearing the thud of a car boot closing, heaved the wooden gate ajar.

'You're here!' she exclaimed, not quite believing what she saw.

'Yes, my darling, I'm here,' Vedat said gently, taking Kaye in his arms and planting a soft kiss on her forehead.

'I thought you weren't coming!' Kaye's voice broke as tears of relief trickled down her cheeks. Hugging him tightly, not caring that rain was dripping from her hair and she was standing in a puddle, she allowed her body to slump against his. Words seemed unnecessary as they gazed into each other's eyes, the longing of years spent apart melting away. As the rain soaked into their skin, washing away the heartache and misery, they walked arm in arm into their new home and their new life together.

Acknowledgements

I would like to thank Rachael Drury, Susan Hobson, Pamela Culley, Karen Andrews, Patricia Zakaria, Julie Lee and Adrian Rees for their encouragement, proof reading skills and suggestions. Thanks also to Paige Stewart, for her technical expertise and Muharrem Celik for his patience, time and valuable insight into Kurdish culture and traditions.

Special thanks go to Cheryl Thomas, Tumay Krugman, Zeynep Dincer, Ceyda Oztekin and Julide Dittgen for being my emotional rocks and support system.

About the Author

Faye Rogan has lived in Turkey for the last fifteen years, initially working in an international school in Ankara and now leading a more relaxed life in Dalyan. She immerses herself in Turkish culture and enjoys an authentic life in a traditional village. Living the dream in this little piece of paradise.

'Seeing the Truth' is her debut novel.

Find her at www.twitter.com/fayerogan101 and www.faceook.com/FayeRoganAuthor.